MW01602259

A CHILLING
ABSENCE OF
LOVE

A CHILLING ABSENCE OF LOVE

Fact-Based Crime Novel

Betty J. Hunt and Helen-Aurelia Smith

0610-AURE

Copyright © 1999 by Betty J. Hunt and Helen-Aurelia Smith.

Library of Congress Number:		99-91419
ISBN #:	Hardcover	0-7388-0764-8
	Softcover	0-7388-0765-6

All rights reserved. No part of this book may be reproduced or transmitted in any form or by any means, electronic or mechanical, including photocopying, recording, or by any information storage and retrieval system, without permission in writing from the copyright owner.

This book was printed in the United States of America.

To order additional copies of this book, contact:
Xlibris Corporation
1-888-7-XLIBRIS
www.Xlibris.com
Orders@Xlibris.com

CONTENTS

AUTHORS' NOTE

To protect privacy, almost all names, descriptions, places and dates have been altered in this true crime story. Events, as told to us by the protagonist, have necessarily been embellished or deleted, and some fiction added for cohesive interest.

0610-AURE

DEDICATION

We dedicate this book to all the children of the world who must grow up with an absence of love.

ACKNOWLEDGMENTS

We could not write without the love and patience of our families and friends, especially Tom Hunt, Lila Cardoza, Sue Birdsong, Troy Westergaard, Al Dial and members of the Riverside Writers' Club. We could not publish without our mentor, Byrd Holland.

Helen and Betty

PROLOGUE

I hurried the new commitment down the corridor to the death
row unit of The California Institution for Women. Catcalls from
hastily locked inmates mocked her: "Baby-killer! Mother-fuckin'
baby-killer. First chance, bitch—you'll see." Although she had not
killed a child, nor ever abused one, the prison grapevine maligned
Anna Louise Anderson with that cruel but twisted version of her
crimes.

As we entered the Special Security Unit I reflected upon the
four years I had guarded the young Manson women. Although
Anna did not receive the death sentence, she was beginning her
own life term under the same extreme security conditions.

Reluctantly I once again switched on the power and pushed
the buttons that electronically controlled the double grille gates
barring six empty cells. Anna moved into the first cubicle and
stood motionless, looking through me, waiting. I left her that night,
hanging on to a copy of prison rules.

For five months I guarded her until her transfer to the Psychiatric Treatment Unit. Five months of psychotropic drugs which
zonked her into the "twilight zone."

I am Betty J. Hunt, former Correctional Officer.

My new patient came to the Psychiatric Unit under stringent protective custody. She was not allowed on the main prison compound unless there were visitors. There were no visitors except
occasionally a lawyer or an M-2 (volunteer) sponsor.

She had developed the Thorazine shuffle to and from the nurses' station. I noted merely the new face with its vapid look of chemically repressed emotions; and the hands which shook so violently that I had to hold her water cup and place her four pills on her tongue. Unkempt. No affect.

The shock of finding out she was a nurse! What frenzy caused this benign, matronly person to commit such crimes? How had that first, brilliantly executed crime led her into the crudely botched murder for which she was convicted? I had to know.

I am Helen-Aurelia Smith, retired R.N.,M.S.

CHAPTER 1

Saturday, May 25, 1974, 7 a.m.

Something was moving in the apartment.

Something other than the rippling of the drapes in the larger of the two bedrooms; partly open accordion shapes shifting just enough to occasionally expose dark, irregular stains within their folds. Something other than the barely perceptible ooze from a damp towel wadded into the bathroom sink; a sticky, pinkish ooze slowly dribbling down the drain while the bulk of the stained towel was drying into a stiff clump. Something other than a small table fan idling from side to side, its whirring blades stirring the emptiness across that corner bedroom.

It was a shadow . . . a child's shadow moving along the apartment corridor and through the living room: first undulating in soft curves past rounded sofas and pillows; then changing into geometrically precise rectangles and bars as it moved into the kitchen. It brushed by the harsh outlines of a chipped table, a grease-encrusted stove, a refrigerator, cabinets and counters, until it finally paused beside the linen closet.

It inched past the partially closed door to the corner bedroom and hesitated. Inside the room an exposed window, overlooking the alley parking lot, allowed in enough daylight to distinguish objects. There was an odd difference about that window. The drapes were drawn back unevenly into unaccustomed pleats. The window now afforded a partial view of the unkempt landscaping across the way, and of the weathered old church which fronted on Victory Boulevard.

It was this view that momentarily caught and held the child's attention. The scene was smudgy because of dirt and rain streaks on the window panes. Katie and her shadow moved into the brightening rays pushing through the dirty window; uneven rays which disguised the dark smears they touched on the dull-white drapery panels.

Now the shadow was moving faster than the small figure to which it was attached. Quickly changing sun ripples created a living thing of her silhouette, twisting it into a huge, gray veil with no definitive shape—and yet—a mass which appeared to breathe on its own. Katie moved uncertainly as light squeezed further through the window.

A tiny form it was to cast such a large shadow which continued to grow as it challenged the morning sun for possession of a dramatic 3 x 6 foot painting covering the near wall. Sudden brightness touched the painting, bleaching many of its iridescent colors into muted tones. The effect could only slightly soften the bold picture.

It came alive. That proud portrait of the child's mother: a lifesize form reclining nude on a red velvet divan; her graceful body partially covered with greenbacks of all denominations. Her lips were slightly parted, seemingly to smile sardonically down at anyone favored enough to be in this small, garishly decorated bedroom.

Little Katie was not thus favored. Her mother had often admonished, "Go on over to Mrs. Gonzales' apartment and stay there until I call you." None of the three children was often allowed beyond this doorway. But somehow today was different. Curiosity overcame habit. Still hesitant, the girl followed her disintegrating shadow into the forbidden room. "Mommy?" her small voice whispered.

"Mommy." Then, more insistent when sunlight brought courage to the youngster, "Mommy!"

No answer. The three-year-old, in oversized slippers and her sister's old, lavender pajamas, padded up to her mother's four-poster bed. She pushed against it.

"Mommy, I'm hungry," she persisted while her lips turned downward into a pout. It was past 7 a.m., long after her mother usually had the coffeepot half empty and doughnuts warming in the oven. And her mother hadn't come in to ruffle her hair or inspect her ears or help her dress.

She lifted her pajama top to cover her nose. "Mommy? What's stinky?" She poked hesitantly at the bedding.

Still no answer. It was so quiet! Sunlight flickered on the walls. Suddenly Katie felt smaller while the room grew bigger. She did not see that the dragging hems of her pajama bottoms were turning dark red, slowly, like a sponge dropped on old tomato sauce.

The bed looked empty. Almost empty. Only the blanket and satin sheets, wadded into lumps toward the middle of the mattress, had at first suggested a sleeping form. Now Katie wasn't sure.

"Mommy?"

The tiny figure became stiff with tension. The petulant stance crumpled, and the insistent voice trembled ever so slightly. Where was her mother? Katie knew she never went away without telling them or leaving a note taped to Corinne's dresser mirror.

She tugged at the top bedding until it was all in a heap at the edge of the bed. No one. But there was . . . something. The bottom sheet was damp with sticky, dark-red stuff sinking into the mattress. Katie reached out a finger to touch the jellied blobs of blood.

With a quick intake of breath she wheeled and ran back down the long corridor, her bloody footprints merging into the worn, maroon carpet. She crashed into her sister, Corinne, rocking the pudgy six-year-old sideways. Corinne dropped her newly acquired nail polish on the rug when Katie yelled in her ear and waved a bloodied finger in her face. She pushed her sister away and tried to retrieve some of her mother's spilled polish. Katie wailed and pulled at her sister's arm.

"Look, Cory, look . . . blood!"

Corinne was dressed—all but one shoe which was hiding under her warped Victorian dresser. She tossed her neat curls and pushed Katie against their bunk beds.

"Boy, is Mommy gonna be mad," she snapped, as she wiped the carpet. "An' be still! I can't even unnerstand one thing you're cryin' about."

"I can't find Mommy," sobbed the trembling youngster. "Cory, come *on*. Now! You gotta come. . . ."

Corinne frowned at her, and for the first time noticed the blood-covered finger. Maybe it was cut really bad. She carefully wiped away the blood and tentatively examined the finger. There was no wound. Katie sobbed louder. It didn't make sense. Corinne called out to their brother, "Bobby, get up! something's wrong."

The boy stirred sleepily. He had watched television all afternoon and evening until bedtime, and his eyes were tired. Even though Bobby was nearly nine he still shared a bedroom with his noisy sisters. He sighed and opened one eye cautiously.

"Bobby, come on," pleaded Corinne as she struggled with the errant shoe. "Please, Bobby."

He dressed hurriedly as the urgency of both girls' cries piqued his spirit of adventure. "Okay, okay," he said. "I'm coming . . . I'm coming. Can't you stop Katie's crying?"

Corinne turned her attention again towards Katie. She hugged her sister once, cupped the cold hand in hers, and gently prodded her back toward their mother's bedroom.

Bobby stumbled along behind his sisters. When he caught up with the girls he sensed their fright and glanced from one to the other. They continued on together.

Soon there were three small figures staring at the mess on their mother's bed.

A desperate urgency nudged at their heightening fears as they began to run around the bedroom calling, "Mommy, Mommy!" They searched behind the armchair and the bookcases filled with knick-knacks and Hollywood souvenirs; inside the shallow wardrobe; even in the pile of laundry stacked in one corner. Maybe it was the source of that awful smell? It took only moments for them to search the whole apartment.

Finally they were still, seeking each other's eyes and hands as they turned and walked slowly back into the bedroom. They stared at each other, then at the very last hiding place.

Their steps were slower and their grip on each other tighter as they moved toward the dishevelled bed. Bobby, trying to be strong for his sisters, sank on his knees beside his mother's bed. He looked back once at Corinne.

And then . . . of course . . . he looked under the bed.

CHAPTER 2

Tuesday, July 9, 1974, 2 p.m.

THE COURT: Next witness.

MR. DURBIN: People call Dr. Forrester.

THE CLERK: Raise your right hand, please.

You do solemnly swear that the testimony you are about to give in the cause now pending before this Court shall be the truth, the whole truth, and nothing but the truth, so help you God?

THE WITNESS: I do.

JAMES FORRESTER, called as a witness by and on behalf of the People, having been first duly sworn, was examined, and testified as follows:

THE CLERK: State your name, please.

THE WITNESS: James Forrester, F-o-r-r-e-s-t-e-r.

THE CLERK: Thank you. You may be seated.

DIRECT EXAMINATION

BY MR. DURBIN:

Q. Dr. Forrester, would you please state to the Court your qualifications to testify as an expert witness in autopsy matters. And, how many autopsies have you performed?

A. I graduated from Stanford University Medical School in 1937. Licensed in the State of California in 1938. I was in general practice for 27 years, including 4 years in the Army of the United States during World War II, Medical Corps.

In June, 1968, I entered the Coroner's office. As a result of training there and by examination, I am certified by the American Board of Pathology in the subspecialty of forensic pathology.

I have performed about 2,000 autopsies.

Q. You are currently employed by the Los Angeles County Chief Medical Examiner-Coroner's office?

A. I am.

Q. Sometime on the 25th of May did you have an opportunity to perform an autopsy on the body of one Rosalind Delgato?

A. I did. It was performed at the office of the Chief Medical Examiner-Coroner. 1104 North Mission Road, Los Angeles, at about—I have it in the file. It was sometime in the early afternoon.

Q. Did you bring the original record with you?

A. Yes, I did.

Q. You may open your envelope. Directing your attention to People's 3 for identification, copies of autopsy, and 25 color photographs marked People's 1-A through Y, are those the notes and photographs of the body and portions of the deceased upon which you performed the autopsy on May 25th?

A. Yes, they are.

Q. Now, could you tell us, please, what you initially observed in performing the specific autopsy in question here.

A. There was an incision in the throat made by a very sharp instrument on the order of a razor blade or scalpel, judging by the wound edges, which cut the . . . partially cut the carotid arteries and the jugular vein; cut the windpipe and the esophagus; and cut into the right side of the fourth cervical vertebra. That's one of the vertebrae in the neck. This would be the cause of death.

There were puncture wounds . . . one puncture wound in the space in front of the left elbow going into the vein, which indicates a hypodermic injection of some sort into the vein. There were two hypodermic wounds in the upper outer quadrant of the right buttock.

There was an incision approximately five inches in length in the abdomen, extending from the navel to a little better than half-way toward the pubis.

On continuing with the autopsy, it was demonstrable that this was, in effect, a classical type Caesarean section: that we had a pregnant womb remaining without an infant or an afterbirth. A relatively firm, but not completely contracted womb. Oh . . . and the decedent's mouth was taped shut.

Q. Judging from the womb, do you have any opinion, Doctor, as to whether or not there was or could recently have been a baby in that?

A. Yes, there must have been a baby in that recently.

Q. Now, was there any bleeding around this classical Caesarean, as you called it?

A. There was hemorrhaging around the classical Caesarean . . . not as much bleeding as I would anticipate from prior experience with C sections, but some bleeding. The minimal bleeding is suggestive that perhaps the "operative" incision had been made after the throat had been cut and the blood pressure had gone down.

Q. Do you have any opinion, Doctor, as to the strength that it might take to produce that wound in the neck? Is that something that requires strength, or merely sharpness of an instrument?

A. Both. A sharp instrument would go through the soft tissue rather well, but neither a razor nor a scalpel nor any conceivable sharp instrument would cut into bone without considerable force.

Q. And you found . . . was it the fourth vertebra that was cut into? Is that right?

A. Yes, on the right side to a depth of about an eighth of an inch.

Q. Now, you, I take it, ascribe the cause of death to the neck wound: is that correct?

A. Yes.

Q. Do you have any opinion as to the quality, if we can call it that . . . the quality of that Caesarean?

A. Well, criticized from a professional point of view, the incision was a little too short. There's no point doing surgery by handicapping yourself to begin with, with an incision which is less than optimum. But, it was adequate enough, and it was an incision such as . . . one must have had some conception of how to extract a baby in a C section. You just can't reach into that size incision and grab an arm or a head. You have to grab the feet to do a breech extraction. Otherwise, you are not going to get the baby out.

Q. Does it appear that the same instrument or type of instrument caused both the Caesarean and the neck wound?

A. The same type, yes.

Q. Did you make any tests to determine the time of death?

A. Yes. We have several tests which help us to some extent in determining the time of death. May I refer to my notes?

A. Yes. The Coroner's investigator who was at the scene at 25 minutes after 12:00 noon on May 25, which is the date of the autopsy, found a liver temperature of 71 degrees Fahrenheit was present, and that there was a four plus rigidity due to rigor mortis in all musculature. He was unable at that time to determine the presence or absence of lividity because the body was clothed, and that clothing was evidence, and we don't tamper with evidence. I determined it later.

Q. Well, based upon the fact that the liver temperature was, you said, 71 degrees at that time, at 12:00 noon. . .

A. Well, let's base it first on the rigor mortis. It would become four plus about nine to twelve hours after death.

The liver temperature concurs with that insofar as it is . . . wait, I misread this. I better correct the record.

The liver temperature was 85 degrees. It was the environmental temperature that was 71 degrees.

The liver temperature will drop on the average of about one degree for the first five hours. That brings it down from 99 to 94. During the next period of time the liver temperature is dropping at about a degree and a half to two degrees. To go from 94 to 85, which is nine degrees, will also take about five hours.

So, both the rigor mortis and the liver temperature put death at, very approximately, within the limits of the tests: at 10 to 12 hours, possibly two to three hours more.

Q. Would you say it was then 12 hours . . . give or take two hours?

A. Oh, yes, or more. We are in the ballpark with 12 hours, and we can slide that up to—depending on other corroborative evidence—up to 18. We can't move it down too far.

Q. Well, it's between 12 and 18 hours? Ballpark?

A. Something like that.

THE COURT: What date was that, please?

THE WITNESS: That was on the 25th of . . .

THE COURT: What date would be the date of death?

THE WITNESS: That's a good question, your Honor. It would be either the 24th or the 25th.

Q. Is there anything else in your report that you feel may have some bearing on the cause of death in this case?

A. I noticed the presence of the adhesive plaster over the face. It was professional type plaster. It had been torn off a larger bolt.

There were the two recent puncture wounds in the right buttock which I mentioned; which may suggest some other premedication . . . or it may not. I have no strong opinion as to what they might represent.

Umm, there wasn't any indication of any blunt force injury. The decedent had not been beaten.

We had no indication of petechiae, which usually will imply suffocation.

We had very little blood sucked down into the lungs and no pulmonary edema, which suggests the death occurred very rapidly: plus the indication that it would occur very rapidly such as when a large artery—in this case the carotid—had been cut.

And . . . oh, yes, we specifically looked in the mouth for possible medication, and found none.

That's about all. I did make a note of the contents of the stomach. There was some digested food; the only thing I could identify with any certainty were large bites of meat. The stomach contents suggest a period of maybe two to three hours after eating as a possible time of death—but that is a very inaccurate estimate.

MR. DURBIN: At this time, your Honor, I would like to move People's 3 and People's 1-A through Y, collectively, into evidence.

MR. WINGATE: No objections, you Honor.

MR. DURBIN: I have no further questions.

THE COURT: You may cross examine.

MR. WINGATE: Thank you, you Honor.

The subsequent cross-examination of Dr. Forrester by defense lawyers, Leonard Wingate and Roland Stokes, although repetitious, is skillful. It elicits some low-keyed emphasis on minor discrepancies by District Attorney Ralph Durbin in slight favor of their client. But damaging evidence remains unimpaired: 1) the conspicuous lack of any signs of coercion; 2) the certain injections of sedatives and anesthesia, possibly hours before death; 3) the taping of the mouth with hospital adhesive; 4) and, most damaging of all . . . the baby issue.

This grim excerpt from the preliminary trial of Rosalind Delgato's murderer reveals a crime sensationalized across the country. Nothing about the case is usual. No fiction can equal the gruesome horrors of the truth. Rosalind, her mangled body and its parts, studied and packed away in formaldehyde, are the end result of the murderer's wayward life style and insatiable needs. The bloody slaughter described in court reflects the final scream of a willful, anguished struggle for love. A struggle that began forty years earlier.

CHAPTER 3

Tuesday, April 17, 1934.

Spring was welcomed early that depression year in Uniontown. Melting snows had washed the hillsides clean and the maintenance crew was busy sweeping slush from the low places. The town boasted scores of sturdy three-story houses, most painted white with blue trim, and all looking remarkably clean for this gray, coal-etched area of Pennsylvania.

"Pride," the town council preached. And, since yearly house painting was a prideful chore the miners vied with one another to get theirs done first. Spring sales of paint to the men were second only to soap and scrub brushes for the wives. Now was the time for "spring cleaning."

On steep Idaho Street one house always sparkled more than any other, inside and out. Some townswomen thought the Mayer home was too clean, not "normal." They often felt sorry for the three Mayer children who looked painfully starched and proper, even dressed in made-over rummage or thrift garments. Neighbors disapproved when the three girls were punished for staining their A-line skirts, or muddying their Buster Browns, or even for running their lisle stockings. But the criticisms didn't extend to the Mayer house, itself. There was a furtive group pride in the attractive, immaculate house and grounds.

Nevertheless, the local tongue-waggers voiced their jealousies. Who did those Mayers think they were? Lording it over the rest of them with the biggest and fanciest home on the street.

Especially that hypocrite, Elsie Mayer, who drove around town, even a measly few blocks, in her shiny '29 Buick. And her grand piano. Why, she played it loud enough to be heard down at Barton's on Main Street. Humph! Everyone knew how poor she really was: that the Buick and piano were gifts from her folks; that she hand-made her own, stylish clothes and most of her family's too; and that she had to take in sewing to pay overdue bills.

And dashing Conrad Mayer, her "fancy dan" musician husband who never worked the mines because he just might get dirty: he was considered weak to say the least. Flitting from one job to another—most of them prestigious sounding but paying little. He was always chasing off to dance and act in vaudeville or to join the "Big Bands" in New York or Boston.

As much for spite to annoy Elsie as for pride, when Conrad was home he brought four-year-old Anna Louise along to bars and and the Odd-Ball poolhall where he'd set her up on a table and sing duets with her. He was proud of the way she could belt out a tune on key, with mischievous body language taught by him when she was barely three-years-old. She knew the hit song of the year and would croon "Blue Moon" over and over while patrons cheered.

A few more observant neighbors did observe that Conrad alternately neglected and smothered his wife. They noticed when Elsie gradually plunged into church and the revitalized W.C.T.U. activities to the exclusion of "sinful" town fairs and dances and movie attractions. But only her minister knew about Elsie's obsessive preoccupation with the sins of sex. Except Conrad. And he just laughed at her insistence for separate bedrooms.

Despite deepening frictions during the years of marriage and children the family did enjoy, many times, a warm evening of closeness. There were fun-filled hours of music right in their own home. Everyone had one or more musical talents. Together they harmonized beautifully, presenting to mere acquaintances a loving group.

Elsie was proud of her daughters. Give her that much thought her neighbors. Just as her mother had done with her, she concentrated on molding her girls into spotless, God-fearing angels. Besides church affiliations and music recitals, she arranged for each to join Rainbow Girls, a prerequisite for becoming prestigious Eastern Star members like their mother and grandmother. It was only Anna Louise who frustrated Elsie: the overactive, unpredictable daughter who was the spitting image of Conrad, certainly not a trait to be proud of in her opinion.

So much of life was now sinful to Elsie that she began to dread the family gatherings which would be followed by conjugal duties. Conrad was her real problem, thought Elsie. All the time penetrating her as if she were just his personal property with no inherent rights. His advances were persistent and often ponderous. She hated herself for the lust he aroused in her until she would cry out and cling to him. Usually, at the height of her response, with no endearing words or caresses, he would simply fall asleep.

It was easy for Elsie to avoid most "sinful" temptations. She kept up a frantic pace of cleaning, baking, and sewing. Her prized possession of the treadle Singer sewing machine contributed greatly to her need to work and her need for money. Her sewing was artistic and meticulous so she had no trouble in attracting choice accounts, even from outlying farm districts. Hard work soothed her. When she wasn't sewing or cooking she was cleaning something. But she could see no way to scrub clean the sin of constant coition.

Elsie's parents, socially prominent church activists in New York state had often chided her about having to sew for pay. "It's so—well, so common." Both of them were unhappy about her choice of a husband. On every rare visit to "dingy" Uniontown her mother would inspect, pry, scold, and belittle Conrad.

"Why couldn't you have married Dr. Dallriver? So what if he was older and not so handsome as Conrad. He really loved you. Do you realize how important he is as Chief of Staff at the hospital? His wife spends all her time at social events or sponsoring charity fairs. You may as well face it, dear. Your Conrad simply doesn't have it in him to amount to a hill of beans. All he can do is get you pregnant and then run off, God knows where."

Elsie paid little attention to her parents' criticisms. It was important to her that the money she earned as a seamstress kept her family financially stable. She didn't need affluence to feel pride. And pride was her powerful substitute for marital disappointments. Hard work came naturally. She chose to scrub her home inside and out with energy enough to wash away its very character. At least a spotless home could not evoke her parents' scorn.

Another spring. So Elsie gathered her buckets and brooms. The April day was balmy and inviting. It was a time for cleaning, gardening, cooking, and greeting one's neighbors. The warmth of the sun added zest to sounds of friendliness.

"Weeds gonna be high this year," a voice floated on a sun ray. And from across the way, "How's Jerry's hernia . . . he gonna be able to plant your garden?" Or, "Hey, Polly, come on over for sweet rolls. Just pulled 'em out of the oven." And from the corner, "Wait a minute, Eb, this letter's not for me. Belongs to Kemper—next block."

Elsie Mayer, with her ample midriff, neat brown hair piled high on her head, and straight back so forbidding to some— ignored the bustling and idle chatter all around her. However, she, too, opened up her house, scrubbed and sterile, to the promise of mild weather.

Gentle, warm breezes drifted through the Mayer screen door and into the large, sunny kitchen which comprised fully one-third of the ground floor. This focal room was brightened by two, long, corner windows with scores of small panes framed in true Pennsylvania Dutch style. Elsie inspected the windows and decided they needed washing again. She sighed, wishing her short, pregnant body didn't feel so heavy today.

With breakfast over, the two older girls off to school, Anna Louise playing in the backyard, and Conrad packing for another trip, Elsie planned her day to begin with outside cleaning chores. The mid-morning sun should have been soothing with its warmth. But, remembrance of Conrad's conquest over her last night grated at her nerves. Repeatedly she guided an old straw broom back and forth across the lye-bleached, wooden floor of her front porch. She imagined herself sweeping away at her husband's sins.

Looking spit-polish clean and smelling of after-shave lotion, Conrad bumped his way through the screen door toward her. Carrying two instrument cases and a bulging suitcase, he followed the busy broom around the porch as he tried to say his goodbyes.

"Guess I'd better catch the next bus to the depot. Only an hour before the train leaves for Boston, where I'm going to join the Dorsey brothers."

Elsie didn't look up. He tried again. "Listen, honey, I think I might be picked to play with the 'Clambake Seven' this trip. Wouldn't that be great?" He smiled wickedly and asked, "You gonna keep your fingers crossed for me?"

Elsie scoffed and hardly looked up. "Don't ask me to be any part of your schemes to go chasing around all over the country with a bunch of ne'er-do-wells. You never have and you never will make anything of yourself by working for people who spend their time playing in dance halls. You know how I feel about that."

"Jesus Christ, woman, there you go again. Why can't you, just for once, say something nice. Like 'good luck,' or 'have a nice trip?' Would that be so hard? My God, it's not like I'm asking you to wrap your arms around me and kiss me, or say, 'I'll miss you, darling.' Hell, I gave up on that a long time ago. It would be nice, though, if you could show even a little interest in my work."

"Your work? You said work? Ha! That's a strange word coming from you. If you want to know what work means, try staying home and taking care of three kids while you're pregnant with another. Yes, and sewing for a bunch of old biddies in town to make a living for your family. And, all because the person you married keeps running off with Tommy or Jimmy, or whomever. You know the Dorseys fight so much that they'll never be a success." She swept furiously as she ranted on.

"It's always the same . . . you leave me with promises and you come back with more promises. But . . . I can keep my opinions of your promises to myself." She glanced up at him. "Why don't you just go? You got what you came home for last night, didn't you?"

"Oh, for Christ's sake, Elsie, why do you have to ruin even

that? Dammit! Do I have to leave feeling guilty about that too?" He tried to grab her around the waist to stop her sweeping.

She pulled away saying, "Just go. Leave me alone. I have work to do."

Conrad and all three cases took the porch steps two at a time and sprinted toward the bottom of the hill. Elsie stood staring after him for a moment then hurried to the railing and haltingly called out to him, "Conrad, wait . . . oh, Conrad." But the cry was lost in the space between them. She looked around to see if any neighbors had been within earshot, and sighed with relief to find no one.

Subdued for a moment, she swept her way slowly off the porch and with continuous motion followed the sidewalk around the house to the back yard. The sight of her youngest child playing "tea party" in the wet dirt of her newly planted flower garden, brought an abrupt halt to her contrite thoughts about Conrad.

"Anna Louise, come here this instant. Whatever are you doing . . . oh, no, not my good china? Look at it! Covered with mud— and you too." Anna started whimpering. "None of that," snapped Elsie. "You've been told, over and over, you're never to play with my things. Why can't you do as you're told? Into the house this minute, young lady. I'd better not find even one chip in my china!"

"I only wanted to make some mud pies, Mama. I was careful. Don't spank. I didn't break any. Okay, Mama?"

Elsie's cheeks were flushed as she flung the broom against the back porch and continued scolding. "Go get cleaned up and don't make a mess in the bathroom. Lord, Lord! You're always pulling stunts like this. Why? A constant worry just like your Papa. I *never* had trouble like this with your sisters. You and your Papa'll be the death of me yet!" Elsie began snatching the pans and dishes from the bountiful supply of "mud dough" before the sun could bake it like glue.

"I sorry, Mama. I sorry."

"Go on! In the house. Take your shoes off on the porch and when you're cleaned up go straight to your room and stay there until I tell you to come out. Do you understand me? You're lucky I don't take a switch to you."

Anna retreated safely behind the screen door before turning to wrinkle up her face and stick her tongue out. When she spied her mother's white sweater hanging by the door she wiped both muddy hands on its inner folds.

Elsie finished sweeping the back porch and rinsed off her mud-caked shoes before entering the house. She immediately scrubbed her hands, dried with a clean towel, and turned to her baking. A battle with morning nausea didn't phase her. In fact, she knew fasting could be helpful because of how much harder it was to keep her weight down with this one.

By noon steady spring breezes through the kitchen caught and swirled the scent of freshly baked spice cookies. The sweet, pungent aroma masked the usual, irritating odor of soot. Coal dust always mingled with fresh air in this urban center of Pennsylvania where high-sulfur coal was a major asset and, a major pollutant. Soot permeated all dwellings, even into the minute cracks in window and door caulking. It to ok a lot of baking to make the air smell sweet.

Elsie rolled out more dough as worrisome thoughts created heartaches she dared not voice. The cookie cutter bit deep into her breadboard and made her grimace. Her thoughts singed her. Pregnant again! How could he? Sinful. That's what it was. And she vowed that she would never sleep with him again.

A low moan caught in her throat as she slammed two cookie sheets into the oven and checked the temperature gauge.

A few minutes later the unmistakable message of something sweet and warm, just waiting to be tasted, found its way throughout the big house. The delicious aroma wafted down the hallway, up two flights of stairs, through a garret doorway and on into the tidy bedroom of the napping four-year old. There the breezes were trapped; circling and dipping and pushing their sweet message again and again at the sleeping child.

Anna Louise, awakened by the tantalizing odor sat up so

abruptly that her baby doll rolled off the bed, protesting, "Ma—ma, Ma—ma." Rubbing her eyes with a great effort to make them stay open, Anna jumped down, swooped up her cherished doll and tenderly placed it back on the bed. She gave it a quick kiss and patted it into the pillow. Only after the covers were tucked around her "baby" did she turn her attention to that oh-so-sweet aroma. "Cookies!" she squealed.

She dashed barefooted down the gold-carpeted stairs, and plummeted into the kitchen. Mama's made cookies for me, was her childish certainty.

There was her mother standing tiptoe at the big, green and white porcelain stove, placing a pan of golden-brown cookies on top of the side oven. She had to really stretch to be sure the pan slid far enough back on the shelf to keep from falling. The tail of her apron rested on the stove's knobby handles that jutted up from a gas pipe running in front of the burners. She pressed her apron back in place and checked the second sheet of cookies. They needed a few minutes more.

Anna skipped about in circles and tried to squeeze her mother's leg in loving greeting. She cried out in joyous anticipation of eating one or more of her favorite sweets— spice cookies.

"Gimmie a cookie, Mama." The little round face beamed up at Elsie; and the pretty green eyes laughed as she danced around her mother's legs.

"Stop that!" cried Elsie. And neither the thin line of her lips nor the appraising coolness of her glance offered affection to her child. She pushed Anna back against the china cabinet. "No, Anna Louise, no!" she scolded. "Of course you can't have one now. They're still too hot. Besides, you'll have to wait until supper."

Anna sniffed—and Elsie turned back to her, explaining in a softer tone, "The cookies are our special treat for tonight—for our music hour. You wouldn't want to spoil that would you?" She laid a hand on Anna's head, but clutched it back to her bosom as if to retract her impulsive gesture of affection.

Anna pouted. Her young mind couldn't understand her

mother sometimes. The cookies smelled so good! Why couldn't she have just one? She watched Elsie walk carefully over to the sink across the slippery, waxed linoleum to busy herself with cleaning a pile of dirty dishes on the sideboard. Anna didn't see the faintest glimmer of a tear in the corner of each eye. She knew only that there were fresh cookies just waiting for her to bite into and enjoy.

Elsie had forgotten her troublesome child for the moment. She lifted her apron to her forehead, mopping at beads of sweat as they rolled out from under her soft brown bangs. A surreptitious movement with the apron also wiped away her tears. As if to conserve energy, or to hide her tears, she swatted at a pesky fly with the apron's folds before she concentrated again on the dishes.

Anna stood close to the stove and sneaked a peek at her mother's unyielding back. Her childish confidence overcame the fear of the heavy-handed strap which was used more on Anna's bottom than her sisters'. She thought she could climb up the stove with all its shiny, white, knobby footholds, grab the biggest cookie, and be back upstairs with her baby doll while her mother still had her back turned.

She pulled a kitchen stool, ever so quietly, into position in front of the stove. It was easy to climb up as far as the gas grill, but she still could not reach even a corner of the pan with the cookies. Glancing over her shoulder she made sure her mother was still busy at the sink. She put one bare foot on the long, porcelain handle of the broiler door in order to raise herself a little bit higher; just high enough for her small fingers to close around her prize. With a determined effort she lunged upward.

All of a sudden, as her finger tips touched the edge of the coveted cookie pan, the heavy door flew open under her weight. With a terrible clamoring noise Anna, the stool, and the flat tin of goodies crashed into chaos around the stove. Cookies slid all over Elsie's gleaming, spotless linoleum.

Anna yelled more in fright than in pain even though she had burned her hand. She reached out for her mother.

"Anna Louise!" Elsie screamed. "Look what you've done!" She half struck her child and pushed her out of the way as she flung herself on both knees beside the overturned cookie sheet. She righted it and quickly scrutinized each cookie which appeared undamaged, peering at it front and back before placing it precisely back on the pan. A few she wiped carefully across the bib of her apron to rid them of some real or imagined contamination. The crumbs she swept into a dustpan.

Tears were sliding down Anna's reddened cheeks, caught by trembling fists, yet seeping through, anyway, to dampen her middy. She sniffed noisily in an effort to keep the persistent dribble from reaching her lips. But the tears wouldn't stop. She couldn't breathe right, and her throat was aching with stifled sobs.

"Shut up!" cried Elsie. "Will you just shut up and get out of my sight?" She got up, spun around toward her smoking oven, and slammed the second pan of cookies—now burned—on the sideboard. All of her pent-up anger and self-pity exploded into words.

"Oh, why must I always have trouble with you? God knows I never wanted you in the first place. It's all your papa's fault —him and sex," she hissed, pausing in her tirade to wash her hands again. "Now look what a mess you've made."

Words tumbled over themselves, sometimes making sense, but mostly rambling and skipping erratically so that the youngster couldn't follow them. One phrase swelled the lump in her throat . . . "I never wanted you." Anna burst out crying, sobs shaking her body.

"Mama, hand hurts. It burns." She wrapped her arms around Elsie's knees and looked up. "See? It got burned. Kissit, Mama."

"You're a bad girl. A bad, bad girl. Now go to your room— right now! And stay there."

"But Mama, Mama, it hurts." Still her mother ranted on, oblivious to her child's needs.

"No indeed. No cookies for you. Such a bad girl. Why you had to be mine I'll never understand."

Anna became still; her cries subdued into whimpers. She stared at her mother and reached out for her once more. "Mama? Don't you want me, Mama?" she asked slowly. "I'll be good— you'll see. Please, Mama, I promise I'll be good. Please, Mama." Her mother's words screamed in her brain, "*I never wanted you . . . I never wanted you.*"

The warm kitchen turned icy cold. The spring day darkened. The air smelled sooty again. Elsie's stiff body leaned against the sink. She kept her back toward Anna while she washed her hands and glared, sightless, out the kitchen window.

Anna's tiny body sagged as she tried to hold in wracking sobs. She half walked, half ran back upstairs to her room. Back to her "baby." Back to her make-believe cocoon of loving thoughts. With all the strength of her young arms she slammed the door behind her. "Shut up!" she mimicked.

She grabbed her baby doll and cradled it against her chest and cried aloud, "I love you, love you, love you."

And suddenly, in that spacious, comfortable home full of potential . . . suddenly Anna Louise felt the numbing chill of an absence of love.

CHAPTER 4

Monday, September 9, 1935.

Opening day of school. Anna wiggled and pranced and bubbled. Starting first grade meant starched, hand-embroidered skirts and long stockings fastened with garters attached to her best underwear. It meant sack lunches with goodies made and packed by her mother; staying at school all day; and making new friends.

"Quit squirming," sighed Elsie. Lord, child, look at you. You're going to need breast binders before sixth grade." She smoothed the new blouse into flat, impersonal planes and made sure it was tucked loosely into Anna's skirt.

Anna Louise twisted to see herself in the long mirror. "Whatcha mean, 'breast binder'?" She stuck out her little chest which already had two, well-rounded nubbins visible under her blouse.

"Will you be still," snapped Elsie as she pulled her daughter around to face her. "And don't say 'breast' in school. That's a very private part. Humph. A part that's growing much too fast on you. So, we'll just have to keep it cinched in until you're of age. I declare, *I* never needed binders. Never even had to wear a brassiere until long after puberty."

"What's poob . . ."

"Quiet. Just get your sweater and go to school with Karen. Mind you don't soil your clothes. And come right home with your sisters, hear?"

Anna soon discovered she was a quick learner. She liked reading about Spot. He looked like her pal, Romer, who sort of lived three houses up the street. She could have written a whole, first grade primer on her pal; a much more exciting story than "See Spot Run."

Anna had discovered him last year, panting and sad-eyed, lying under a rhododendron bush in their front yard. His paw was raw with one nail torn off. Anna dragged out her mother's first aid kit and spread gauze and tape in the dirt beside him. He let her smear Mercurochrome over his foot without one whimper. Her bandaging used up most of the gauze and dirtied the adhesive tape. But, she was proud of the results, and delighted at playing nurse. For about a year Romer was Anna's best friend and confidant. He took the place of the pet she was never allowed to own.

Learning to read and write was fun. Reading Elsie's list of rules posted in the kitchen was not fun. Every other line referred to cleanliness in some way. If Anna stood on tiptoe she could read the last four lines of the list, one of which said, "Always Keep Clean in School."

Even when she stayed late to clear off the blackboards she tried to keep clean to avoid her mother's wrath. When the clapping of erasers inevitably got chalk on her sweaters she carefully shook off the dust and cleaned her hands before starting home.

Her enthusiasm did not emulate her sisters' outlook toward schooling. If Karen had to wait more than ten minutes for Anna it made her cross. Ultimately Karen and eleven-year-old Florence would skip home as soon as the 3 o'clock bell rang, leaving little sister to fend for herself. Their mother would have warm sweet rolls ready for her girls while she helped them concentrate on their homework. A constant conflict for Elsie was anger at her third daughter's defiant disobedience, versus pride in her sparkling academic accomplishments.

Whenever Anna Louise bounced in hours late, usually breathless and full of stories, her sisters paid little attention. If she sneaked a roll right before supper Elsie scolded. When she dumped her homework and books on the dining room table her mother would scoop it all up and pile it on a bench in the foyer saying, "Take your books upstairs . . . how many times do I have to tell you?"

If Conrad was home Anna would wave her A+ homework at him and perch on his lap to tug at his red moustache. Gently. The curled and stiffened ends were his pampered trademark. He liked to believe his high cheekbones were handsomely framed by the moustache and his huge halo of red hair.

"Come on, kid," he'd laugh. "Let's you and me show 'em what for." And they would harmonize a duet of popular songs such as "Lullaby of Broadway." Every now and then a bawdy ballad screeched into the kitchen where Elsie and Florence would be preparing the evening meal.

"Conrad!" she'd call. "Stop that this instant and take your place at the table."

"Ya, ya, liebchen," he might answer. "Right away, my darling." And he'd wink at Anna Louise. Sometimes he'd swing through the kitchen and pinch Elsie's bottom.

"Stop that," she'd say, "or you'll be sleeping alone tonight."

After supper Elsie would follow her husband's lead and accompany him skillfully on her piano as he played a variety of wind instruments. All the girls could sing in a wide range with true pitch. Elsie would even catch herself having fun unless she thought about bedtime. Separate bedrooms did not always deter Conrad. So she would prolong the evening with ponderous hymns until one by one the sisters went to bed, and Conrad dozed in his easy chair.

During the lean '30s while Anna Louise was mastering the three Rs, Conrad tried several jobs around town, staying the longest at Anchor-Hocking. But his steadiest and most enjoyable job was the yearly, holiday tutoring of the various choirs at Uniontown's protestant churches. Occasionally he traveled as far out as Chalkhill and Farmington for special concerts. During slack months he spent many an evening entertaining with transient groups performing at Mt. Washington Tavern east of town, but tips and drinks were his only pay.

His favorite but infrequent work was playing with Ray Noble's band during the time when a young fellow named Glenn Miller was conceiving his characteristic sound of a clarinet over four saxophones. Conrad could play almost any position in the jazz or swing bands. When invited he would drop everything and hop a bus to Pittsburgh for a Big Band booking in Heinz Hall. At those times he wore new, tailored suits appropriate for whichever band he joined. Often his wardrobe looked expensive, and his elegant appearance attracted many an affluent coquette in Pittsburgh.

His pals kidded him about one "grande dame" he would always visit in nearby Sewickley. Her Victorian home on the banks of the Ohio River was murky and cold . . . but she was voluptuous and warm and giving. Occasionally, when he stayed behind too long the band moved on without him. But, when his pay was gone, Conrad would kiss his paramour's finger tips as gallantly as a Renaissance cavalier, and return to the stability of his family.

On "special" evenings in Uniontown Anna would run down the hill to keep pace with the long stride of her father and march into the Odd-Ball Pool Hall shouting with him, "Onward Christian Soldiers." Once inside the smokey building Anna heard and memorized such bawdy songs as "Roll Me Over in the Clover," "Them There Eyes," "Clap Hands! Here Comes Charley!" and her favorite bouncy 'Vo-do-de-o' tune, "Crazy Words—Crazy Tune." One night she blew into her home swinging her little hips and singing,

"If the ocean were whisky an' I was a duck,

"I'd dive to the bottom an' NEVER come up!"

For that exhibition she had her mouth washed out with yellow soap.

A traumatic incident occurred just before Christmas that first year at school. Anna rushed into her mother's austere living room where the church music committee was having its pre-holiday meeting. Her face was wet with tears, her hair flying out from under her crocheted hat, and her overshoes tracking in gray slush.

"Mama, Mama, come quick!" she shrieked. "There's two dogs stuck together across the street at Helga's house—right near her front door." Her gestures were frantic. She tugged at her mother's crisp white blouse. "You gotta come. They're makin' an awful fuss, an' everything. I know they're hurtin' real bad. Mama, please come help!"

Elsie moved quickly to closet them both in the pantry away from the gasping women. Her look seared Anna. She spoke low into her daughter's ear; with her grasp squeezing her child's shoulders until her fingers whitened.

"How dare you embarrass me like that? Dear God, can you *really* be my child?" She choked. "Anna Louise, you are never again to mention what you saw at Helga's, you hear me?"

"But why, Mama? I didn't make it up. Honest! They're really stuck, an' everything."

"Hush. You listen good, young lady. What you saw had something to do with sex; and how many times have I told you nice people don't talk about such things?

"Go on and get cleaned up. Back stairs, mind you, and not one word to Karen. You hear me?" She opened the pantry door.

Anna ran upstairs as fast as her sturdy legs could move. New tears dried on her lips with a caustic sting. Between sobs she promptly told Karen everything.

"Don'tcha know?" chided her worldly eight-year-old sister. "It's the boy dog sticking his thing into the back of the girl dog. It's how they make puppies, silly."

Anna's eyes widened as she thought about sex really being as terrible as her mother had always taught her. Karen's immature lesson impressed her with its importance. But, why hadn't her mother been able to explain about the dogs? Why couldn't her mother ever really talk to her?

On Easter break she was sent to stay with her Aunt Emily and Uncle Dooley in Casselman. She often visited them, delighting in watching the rural craftsmen who were adept at coopering and applebutter making. The air was clear and sweet- smelling in the mountain valleys. Her aunt and uncle, barren for all of their marriage, always welcomed Anna Louise as if she were their own, longed-for daughter. She ran to them from the bus.

Dooley wrapped his long, skinny arms around her and pivoted until she yelled for him to stop. They all laughed and hugged each other. They were so tall! Anna stretched until her flour-sack bloomers were showing. Dooley's eyes sparkled and he swept her up in his arms again.

Anna loved her father's relatives, but, maybe more, she loved her freedom during the long bus ride from her ho me to Somerset where they met her. It was almost like runnung away.

At night she was used to wriggling in between Dooley and Emily where she felt warm and loved. She had always slept with them in the large, specially crafted bed. This time her first night with them was different. Uncle Dooley was sweating and she heard him groan twice. Sometime during the night she woke up feeling her uncle's hand stroking her. When he saw she was awake he pulled her hand into the opening in his pajama bottoms. "Here," he whispered. "Touch it. Come on—I'll show you." He kept placing her small hand around his penis.

But Anna rebelled at touching the hard pulsating thing. She pulled away and tried to put her arms under her body—and she was afraid. She knew she must be committing a sin.

Uncle Dooley persisted in running his hand up and down her stiff body until his fingers settled in one spot, moving and pressing her smooth vulva. All of a sudden he jammed a finger into her tight vagina.

"Stoppit!" she shrieked.

Suddenly the room was bright, as if lightning had struck and frozen there to illuminate her shame. Instantly Emily threw back the covers and stood there glaring at them. Anna sat up, tugged at the hem of her nightgown and began to cry.

Not one word was uttered. Emily pushed her niece to the edge of the bed and settled herself in the middle. There were strident whispers, staccato exchanges that Anna didn't understand. She lay there all night, chilled and frightened.

What did I do now? Will Mama be mad at me again? Why did Uncle Dooley have to do that?

They took her home the next day. Driving for three hours in a borrowed truck which smelled like chickens. Anna was sick twice along the roadway.

She was hurried up to her room by Florence who kept scowling at her and asking her what she had done to be brought back home so soon. The faint, whispered words from downstairs, "couldn't help himself," and "precocious brat" frightened her further.

She never saw her Aunt Emily or Uncle Dooley again and to her surprise no one ever mentioned that trip to her.

By June, near the end of the school term, Anna had become notorious for her wild antics. One day before recess, when the teacher caught her shinning up a pole in the classroom, a hard knock from a ruler brought her down with a crash. An inkwell broke on one of the student desks, splattering herself, the teacher, and several classmates. All but the teacher were favorably impressed with Anna, and, they told of her brashness around school.

Her neighbor, Lela, a buxom, loud teenager prone to lipstick and rouge when no adults were nearby took a shine to the precocious six-year-old. She started hugging Anna at every meeting. The delighted child responded with hugs and kisses of gratitude for the affection from the older girl.

Lela and her friends bragged to the youngster about secret delights that were absolutely taboo for adults to know about. "Your folks will kill you if you tell them," they said. Finally one day after school they invited little Anna to join their games. She was overjoyed.

"I'm comin', Lela." She grabbed her friend's hand. "Where are we goin'?"

"To that old, deserted garage beyond the schoolhouse. We're going to show you some fun." Lela smiled at her girlfriends and they all giggled as they ran through the yard. She locked them in with a rusty skeleton key which she carefully re-wrapped and pushed deep into her pocket.

"Okay, now, we're going to play our very secret game."

"What'll I do?"

The older girls continued to giggle as they pulled up their skirts and took off their bloomers and lay down on various tattered blankets brought there ages ago by others bent on their own secret games. Lela pushed Anna down on her knees. "Okay, gooney, here's what you do. You got to kiss each one of our privates before we let you out."

"No, Lela, no," whimpered Anna. She was frightened like that night with her Uncle Dooley.

"Do it! Do like I say or we'll never let you out and you'll starve to death with maggots eating your skin—and you'll rot in hell."

The next hour Anna was pushed and pinched and threatened. The taunting laughter infuriated her and she tried to hit Lela with a board. But, the older girl trounced her good and only laughed louder. Ultimately she was forced to do what they demanded. She thought she must surely be struck dead. Never could she tell anyone how sinful she was.

That night she ran away from home, at least for five blocks and for two hours before her father found her.

Conrad went away again, playing reed with the "King of Swing." He sent home presents and what little money he could, while Elsie was still sewing the latest fashions for her customers as well as looking after the new sister. But, without her father's affection and protection Anna felt alone and angry.

"Shush," she whispered to her baby doll, "We'll go far away some day."

She was being called "incorrigible" by the time the second grade began. She often took money from the bottom drawer of the Singer—Mama's secret place—to go to the new movie house. She saw Bette Davis in "Dangerous" four times, before Elsie realized her secret stash was being tapped. By the time "Mutiny on the Bounty" got to Uniontown Anna had discovered how easy it was to sneak into the show without paying. It was the most thrilling movie they had ever seen, and, since all the older girls fell in love with Clark Gable, Anna idolized him too. Going to the movies became a temporary substitute for running away.

In November of her third year in school she met the new girl, Mary Vicenti. Mary's raucous home became a refuge for Anna. It was the "Happy Family's" home. Count Vicenti, a proud immigrant who kept his aristocratic title when he fled to the United States, had created an Italian paradise at the foot of Idaho Street.

He and his sons had built a large, oblong, brick oven against the wall of his property where, daily, the tempting aroma of home-made, Italian breads filled the neighborhood. Through the middle of his garden was a latticed archway, about ten feet long, for hanging and drying peppers, herbs, garlic, and exotic foods not known in the region.

They were musicians, carpenters, cooks, and fierce workers in the coal mines: a happy group always. They welcomed Anna as one of their own. She sat at their long, hand-hewn table and shared wonderful cheeses and dago wine. Most of all she loved the way they trusted her to hold and feed their baby, the 12th child in the family. Where Anna was denied closeness to her own baby sister at home, here she was handed a newborn without question. It was a haven of love and merriment, and it became her favorite hiding place.

That year, on New Year's Day, Anna was beaten by her father for the first time.

Conrad awoke in a mean mood with aching temples and blood shot eyes when sounds of screaming jarred the early morning calm. He heard Elsie run from her bedroom and dash upstairs to the large, third story room which Anna Louise and two-year-old Margaret shared. He pulled on his robe as he climbed the stairway.

Elsie was holding Margaret while Anna stood in a corner of the room. "Hush, hush," crooned Elsie. "Mama's here. It's all right now." Margaret's tears plummeted off her shiny cheeks onto the soft flannel nightgown as Elsie held her close and lovingly. She turned to her husband and her eyes narrowed.

"Just look at these marks on Margaret's forehead. You can see Anna Louise has been hitting her with something—probably the hairbrush. Now I'm telling you, Conrad, this simply can't go on any longer. You're too easy on that child! You've got to teach her a lesson! It's about time you take over some of the discipline. I just can't handle her anymore."

Anna yelled, "Papa, Papa, no Papa! I had to hit her. She took my doll and threw it in the stool. She did it on purpose, and then she *laughed* at me." Anna stamped her feet in a fit of anger and struck out at a bedpost with her hairbrush.

Conrad growled, swooped her up, and carried her down to the basement. He unclamped the washer drainhose as he held her against him.

"Don't, Papa, please, I'll be good," sobbed Anna.

"Shut up, you've had this coming for a long time."

"No, Papa!" But Conrad methodically beat her back and legs until there was blood showing through her nightgown. His anger softened when he saw this and noticed she was no longer crying. He sat her upright on his knee and tried to kiss her cheek.

"No," she said, and slowly limped back upstairs to take care of her doll.

Later at church, while she sat on the pillow Elsie had brought from home, Anna sniffed and bumped her feet against the pew in front. When she didn't heed her mother's admonitions Elsie tried to dig her fingernails into her daughter's thigh. But the heavy underwear and wool skirt absorbed the intended effect. The youngster continued to wiggle and pout. They sat alone in the last occupied pew toward the rear of the church, so that Anna could not pinch her baby sister.

While parishioners crowded together for the usual greetings Anna slipped away, grabbed her overcoat, and darted along Main Street. It was two miles, at least, to the Vicenti home. She watched from the alley beside Barton's Drug Store as the Buick cruised slowly by, and stepped back onto the sidewalk only when her folks were out of sight.

Her chubby legs raced, then slowed, and finally dragged before she spotted the Vicenti house. No one was at home. Of course, she thought, they haven't gotten back from mass. She perched on the rough, brick oven, tucking one foot under her while the other rhythmically chipped at the harsh surface, effectively scuffing her brand new shoe.

Her lips quivered as she kept her foot swinging in its destructive arc.

Why don't they come home? They don't love me, either. Should I run away . . . or just go back home?

Her body tired of sitting on the rough bricks. Before she left Anna grabbed a hoe and struck at the garlic and spices hanging from the archway until all were dipping and whirling in crazy patterns.

School was okay, she thought, as she slowly trudged up Idaho Street, but growing up was hard.

CHAPTER 5

Tuesday, July 9, 1974, 10 a.m.

VAN NUYS, CALIFORNIA

THE COURT: This is People vs. Anna Louise Anderson, AKA Maxwell, Case no. A-3062146M.

MR. WINGATE: Good morning, your Honor. Leonard Wingate and Roland Stokes appearing on behalf of Miss Anderson, who is present, your Honor.

MR. STOKES: Good morning, your Honor.

THE COURT: Good morning.

Miss Anderson, the Court advises you of your constitutional rights as follows:

You have the right to a speedy and public trial.

The right to a trial by a jury or, if you wish to waive that right, to a trial by a Court without a jury.

The right to be confronted by and to cross-examine all witnesses testifying against you.

The right to the compulsory process of the Court for obtaining witnesses in your favor.

The right to have the assistance of an attorney of your own choosing, for your defense at all stages of the proceedings. If you are indigent and unable to afford an attorney, the Court will appoint an attorney to represent you.

You have the right to testify in your own behalf.

However, you have the absolute right to remain silent. If you do remain silent, no inference can be drawn from that fact. You cannot be compelled to be a witness against yourself. However, if you do testify, then you will be subject to cross- examination by the People.

You have the right to be released upon reasonable bail if the circumstances so indicate.

Do you understand your constitutional rights?

THE DEFENDANT: Yes.

THE COURT: Do you have any questions in reference to your constitution rights?

THE DEFENDANT: No.

THE COURT: The Court now advises you that you are charged with the following:

That on or about the 24th day of May, 1974, at and in the County of Los Angeles, State of California, the crime of murder in violation of Section 187 of the Penal Code, a felony, was committed by Anna Louise Anderson, who, at the time and place last aforesaid, did willfully, unlawfully and feloniously and with malice aforethought murder Rosalind Delgato, a human being.

Anna raised her head abruptly.

No! That isn't true. What's he saying? That I meant to hurt Rosa? No, what . . . ? Oh, Papa, why can't it be like it was?

Her head ached. The tranquilizers fuzzed her brain. For a moment she felt as if she were a child again, on the old county road, bumping along over the ruts in the family's 1929 Buick. That long road to the farm; a dirt road which dusted the shiny green sedan into a dark, muddy gray. Clouds of the clay dust settled on the running boards as if purposefully tossed there by a shovel. As the judge continued Anna absently brushed at her dress.

It is further alleged that the murder of Rosalind Delgato was willful, deliberate and premeditated, and was personally committed by defendant during the commission and attempted commission of a kidnapping, violation of Section 207 of the Penal Code.

In the very last row Captain Freeley sat unobserved, flanked by curious spectators eager to hear the gory details of the murder. His face was stiff with suppressed emotion as he thought about the warm, affectionate victim. How often she had nagged at him about marriage. All that sensual, unselfish vibrance gone in a moment of madness. His body cried.

Are the People ready to proceed at this time?

MR. DURBIN: Yes, your Honor, the People are ready to proceed.

I would advise the Court that we have two physicians at Metro Municipal Hospital that we have on call, within a half hour's call. Other than that, we are ready to proceed.

The voices droned on. Anna stared at her father . . . or was it her father over there? That man in the black robe—the judge? And the tall, handsome man with gray sideburns, the familiar face which stared so intensely at her from the back of the room. She knew him. Dancing—that was it. Dancing with Rosa. Where?

It was so confusing. What was she doing here? All of a sudden the county road looked waxy smooth and polished; the car was bigger and made of varnished wood; the clouds of dust were gray people-faces; and she was—old? Old and alone? And with her father dead? Was he really dead?

What's wrong, Papa?

MR. DURBIN: I have a few preliminary things, your Honor. I would like to mark the evidence.

I have 25 autopsy photographs in color. May they be marked People's 1-A through Y?

THE COURT: Just a minute. People's 1-A through Y?

MR. DURBIN: Yes.

THE COURT: For identification. Those 25 photographs will be so marked.

Wait . . . 25? What 25? Of course. It's 25 miles to the farm.

Anna's eyes focused on an ornate knob atop the dividing pole between her and the jury box. It widened and circled into the steering wheel of the Buick. There were voices around her, words directed toward her, eyes shifting between her and her father. Why couldn't she just stay on the old county road? She sat immobile, mute, rejecting the cruel words, reaching for happy times . . . the farm.

John! Papa? Where is everyone? The unfamiliar voices again intruded.

MR. DURBIN: Incidentally, your Honor, since the doctor has come, I have an additional item of evidence that perhaps we should mark. It's a photocopy of his records, Dr. John Forrester's records, concerning the alleged victim, Rosalind Delgato. May that be marked People's 4?

THE COURT: It will be so marked.

MR. DURBIN: May I call my first witness, Dr. John Forrester?

THE COURT: Yes.

MR. DURBIN: People call Dr. John Forrester.

THE CLERK: Raise your right hand, please, sir.

You do solemnly swear that the testimony you are about to give in the cause now pending before this Court shall be the truth, the whole truth, and nothing but the truth, so help you God?

THE WITNESS: I do.

But he's not John! "Hey," she said, and started to rise. Her attorney held her back and cautioned her not to speak.

What was the matter here? Sweet John was young and strong and smart. Something was very wrong. That man wasn't her John. Where was he? She gazed out a window high up against the ceiling, and her mind slowly floated into the outside clouds. Clouds of dust. Peaceful clouds blotting out the bad words and strange faces. She concentrated on that outside scene and smelled the freshness of Pennsylvania farmland.

"How much further, Papa? Aren't we 'bout there?" Anna's elation heightened and she tried to spin clockwise to see out all the car windows at once.

"Well, about another ten minutes, I'd say." Conrad patted Anna's knee. Sometimes he wondered at how much he loved his contrary nine-year-old so full of mischief and energy which earned her stiff punishments. His other daughters were sedate, lady-like, so much the image of their mother. Maybe that was why he took to Anna Louise, his wayward child who might have fared better as a boy. He glanced at her reddish-blond hair, and at the curve of her mouth with the left dimple just like his own.

"Sure you want to stay *all* summer? You know Uncle Joe is gonna work your socks off." He laughed at his daughter's impatient shrug.

"You imp," he said, "you think it's all fun and games, don't you? Well, farm folks believe in hard work. I mean *hard*. Everybody works—you know that. This year you're old enough to do some sweating along with your cousins, out in the fields. Better listen to your old papa and think about it good 'cause once I start back home that's it for you until fall— after the crops are in.

"There'll be no running away, either."

"Oh, Papa, you know I wanna stay. It's all gonna be fun. An' Uncle Joe'll teach me 'bout crops, and everything. I'm big now— an' I can do anything that smarty ol' John can do."

Conrad's eyes crinkled and his dimple twitched with amusement at this cute, buxom youngster trying to pretend she didn't really admire her cousin, John, a strapping fourteen years old last winter. He suddenly remembered his own precocious youth, and grimaced. Was his little tomboy growing up too fast, too soon . . . ?

Anna settled back and leaned against her father, eagerly watching for the sharp turnoff.   .

"And, Papa," she bubbled, "I'll help Aunt Clara, too, every day if she wants. Gosh! I'll be so good they'll want me to come back every summer. I'm so happy, Papa!" She hugged him and kissed his cheek.

"Hey, easy now—save some of that energy. You're going to

wear a hole in the seat and we know what Mama'll say about that."

He tapped her shoulder and pointed to a huge white house with an even bigger barn near it. Anna had her door open and a foot on the running board before Conrad could fully stop. There it was . . . all of it, just as she had remembered for two years: white rail fence covered with roses; sweet peas twisting against the white house; chickens scattering to one side; and, of course, the huge-footed horses she loved, standing in the barnyard.

It even smelled good. Not like home where even Mama's neatly kept garden had the odor of stinging coal dust.

She ran for the big iron bell hanging all by itself in the yard, stumbling over a pile of chopped wood stacked by the kitchen door. A hard tug on the rope set the bell to clanging. Again and again it pealed, "*Anna Louise is here—she's here— she's here!*"

It woke Jake.

That old, blue tick hound came tearing out of the barn baying as if he were coon hunting. Anna squealed with delight. "Jake, it's me, come on, Jake . . . oh, hush, it's only *me*."

Conrad pushed in between the two. "Anna Louise, watch out! It's been a long time since Jake's seen you, and he might just snap at you."

"Papa, no, he's my friend."

"Just the same, go slow until he knows you again." After Jake wagged his tail and licked Anna's face Conrad turned back toward the house. He stroked his moustache and pulled a comb out of his shirt pocket to flatten his thick hair. His hands fumbled and sweat dampened his armpits. After all, these were his wife's land-rich relatives. Always cordial enough to him, but sometimes hinting in a subtle, not intentionally unkind way, that Elsie had married beneath her. His pacing wrinkled the scatter rugs on the front porch.

At last he heard Clara calling to him from the south field, "Conrad . . . and Anna Louise! My it's good to see you both." She looked back and yelled, "They're here, Joe. I'm going on to the house."

Anna knew that her Aunt Clara was always good for a big, soft bear hug, so she took off across the field, with the ecstatic Jake, to meet her. Clara grabbed her niece and hugged her into her large bosom. The feeling of love, of belonging, was wonderful. Anna squealed again.

"Oh, Aunt Clara, I get to stay all summer! And this year Papa says I'll be able to help with the big chores, inside and outside, and everything. I love it. Oh, I just *love* farmin', an' I'll help out everywhere."

Clara laughed loudly and responded with another big squeeze before turning to Conrad. She gave him a short, reserved hug and invited him in for a glass of her own, 40 proof elderberry wine. She handed Anna some grape juice.

There followed an uneven flow of constrained chit-chat while Anna flitted around the long, airy kitchen, making sure she remembered where everything was kept. She found the big, carry-out jug in a bottom cupboard.

"Fill it up for me, Aunt Clara. Now! Hurry—I wanna take it to Uncle Joe and the kids. You fix it," she demanded. "Do it now an' I'll finish my juice. I wanna hurry an' get out there."

Conrad shrugged at his daughter's demands and poured himself another few swallows of wine, letting Clara take over. Clara glanced at him with her lips pressed in a thin line; the same look her sister had when she disapproved. He hurriedly finished his wine and got up.

"Anna Louise, come say good-bye to your old papa. I gotta get going. Be on the road next week, probably all summer. Come on and get your suitcases before you go running off." Anna pouted and turned her back.

"Hey, you going to leave me your baby doll?"

Anna reacted instantly and ran to the car for her bags. Conrad thanked his sister-in-law for inviting Anna to the farm all summer and hurried out to help his daughter. They hugged and exchanged a wink. "Be good, hon," he said and waved good-bye.

Anna Louise learned a lot that summer. Sundays were a day

for rest and play on the farm. After a bible quote from Joe and some prayers from Clara the kids were on their own. In summer playing usually meant "ye olde swimming hole."

The cousins had a favorite spot right on their own land: a perpetual creek with a few deep holes good for swimming and skipping stones. Joe had diverted one section of the creek into a watering pond for his cattle. With a system of wooden locks he kept the water at a constant level and surprisingly clean all summer.

Just downstream from the pond overflow was a wide, deep place which dropped off steeply from the bank. Here was the biggest, oldest, and most majestic oak tree to be found along the entire creek. The boys had hung a strong rope on one limb that jutted out over the embankment. All of them, including the girls, Anna and her cousin, Grace, would take turns straddling the hay-filled gunny sack tied securely to the end of the rope.

They would holler at the top of their voices while kicking and pumping to get the swing going. It had to be fast enough and high enough to soar over the deepest part before turning loose to go plummeting down with a thrilling, spectacular splash. There were screams of glee and hours of fun as they shared the happiness of their special place.

One particular Sunday afternoon at their spot Anna got her first unobstructed, scrutinizing look at a penis. All six cousins were sitting in the old oak tree—wet, happy, and tired when Dave, the youngest, said, "I gotta pee."

"Well, don't pee on our swing," fussed Grace. She turned her head so as to look out toward the foothills.

"Say," Dave bragged, as he took his `task in hand.` "I betcha I can pee way out to that big rock past the swing."

"Nah, you'll never make it," quipped one of his brothers. "But go ahead and try. Then I'll show you some real distance."

Soon all four were poised and ready for the big contest. John bragged, "You guys don't have a chance. You can *see* I've got the longest `gun barrel' here and so can shoot the farthest."

The contest was on and Anna was taking it *all* in. She swung around on her limb and piped up, "I wanna try too." But the raucous laughter at her pitiful trickle straight down onto the bank prompted her to be still, to quell her sudden anger, and just watch the show with childish excitement. What she saw on that happy outing clarified her awareness of the anatomical difference between the sexes.

She was eager to learn more. By now she knew sex was a daily, essential part of farm life. Her cousins took it for granted. However, since the subject could not be discussed in Anna's home, her curiosity was inordinately piqued in an atmosphere of acceptance. Heretofore forbidden words were refreshingly commonplace on the farm, and Anna was impatient to know everything. But some of the lessons were not easily understood.

When she first saw Clara's big rooster jump on top of a hen and grab her head in his beak Anna rushed into the kitchen screaming, "Aunt Clara, Aunt Clara, come quick! Do something. The rooster's killin' one of the hens!"

Clara laughed indulgently as she hugged her, and gave her a cookie before explaining. "It's all right, child, shhhhh. He's not hurting the hen at all. Why, he's doing just what he's supposed to do. He's a darn good rooster, that one. Earns his feed, yessiree. That's why we have lots of little chicks every summer."

"How do you mean?"

"Guess I'd best set you straight," mused Clara. She knew her prim sister very well, and guessed her niece had never been exposed to the facts of life. Slowly and carefully Clara explained what the rooster was doing to the hen, and how it contributed to the hatching of the eggs into baby peeps.

Anna sat silent on the porch. Even her feet were still as she stared intently into the smiling eyes of her aunt.

"Does it hurt?" she asked hesitantly.

"No, no, dear. As a matter of fact, they like it—most of the time. Of course every now and then a hen will refuse the rooster and run away. But he gets her eventually. Some pullets squawk like mad at first . . . but he keeps chasing them until he gets them all—several times."

Anna was quiet for such a long time that Clara wondered whether she had told the youngster too much. Finally Anna looked far out across the fields and asked, "It's not bad, then? I mean, havin' sex, and everything?"

"Why no, child. Of course not. You poor thing. Honey, God made sex feel good so all his creatures would use the miracle to make babies. But remember, *people* must be in love and get married before they have sex. That's what makes us different from animals."

"But . . . Mama doesn't like it. I know! I hear her, and everything. She doesn't love Papa."

"Hush, child, of course they love each other."

"But, Aunt Clara, I know Mama doesn't like it 'cause she's told me over and over that sex is dirty and sinful, an' it hurts. She said havin' me and my little sis was Papa's fault, and she wouldn't have had us if she'd known how to keep from it."

Clara pressed a hand to her heart. She knew her sister wouldn't sleep with Conrad anymore, and she knew all about the "hellfire and brimstone" lectures to the girls. She also knew about Anna's disobedience and her running away. Clara had long ago understood that her rebellious niece needed affection more than anything else in her world.

"Come on," urged Clara. "Let's you and me take a turn around the hen house and check the eggs."

Anna had often watched the little peeps hatch. They would cluster around their mothers all day and crowd in under them at night. As the two walked toward the hen house they noticed that one old hen kept chasing away her new baby chicks. Anna was distressed and repeatedly nudged the tiny peeps back toward their mother.

"Won't do any good," soothed Clara. "That old hen has no mothering left in her. Happens that way sometimes. Don't really know why. But, we can solve that problem tonight. You can help me. We'll slip these chicks in with some of the good mothering hens. They'll take care of them as if they were their own. Never know the difference."

"Will the peeps know they got a different mama?"

"No, dear. They'll just be glad they're wanted." Clara kept Joe awake that night with her restlessness.

"Will you settle down?" he grumbled.

"Can't. I'm too worried about Anna Louise." Her thoughts took her back to the first day of Anna's arrival. She was helping her niece unpack when she came across six, hand made breast binders.

When questioned about them Anna explained, "Oh, Mama says I have to wear them so's people won't know how big I am. She says I'm too big up here." With that she lifted her blouse, unhooked her binder, and cupped two full, beautifully rounded breasts in her small hands. "See? They're too big, so I have to keep them flattened with these ol' scratchy things Mama made for me. I don't like 'em 'cause they're too tight. But, Mama says they're s'posed to be tight—so I just wear 'em an' try to forget about 'em, and everything."

"Not here, you don't," said Clara. "I never heard of such a thing for farm folks." And she packed away the binders in one of the suitcases until time for Anna to go back home.

While Clara tossed and turned, Anna slept, peacefully hugging her doll. She had gone to bed thinking that sex might not be so bad after all.

Anna had yet another lesson in mothering that summer. She had pleaded with her Uncle Joe to let her watch when one of the sows was about to have her litter of pigs. In late August she finally won him over. Early one morning she was allowed to stand outside the pigpen to watch the big event.

"I have to warn you; it's not a pretty sight," cautioned Joe. "Not like cows or mares." He grabbed a long, heavy piece of wood that was always kept by the pig enclosure. His sow was lying in the only dry corner of the pen; her breathing so heavy it was stir-

ring up dust in front of her round snout. Joe jumped into the pen
with his club.

"Uncle Joe," cried Anna, her eyes wide with apprehension.
"You gonna beat her to get the baby pigs out?"

"No, sweetie, it's not like that. She'll shoot 'em out easy enough.
But . . . well . . . it's hard to explain." Joe looked sideways at Clara
who nodded encouragingly.

"You see . . . uh . . . uh . . . well . . . sometimes an old sow
will just turn around and grab one of her newborn pigs in her
mouth and almost quicker'n you can see . . . uh . . . she'll, well . . .
she'll kill it and then eat it."

Anna stepped back behind Clara and grabbed her aunt's hand.

"So, if she tries that I'll just whop her across the snout 'til I can
get the pig away from her, 'cause she'll never let it be once she's a
mind to kill it."

Clara clutched the girl's hand tightly. "You see," she explained,
"Once in a while, something inside a sow keeps her from accept-
ing one of her pigs. Nobody's ever been able to figure out why it
happens . . . it just does."

Anna peeked out from behind Clara's skirt and whispered,
"You mean, uh, kinda like with me and Mama?"

"Hush, child, you mustn't think that."

That warm and wonderful summer on the farm, filled with
learning about life and love, was passing much too quickly. Anna
wished it would never end. However, she knew her father would
soon be coming for her.

She rushed into every day, now, cramming all the fun, excitement, and happiness she could find into the recesses of her mind . . .
storing up her harvest of love to see her through the long winter at
home. She dreaded leaving this place where she felt wanted. Where
her cousins accepted her and shared hidden places and secrets with
her.

Time was closing in on her; the leaves were turning and beginning to fall, and the days were shorter. At night, Anna's thoughts
dwelled on the inevitable questions: would her mother be any

different after being without her for so long; had she missed her; would they be able to love each other even a little?

Each day the dark, chocolate-brown earth was being shaved of its lush, undulating, green cover, leaving only an amber stubble to keep a tight grip on the land until spring would soften it again for another summer. Storing up the bountiful harvest was almost complete.

Labor day was not a holiday for the farmers. It warned of fall with its threats of rain and frost. Joe was hurrying. Anna sat proudly on her uncle's lap as she steered the clangorous tractor across the fields toward the barn. Bouncing along behind was a wide, flat-bed trailer loaded with hay. A few dark clouds had been forming overhead all day. Pungent odors of exhaust mixed with new mown hay mingled heavily with the humid air.

"Sure be glad to get this last load safe under a roof," Joe shouted. "Then I'm gonna quit for the day. Too damn hot and sultry."

The noise of the laboring motor almost drowned out Anna's young voice as she yelled back, "Can I help unload? Can I? Auntie doesn't need me. Please, Uncle Joe!"

"Okay, okay. Get on up in the loft and help John. That is, if you're sure you're not too tired. Girls really shouldn't work as hard as boys. They're not built for it."

"Gosh, I'm not a bit tired! Don't you worry 'bout me bein' a girl. I can work just as hard as John."

"Well, we'll see about that. Mind your feet!" Joe steered in close under the loft. Anna leaped from the tractor and scrambled up the sturdy wooden ladder just inside the barn doors. She struggled to pull her short, chunky body up the steep, widely spaced rungs as John, right behind, urged her on by pinching at her bottom.

"Hurry up, Shorty!"

"I'm goin', I'm goin'," she squealed.

"Okay, haul 'er up," shouted Joe. They both tugged at the rough, hemp rope which was threaded around a pulley dangling outside the loft window. The slack was quickly taken up as their hands pulled the rope toward them, letting it curl in big circles at their feet.

The weight of each load seemed to increase as the afternoon waned. Their arms tired, the rhythm faltered, the rope curled more slowly, and the fun turned to sweaty work. By the time the last bale swayed outside the opening they were both exhausted.

"Thanks, kids," Joe yelled. "When they're all stacked up come on in. See you later."

John reached far out with the hay hook and guided the last rectangle of hay through the loft opening. He sighed with relief as he closed and fastened the big shutters.

"Grab that pitchfork, gal, and help me get these all stacked toward the back," urged John.

"Gosh, these ol' bales are a lot heavier'n they look."

"Maybe you oughta quit."

"Watcha mean, quit? I can do it. All I said was it's heavier'n it looks." She knew she wouldn't quit even if she were dying.

After awhile they were both puffing and panting. Bits of hay that swirled about them clung to their sweaty bodies making their skin red and itchy. John yanked off his shirt and wiped at his face and chest with it.

"Damn, it's hotter'n the hubs of hell up here," he muttered as he spat, trying to rid his mouth of the pesky chaff. "You sure work good for a gal. How come you like doing hard work so much?"

Anna, panting in great gasps, looked over at him and spat also. She grabbed the tail end of her sweatshirt, tugging at it until it skinned over her head and down her arms, falling inside out on the pitchfork. She swooped it up and began brushing at her face and breasts complaining, "Damned ol' scratchy hay."

John stared at her in disbelief.

"Whatsa matter?" asked Anna.

"Damn, Shorty, you sure have some big titties for a kid your age. Ain't sure you oughta have your top off. Christ! A feller could get so bothered he wouldn't be able to work worth a shit."

She was puzzled by John's outburst—also excited in a way she couldn't define. She felt kind of proud as she strutted closer and paraded in front of him.

"For Christ's sake," he blubbered. "You oughta know seein' a sight like that makes a guy want to play house. Jesus!" He stared at her naked breasts in a stupefied trance.

"Whatta ya mean, 'play house'? Aren't you pretty big to play house?"

"Boy, you sure are dumb, gal. Didn't you ever get all naked and play house with a boy? You must have seen other kids do it."

"Nope. But . . . that's not sayin' I'm dumb. Tell me how. What do we do?"

"Well . . . uh . . . well, okay. First we take off all our clothes. And then, we just lie down in the hay and pretend we're mama and papa in bed. See? And you oughta know what mamas and papas do in bed. Huh?" By the time he finished his inadequate explanation his trousers and shorts were in a heap and he stood looking at her.

Anna was so amazed her words tangled together in a burst of excitement. "Wow! It's only the second time I ever saw a boy's . . . you know . . . thing. Other time was at the creek. 'Member? Does it always stick out like that when you take your pants off? What are those little sacks for? They look funny. What are they for, John? Why do they . . ."

"Shut up, Anna Louise, just shut up," he said impatiently. "I look just like any other guy, and, no, it don't always stick out. Quit askin' so many questions and get your clothes off if you want to play this game."

Something sounded like squeaking hinges.

"John," whispered Anna. "Someone's comin' in down there."

"Will you hush, gal, and stop being such a scaredy cat? There's no one out there." He touched her gently. "Come on get your clothes off. It's only the wind rattlin' the slats." Awkwardly he rubbed his hand across her nipples. "Don't that feel good?"

"I guess so."

"Well, come on. Papas like to feel mamas' titties."

She looked curiously at her stiff nipples. John grinned. His eyes sparkled with mischief and anticipation. He was a wise four-teen-year old, and he felt very superior at this moment.

"Hurry up," he urged. "I'll show you some other places where it feels good too. 'Course, we won't do nothing but touch 'cause you're too young for anything else. Besides we're kin folks and you never do the real, all the way thing with your own kin. But touch-ing and fooling around is almost as good. Can't you hurry it up?"

"Wait a minute. It's these ol' bloomers. Mama made the 'lastic so tight they're hard to get off over my shoes. But I do wanna play the game."

John was running his fingers in circles around her breasts when again a noise intruded. This time the noise brought with it the certainty of the barn door opening. Fresh air nipped at their bare bodies.

A shadow loomed crookedly across the barn floor. They both peered down the ladder and into the apoplectic face of Anna's mother.

Elsie's whole body was shaking. She glared at her daughter with chill enough to freeze her into oblivion. Her words were slowly enunciated, painfully deliberate, and chosen for maximum effect.

"Get your clothes on. Not a word. Get down here—this in-stant! We're going home—now! No! Not a word out of you. Either of you. So this is how you've spent your summer!"

"Aw, gee, Aunt Elsie," John stammered. "Don't be mad at Anna Louise. We were only playing. Nothing bad happened. It was all my fault. But, we didn't do nothing bad . . . honest!" He hur-riedly got his "bothered" part back to normal and stuffed into his pants.

Anna struggled with the tight bloomers which were half off and half on. Tears became wails of fear and futility.

"Mama, please! We were just seein' and touchin'—nothin' else. First time ever, honest."

"I told you—not a word. I don't want to hear your lies."

She clutched the ladder so fiercely that John feared she would somehow yank it from the loft floor and pull it out from under them. Her fury pronounced hellfire for Anna; and her silent scorn for him was just as searing. He followed along meekly.

Elsie pulled away from Anna's hand, whirled around, and marched stiffly out the barn door.

There she turned and said, "You're never to speak of this, either of you. I'm too ashamed." She marched on, mumbling about redemption and sin. "Hurry and pack," she commanded as Anna rushed ahead, sobbing uncontrollably.

A mother hen with her chicks was scratching in the dirt around the porch steps. As Anna ran past they scurried to get out of her way, but one wasn't quick enough. As the distraught girl ran up the steps her heel caught on the edge of the second one. She fell with a scream, landing on the chick. She rolled over, picked up the dead chick, and held it against her tear- drenched cheek.

Clara quickly came to the rescue. She was alarmed at her niece's wracking sobs. "Whatever is wrong, child?"

"It's the little peep—see—I killed it. Poor little baby. I killed it. I killed it, Auntie." The wailing continued.

Elsie and Clara argued about Anna for several minutes, but not once did Elsie confide in her sister about the incident in the barn. While Elsie glowered and tried to rush her daughter into packing, Clara promised there would be time for a grand funeral for the little peep.

And there was. The casket was a wooden match box lined with soft grass. Her cousins never would have bothered with such ceremonial sentiment, but they were there with sorrowful faces because they knew it was important to Anna. She pulled the box half way open and whispered to the little yellow form inside.

"I'm so sorry little peep—sorry that my Mama had to come when she did. If she hadn't got so mad at me you'd still be alive."

She straightened up and spoke aloud, "Bye, little one, now you can stay right here in the flower garden near Aunt Clara forever. I love you. Amen." With one thrust of the spade she lifted enough dirt to bury the small box. She and each of the children heaped brightly colored blossoms on the tiny mound and then ringed it with rocks.

Anna's heartache was warped with anger. She wondered whether her mother had ever had a summer. A summer of happiness and love.

The goodbyes were short and somewhat strained. It was not at all the way Anna had wanted to leave her "Shangri-La." She waved a half-hearted farewell. The car pulled away with Elsie clutching the steering wheel and looking straight ahead. Anna huddled in one corner of the back seat, head down with knees clasped in her arms. The smell of spent gasoline drifted up through the floor boards of the majestic sedan and mingled with that unique odor of a car's upholstery. Anna sat back rubbing her hand back and forth across the velvet like surface of the seat. Her silent tears were the only evidence of the tortured feelings welling up inside her.

She tried to remember the day when she and her father had come down this same road on their way to the farm. It had been so much fun sitting beside him, laughing and talking about farm life. But now . . . now everything had gone wrong. Finally she couldn't stand to hold it in any longer and the crying questions burst out at her mother.

"Mama, why didn't you send Papa for me? Why'd *you* have to come and ruin everything? You hate me, I know it, so why'd you come to get me, anyhow?"

"Shut up, Anna Louise! Just sit back there and keep your mouth shut. You're in enough trouble already. Your Papa didn't come because he's still off gallivanting around the country with some vaudeville group. No telling what he's been doing all summer, either."

They traveled the rest of the way back in silence, each occupied with the impressions of Uncle Joe's hayloft.

Anna could hardly wait to get out of the close confinement of the car and upstairs into her room. She ran past her sisters with hardly any recognition, and stayed in her room, refusing even supper. She curled up with her doll and cried out softly, "Please, God, can't you make us love each other— just a little bit? If you don't, Mama's not ever gonna let me go back to the farm again . . . not ever. Please."

CHAPTER 6

Thursday, July 11, 1974, 11 a.m.

THOMAS WALTERS called as a witness by and on behalf of the people, having been first duly sworn, was examined and testified as follows:

THE CLERK: State your name, please.

THE WITNESS: Thomas Walters, W-A-L-T-E-R-S.

THE CLERK: Thank you.

DIRECT EXAMINATION

BY MR. DURBIN:

Q. Investigator Walters, I want to direct your attention to approximately 12:45 p.m. on the afternoon of the 25th of May of this year. What was your occupation and assignment?

A. Police Sergeant for the City of Los Angeles, assigned to Robbery Homicide Division under Captain Freeley.

Q. Were you working on this particular case?

A. Yes, I was.

Q. Were you at Metro Hospital at that time?

A. Yes, sir.

Q. Where was the defendant when you first observed her?

A. She was in a hospital bed.

Q. Did you tell her who you were?

A. Yes I did.

Q. Did you give her her constitutional rights?

A. Yes, sir. I read them from a card, as per LAPD Form 15.03. I then asked her three questions. First I asked her: "Do you understand each of these rights I have explained to you?" She said, "Yes."

Then I asked: "Do you wish to give up the right to remain silent?" She said, "Yes."

Then I asked: "Do you wish to give up the right to speak to an attorney and have him present during questioning?"

She said, "Yes, but what's this all about?"

Q. Wait, could you tell us, please. what the defendant looked like and acted like at the time, your impressions of her at that time?

A. She appeared to me to be alert. She was sitting up in the hospital bed. She didn't appear to be under the influence of anything—any drugs or alcohol or anything. She was coherent; no slurred speech.

Q. After you gave her her rights and elicited the answers to the questions that you just gave the court, did you then have a conversation with her?

A. Yes.

Q. Did you reduce that conversation to writing, here as People's 5 for Identification?

A. Yes, sir.

Q. Now, Sergeant Walters, I want to start—well, let's start where you apparently put the defendant under arrest for murder. Do you recall when you did that?

A. Yes.

Q. What transpired between you and the defendant after that?

A. She—to begin with, she asked me if she was under arrest. She demanded to know if she was under arrest. And I said, "Yes, you are." I said, "You are under arrest for murder." And she said, "Who did I murder?" And I said, "You are under arrest for the murder of Rosalind."

She said, "Well—," she says, "I see, and you are threatening me. You are going to get a Court order to get me examined." And I said, "No." I said, "Nobody is going to put any pressure on you at all for an examination." And she said, "Well, I think that if I am under arrest, then I am not going to say any more before I talk to an attorney."

I ceased questioning, and advised her after that.

Q. What did you advise her of?

A. I said, "Well, that's your privilege." I said, "You have been warned of your rights, and I believe you understand your rights fully." I said, "No one is going to put any pressure on you to consent to any medical examination. If you do that, you are going to do it on your own."

Q. Now, after the defendant indicated that she wanted an attorney and you stopped the questioning, what then transpired?

A. Well, I talked to Dr. Hanamoto and Dr. Crane, and I explained to them what our situation was and asked for expert opinions as to what they could tell about her by, you know, examining her.

Q. Now, when you explained what the situation was, what was the situation that you explained?

A. Well, I told the doctors that the baby Mrs. Anderson had brought into the hospital—there was a very great probability that it was not her baby and that the baby had been taken from a dead woman, and I wanted to know if they could tell by examining her whether she just had a baby or not.

And Dr. Crane, a pediatrician there, was concerned because of the health of the baby. He said that Mrs. Anderson had some problems with the baby and he wanted to know whether or not she was the mother.

Q. Did the three of you discuss this?

A. Yes. Officer Mallory was also present. Mike Mallory, myself and Dr. Hanamoto and Dr. Crane.

Q. For the record how do you spell those names?

A. Mallory, M-A-L-L-O-R-Y. Hanamoto, H-A-N-A-M-O-T-O. Crane, C-R-A-N-E. Oh, and Captain Freeley had arrived. That's Freeley, F-R-E-E-L-E-Y.

Dr. Crane was the pediatrician in charge of the baby, and Dr. Hanamoto is the gynecologist who was responsible for Mrs. Anderson.

Q. Now, after this discussion, what did you and the other officers do?

A. Well, Dr. Hanamoto proceeded to examine Mrs. Anderson, a pelvic examination, and we stood by outside the examination room while this went on.

Q. After Dr. Hanamoto examined Mrs. Anderson, the defendant, did he come out and tell you the results of his examination?

A. Yes, he did.

Q. And you had, I take it, previously already arrested the defendant?

A. Yes.

Q. What happened after that, after Dr. Hanamoto came out and told you the results of his examination?

A. Officer Mallory and myself were assigned by Captain Freeley to go back to Mrs. Anderson's residence next day: and two other officers transported Mrs. Anderson to the Van Nuys police station.

MR. DURBIN: I have nothing further.

THE COURT: All right. You may cross-examine.

MR. WINGATE: Thank you, your Honor.

CROSS-EXAMINATION

BY MR. WINGATE:

Q. Sgt. Walters, I have People's 5 here which is a four-page transcript. Do you have that before you?

A. Yes, sir.

Q. Did you show it to Mrs. Anderson after you prepared it?

A. No, sir.

Q. Did you offer her the opportunity to make any corrections on this transcript?

A. No.

Q. Did you ask her at any time if this transcript was what she recalled the conversation being between the two of you?

A. No.

Q. In other words, this is your sole product, referring to geople's 5; is that correct?

A. That's correct.

Q. Now, sir, the first part of the admonition is, "You have the right to remain silent"; is that correct?

A. Yes.

Q. And you told that to Mrs. Anderson, didn't you?

A. Yes, I did.

Q. And then the second is, "Anything you say may be used against you in a court of law"; is that correct?

A. Yes.

Q. Where on page one did you say that to Mrs. Anderson?

A. When I wrote on this report that I advised her as per LAPD Form 15.03, those are the rights—

Q. Yes, sir.

A. —as they are written on the form.

Q. Yes. But what I am pointing out, Sergeant, is: After you read her the rights from LAPD Form 15.03, you asked her if she gave up the right to remain silent, and she said, "Yes." Then you asked her if she wished to give up the right to speak to an attorney and have him present during questioning, and she said, "Yes." But you did not ask her or you did not inform her, after you read her the rights, that if she could not afford an attorney, that one would be provided for her. Am I correct?

A. You are correct. The questions posed are written on page 1. Those are the only questions I asked her about her rights.

Q. Yet, there are four parts to the rights; is that correct?

A. That's correct.

Q. And you only asked her about two of them after you read her rights?

A. No, I asked her if she understood them first, and then I asked her about two parts of them.

Q. Why didn't you ask her about the other two parts?

A. The rights—I understand the case law now, and the reason that this one is printed is that this is what we advise the defendants of at this time—and this covers them. We don't ask, as a matter of policy, any more questions about the rights.

Q. Why did you ask her the two rights after you read her the card, then?

THE COURT: Mr. Wingate, I think you may be confusing the witness when you say, "Why didn't you ask about the two questions?" You might specify the two questions you are referring to so that he will know what you are referring to.

MR. WINGATE: Yes, your Honor.

Q. After you read Mrs. Anderson her rights, you then asked her if she wished to give up the right to remain silent, and she said, "Yes." You asked her if she wished to give up the right to speak to an attorney and have him present during questioning, and she said, "Yes."

A. Yes.

Q. Why didn't you ask her if she understood that anything she said might be used against her?

MR. DURBIN: Objection, your Honor. It's irrelevant and immaterial.

MR. WINGATE: It goes to impeachment, your Honor.

THE COURT: I'm going to overrule the objection on the basis that this conversation was gone into and he can be cross-examined as to that conversation. You may answer or have the reporter read the question back.

THE WITNESS: I'm not sure I understand—

THE COURT: The reporter will read the question.

(Pending question read by the reporter.)

MR. DURBIN: Objection, your Honor. It's argumentive. He didn't advise her again, period. Why he didn't is irrelevant, immaterial and argumentive.

MR. WINGATE: Well, your Honor, there's nothing argumentive about it. He has given her part of her rights after he reads from the form, and I'm asking why he didn't give her the others. There's nothing argumentive about that. This is cross-examination.

THE COURT: Objection will be overruled. You may answer.

THE WITNESS: Well, I didn't ask her because at the present stage of—at the present time the District Attorney and the Police

Department—has determined that the requirements that are written on the LAPD Form 15.03 meet all of the Miranda requirements, as case law has it today, and I'm not—I always read the form verbatim.

BY MR. WINGATE:

Q. Sir, I understand that.

My last question, I hope, on the subject is: if it's your understanding and the D.A.'s understanding that the reading of the form 15.03 is sufficient, then why did you ask her if she understood only two of her four rights that you read her from 15.03?

MR. DURBIN: Objection, your Honor; that's argumentive.

THE COURT: It's already been asked and answered.

MR. WINGATE: I don't think I have gotten an answer yet, your honor. I really don't.

THE COURT: I think you did.

MR. WINGATE: Does your Honor recall an answer?

THE COURT: Yes, I do.

MR. WINGATE: You always were smarter than I, your Honor.

THE COURT: He said he didn't, apparently because he read from the form, and because the District Attorney and the Police Department have determined that the form meets all the Miranda requirements. That is the answer, as I see it, to the question.

MR. WINGATE: Thank you, your Honor.

BY MR. WINGATE:

Q. Now, when you asked Mrs. Anderson if she would consent to an examination, what did she say to you?

A. She said, "No! I won't. I can't!" She said, "It's the principle of the thing." She said, "I consider a vaginal examination an assault on my body!"

Q. Then why . . .

The defendant burst out crying; a rocking, wailing display of anguish. Questioning was suspended while Mr. Stokes tried to restrain her. She couldn't see through the tears, and her headache blocked the voices around her.

Only that terrible day when she was nine years old, and the doctor explained "examination" to her, only that day was clear in her memory as if she were there again. There in the tiny, square office of Dr. Webb. There, too, she was rocking with apprehension and anger. There her crying didn't show, but its tearful pressure within her threatened to choke her breathing. Now—and then . . . then—and now. She was still haunted by that word, examination.

It was Monday, September 11, 1937, early.

Anna awoke tired and unhappy. Her eyes burned from the sudden re-exposure to coal dust, and her stomach protested its emptiness. Every detail of her last day on the farm pushed at her brain like tiny awls trying to poke holes of escape for the aching pressure. The drive home, with the stubborn ambiance between mother and daughter, had been exhausting for both.

But, by dawn she was hungry and couldn't resist the aroma of bacon broiled to the amber crispness her mother preferred. Yesterday's depression was tempered, not only by the anticipation of a good breakfast, but by the realization that today was the start of a new school term. While Margaret was in the bathroom Anna took the time to carefully tuck away her doll in a back corner of the closet before venturing downstairs to face her mother.

She eased into the kitchen, dressed for school and eager to eat and be off. Her sister, Florence, was already finishing her poached eggs.

No one said, "Good morning."

Elsie pushed a basket of warm, buttered toast toward her without looking at her, and set down a plate of bacon and eggs, scrambled eggs. Anna looked up in surprise. Her favorite breakfast. *Is Mama going to forgive me?*

"Eat up," commanded Elsie. "I'm glad you're up early. We have a big day ahead of us." She turned her back to wash her hands while she continued. "As soon as you're finished I want you to bathe, real good, mind you, and put on the new underwear I made for your birthday. It's in your bottom drawer. Wear a clean skirt and blouse."

"But . . . I *am* clean. I put this dress on special for the first day of school."

"You're not going to school. Do as I say."

"I can't. I'll be late for school, and I am so going." Elsie dried her hands on a clean towel and turned to glower at her daughter. "Young lady, you are not going to school today," she said with quiet, measured firmness. "You are going with me to the doctor."

"But, why? I'm not sick. Why do I have to take a bath? Why, Mama, why do I have to see Dr. Phil? I'll be late for school!"

Entreaties failed, and Anna did as her mother directed. She could only watch, helpless and frustrated, as her sisters marched off to a new school term.

It was a short ride to Dr. Webb's clinic. A silent ride. Anna managed a sad wave to Mary as they turned right on Main Street. She wished her friend could be sitting beside her. The Buick crunched around to the back of a red brick building on a gravel side road. The clinic was old with old equipment. Even Dr. Webb was "old."

Anna dangled her legs from the overstuffed couch in the waiting room and tried to read the various framed diplomas. Her mother whispered to Mrs. Webb who was the doctor's wife, receptionist and nurse's aide.

"Sure, sure, Mrs. Mayer, he'll see you right now. Anna Louise can wait here with me."

Phillip Webb had been the Mayers' family doctor for years: delivering all four girls, and regularly caring for Conrad's aging parents. He was a kindly man, a social friend of the Mayers, and, an excellent general practitioner. He peered at Elsie's flushed face. "Say," he asked. "You still taking those little white pills I ordered for your nerves?" He tried to take her pulse.

"It's not me, Phil." She hid her hands under her purse. "I mean, yes, I am nervous—worried sick about Anna Louise. It's so embarrassing." She paused, then looked him straight in the eye and stammered, "I've brought her in for an examination. You know." She shuddered and looked away.

"Hey, come on, now, what are you saying?"

"This summer . . . this summer, Phil, Anna was up to the farm, and, well you know how—how—*developed* Anna is. Well, I'm worried that her older cousin may have taken advantage of her."

"Wait a minute. Elsie! You trying to tell me your little girl was raped?"

"Well, maybe—not exactly—I mean, *yes*, that's what I think. I want you to examine her and tell me if she's still, uh . . . uh . . ."

"Still a virgin?" he interrupted. "Come on, now, Elsie, she's only nine years old. How can you think like that? What's made you want to put a child through that? Did she tell you a boy hurt her?"

"No, no, Phillip. It's too personal to explain. Please, I've got to know! Is she . . . is she . . . still pure? I've got to know."

"Okay, calm down. I can do the examination if you're sure she's, I mean, if you really feel she's been . . . involved, sexually, let's say." He looked sideways at her rough, reddened hands.

"Look here, Elsie, I don't mind telling you I don't like this. Not at all! It's too uncertain. Liable to shock the hell out of the youngster. Only nine. We might do her a lot of psychological harm. Are you *sure* you know what you're asking? What the exam might do to her mind?"

"Yes! For God's sake, yes—it's got to be done, I tell you. I've got to know."

Dr. Webb and his wife were gentle and compassionate with Anna. They wanted to reassure her about what came next.

"It'll be just fine," murmured the doctor. "A pelvic examination doesn't really hurt."

"But, what's that?" asked Anna. "Is it shots again? I'm going to be late for school. What're you gonna do?"

Mrs. Webb shook her head as she helped Anna undress from the waist down. "Honey, your mother is worried about you. She cares. She thinks some boy may have done something bad to you, so Dr. Phil is going to examine you; he's going to check your private place to make sure no boy has harmed you."

"No! No, doctor, I told Mama me and John were only playing. He didn't hurt me. No one hurt me. We didn't do anything bad. Honest. Tell Mama. We didn't do anything! Please!"

"Shhh, honey," soothed Dr. Webb. "It's going to be okay. Won't hurt a bit. I promise. So, since you're here, and your mother is paying for a check-up, let's do it right and examine you like she wants."

Anna stiffened and pushed away his hand. She flounced down on the hard table and put up her feet as directed.

"Go ahead," she said. "Do whatever you want. I don't care. Just do the zamination and see if I care." She lay perfectly still, staring at the ceiling through escaping pools of humility.

When Dr. Webb finally straightened up he felt disgusted that he had been coerced into being a party to Elsie's neurotic suspicions. He tore off his glove and charged into his office.

"Damn it, Elsie, of course your daughter is still a virgin to everyone but you. I'm sorry as hell I had to force the girl into such a traumatic experience." He grasped her around the shoulders and spun her around to face him.

"Now, you tell me, Elsie Mayer, *are* you still taking your pills?"

She frowned and looked away without answering. Once again mother and daughter were confined in the small space of the automobile. Neither could speak, nor could either even understand the needs of the other.

Anna ran from the car and stumbled up one step after another until she burst into her bedroom. With a violent wrench she flung open the closet door, and propped herself into the dark corner. Pulling her doll in close under her chin she sat there, rocking back and forth, banging her head against the wall.

There were no tears. Her empty eyes, much like those of her doll, stared into the blackness until the hypnotic rhythm lulled her to sleep.

Downstairs Elsie changed into her cotton housedress and slowly plodded her way into the kitchen. There she stood at her sink washing her hands until the knuckles were bleeding.

But, she didn't notice.

CHAPTER 7

Sunday, December 17, 1944, evening.

It was a crisp, cold night with bustling people along Main Street finishing their Christmas shopping. Anna Louis was getting Mary a soft, lavender scarf; and Mary was at Barton's choosing a risque pair of black underpants for Anna. It was barely an hour before Christmas choir practice, and Anna had to hurry to reach the church in time.

She had browsed longer than she had intended in the shoe store to flirt with the new clerk. The young man had responded eagerly by suggesting they meet at the movie house when the store closed. But, she couldn't risk the wrath of her father, and more especially that of her mother, if they should ever find out she was seriously dating.

At fourteen Anna Louise knew more about life in general and sex in particular than her mother. And she was no longer the naive tomboy her father used to show off: after she was about nine Conrad seldom paid attention to her other than starring her in the church choir. Anna worried about her father not liking her the way he used to. It seemed to her the more she matured the more distant he became.

Elsie continued to insist her daughter wear the flour-sack breast binders and youthful A-line skirts with middy blouses. Anna despaired that her last pair of sturdy, black, ankle-high shoes would ever wear out, and she would have to use them all through high school. All except Florence still grumbled about having to wear the hated lisle stockings; and none of the girls was allowed to use makeup.

However, Anna's best friend, Mary, "Miss Popularity-Plus," owned a wonderful leather case full of lipsticks, mascara, rouge, powders and perfumes. There was even a cherished eyelash curler and a pointed eyebrow tweezers. The friends felt closer during their teens, thinking alike and shutting out grown-ups who didn't accept new ways. Mary's folks were not as traditional in their criticisms of teen morals as were Anna's; thus the freedom at the Vicenti home for makeup and dating.

On special evenings, when Anna's parents thought she was safely out of mischief at Papa Vicenti's, the young girls would discard their thick stockings and spread on the popular leg makeup which came in various shades of tan. They spent hours with the newest cosmetics before they sneaked out to meet the boys. No breast binders on those occasions.

Sometimes Anna had to squeeze her body out of her third floor window and skid down the rough, decades-old oak in order to join Mary for roller skating. That sport became a great ploy for both girls to hang around the boys. They almost always got a soda out of the older ones who were making money in the mines. By 10 p.m. Anna would flee like Cinderella to get back to her room in time to clamber up the old tree before her father got home.

A brash lad whose uncles owned the hardware store had pierced Anna's virginity when she was barely thirteen. She had quickly learned from him how to entice boys with her provocative body, and she soon realized that her perpetual smile and aggressiveness delighted most of them.

However, when her two, most ardent boyfriends went off to college that fall, never writing, or visiting her when home on weekends, Anna's anger at them soured into doubts about herself as a desirable person.

"I'm so depressed," she had told Mary during Christmas school break, with her pretty face pinched into despair.

"I'm just not a worthwhile person. No, I'm not. Somehow I'm not loveable . . . and I don't know why . . ."

"*I* love you. You're my very best friend!"

"Oh, I know that. I mean, Mama and Papa, and the other kids, and everything. I want to be in love with a boy who really loves me back. You know?"

"Sure, but we're not old enough to be serious about *love*," protested Mary. "Come off it. Let's just have a good time until our shining knight wheels into our life in a gold Cadillac. It'll happen some day." Mary had an enviable way of gliding through her teens with regal composure and serene confidence.

"Well, I'm going out looking for *my* knight."

Trouble was, some of the boys at school had found out that she was "easy," including the eight seniors in Conrad's local choir. They were waiting for her behind a snow bank late that December night after choir practice. A light smowfall had dusted the streets. When Anna came bopping around the corner at Main and Saugus Streets the eight firmly circled her, and pushed her through the jimmied back door of the empty railway station which always closed at 6 p.m.

"Hey," she protested, "cut it out. No new adventures for me tonight—I've got to get home."

The boys kept up a volley of chatter as one skillfully removed her woolen scarf and unbuttoned her coat. Grid, the sheriff's son, began fingering the tie of her embroidered Christmas blouse with its high crinoline collar.

"I said stop it! And I mean it." Her voice became loud and shrill. "Leave me alone! I've got to go."

"Aw, not yet, sweetie," said Grid. His leering stance was threatening to Anna. "We want to see your stuff."

"Whadda you mean?"

"Come *on*, Annie Lou, you know exactly what we mean." Suddenly Anna's eyes widened as the boys' intent became obvious to her.

"Oh, no, you don't!" she screamed and swung at Grid with both gloved fists. He ducked and grabbed her flailing arms.

"Get her." he panted. Two boys knotted her scarf and jammed the lump into her mouth as they struggled to tie the fringed ends tightly around her head. It took three of them to get her coat off while Grid tore at her blouse.

"Jesus, you wear a lot of stuff under your clothes. What's this band?" He tugged at the breast binder which defied his strong grip. Meanwhile the youngest boy had unhooked her skirt and shoved it down around her ankles. Eager hands pulled the skirt free from each foot—not without sustaining a few bruises.

Their excitement heightened the harder she fought them. But she hadn't been her father's favorite shadow without learning some of the arts of self-defense. Sneaky, dirty tactics she had picked up watching the Vicenti sons scrap. Now was the time to fight dirty. She kicked upward with her left foot. It connected forcefully with Grid's erect penis bulging out from inside his trousers.

He doubled over, loosening his grip on her as he blanched and grimaced with pain. The others hesitated long enough for Anna to pull away, leaving the ripped blouse in their hands.

She stumbled toward the station entrance, unbolted the lock, and slammed open the door. Free! She sprinted outside where icy winds hit her body clad only in breast binder and petticoat. She gasped and tore at the knotted scarf. That one second's hesitation lost her the battle.

Little Roger, the gentle "four-eyes" she had always liked, tackled her with his short, wiry body. Anna fell hard onto the snow-covered platform. Many hands dragged her inside despite her desperate grasp at the doorjambs. Her fingers stung with splinters; her breathing labored to suck oxygen through the gag; her face, dirtied with coal dust on the floor, was etched with irregular paths of white—a blotched map of dust and tears.

Her struggles infuriated Grid. He slapped her face and pummelled her body into weakened submission. The other boys stripped her entirely and roughly laid her on her own coat. Only Roger showed compassion by rolling up his jacket and placing it under her head.

Grid declined to go first and waved on the others while he hung back to inspect his injured penis. He dropped his pants and decided he would be okay in another few minutes. Meanwhile he joined the fun by biting Anna's nipples which were sticking far out because of her chilled and frightened shivering.

"Umm, good," he teased as he swept his hands over her naked body. "I mean it, toots. I've been excited by you for a long time, thinking about how it would be. Guys have told me how good you are . . . now I aim to tell *them*."

Bastards! Church goin', hymn singin' bastards. Papa's good little choir boys. Damn you, you scabby-faced fuckers!

Anger and pain vied for her attention as the orgy of the inexperienced, impatient boys continued into the night. Finally they began to leave, one by one, subdued in their retreat, until only Grid and Roger were left.

Grid lay on top of her for several minutes after his grand passion subsided. He looked up into her accusing eyes and said, "You're such a bitch. Don't blame us 'cause you're a bitch." He jumped up and faced Roger who appeared to be frozen in place. "You comin' or are you gonna have a go at her? I don't remember if you did or didn't already."

Roger, still holding Anna's shoulders, answered haltingly, "Uh, no, I'm all done. You go ahead. I'll be comin' along, too, in a minute." As Grid ran out the back door, pulling at his pants, Roger picked up Anna's petticoat and skirt and gently covered her. He knelt down, untied the gag and whispered, "God, I'm sorry, Anna. I couldn't do *that* to you, but I was a part of it. Don't know why. I . . . uh . . . uh , I just was and I'm sorry . . . really sorry."

Anna sat up and wiped at her stomach and thighs with the petticoat. "Go away and leave me alone, Roger. Go on and chase after your friends. No need to worry about tonight. Remember what Grid said. I'm only a bitch. You shouldn't feel bad about hurting a bitch. So, go on, get out of here. Go tell everybody about your night with a bitch. I don't care anymore. You hear me? I don't care!"

Multiple rape. Not fun, not loving, not gentle, not romantic. It was ugly, forcible rape; and when it finally ended, and Roger had slinked past her out of the door, Anna sat torn and bloodied. She couldn't move. How she hated the sight of her own naked body. But greater hate for the boys burned at her soul; a hate which was more scarring than her shame.

She couldn't go home. It was unthinkable that she could tell Dr. Phil, and especially the sheriff. She knew it would be all over town and she'd be blamed for it. Her Christmas blouse was ruined, the embroidered bodice ripped, and her skirt soiled beyond repair. She couldn't face another beating from her father and a humiliating confrontation with her mother.

She hurt. And she was frightened. The bleeding didn't stop for an hour. She painfully untied the knotted scarf, retrieved her winter coat, and buttoned it up to her chin. It was hard to walk even slowly on the icy streets, but she made it to the Vicenti home sometime after 11 p.m. The whole house was dark. She threw snowballs at Mary's window until her friend saw her and came out.

"Jesus, look at you," whispered Mary. She hugged Anna and eased her sore body into the darkened kitchen. "Hush, now, or you'll wake somebody." She wrapped her shaking friend in her grandmother's crocheted afghan and heated some coffee.

"Here. A hefty dose of dago wine first, then hot coffee. Now, tell me."

Anna did tell her. All of it. Including the presence of the sheriff's son as one of her attackers. Mary let her sob into several, huge, muslin squares that the Vicenti men used as handkerchiefs. She then helped her into the bathtub filled with steaming water and suds, and quietly woke her sixteen-year-old brother.

When Anna was dressed in a clean, warm robe she was able to relax with her friends. Her sobs lessened but couldn't stop entirely.

"But, Mary, I can't go home. Not ever. What'll I do?" Sister and brother looked at her—and had no answer.

"I'll have to run *far* away this time, and make sure I'm never caught. God, I hate this damn town. I'm *never* coming back."

"Oh, Anna, do you have to leave? Forever? I'll miss you so much! It's not fair. But that pimple-faced gang of delinquents *would* get off scott free even if you did have the courage to report them. I

know how you feel. Guess I'd do the same thing, about not reporting them. But I wouldn't have to run away.

"Gee whiz . . . well, if you're sure, well, I've got some money.
Maybe four dollars. You can have it all!" And she squeezed her
friend's hand.

"Me, too," offered Gueseppi. "Got a five-dollar-bill hidden
away. And, listen, give me the names of every one of those sons-a-
bitches and me and my brothers will drop your name on them as
we beat the shit out of each one."

"Gosh, thanks. You're swell friends, and I just wish I could
stay and live with *you*. But, Mama would never let me. Don't ever
let her know what happened! Promise!"

"Sure, sure, Anna. Now, let's be practical. You can be on your
way before dawn. Honey, look at me! You're plenty smart, and a
girl can make it out there on her wits. Say, with your knack for
making out—well—you'll be okay. Just get to a big city."

"You bet," said Gueseppi. "I'll help. Just tell me how."

"Hmm, she'll never get far as a girl. Maybe . . ."

The two dressed Anna in a warm miner's cap with ear flaps,
piling her blond hair up under it; and pushed and pulled her into
a pair of boy's work pants. The hated breast binder was a necessity
for their plan to work. They cleaned blood off of Anna's own shoes,
polished them with boot black, and gave her a pair of striped boys'
socks. An out-grown wool jacket over two sweaters completed the
illusion.

"There, kid," laughed Gueseppi. "You're a tough dago boy
out to see the world." The girls laughed, too, and embraced with
parting promises to write and to be friends forever.

"Wait," cried Mary. "Here, here's the eyelash curler you always admired. No, take it, honest. It's for good luck—and to remember me by."

Brother and sister escorted Anna through narrow back alleys,
skirting the sheriff's station and ducking out of sight of headlights
until they were well east of town. They knew that Stuckey's had an
active, 24-hour truck stop. They watched Anna saunter up to a

middle-aged trucker who was eyeing his tires while pulling on leather gloves. They saw him boost her up into his cab then climb in himself. Mary and Gueseppi waved frantically as the trucker gunned the motor and headed out with his white exhaust spitting back into their faces.

"Bye," called Mary softly.

The trucker introduced himself only as Sill, and she volunteered her name as John, telling him she was hitch-hiking to New Jersey to spend Christmas with her grandparents. He didn't quiz her, just accepted her as a young boy needing a lift.

About five hours later the interstate semi half-skidded into a huge truck stop near Carlisle.

"Hey, kid I'm gonna grab a cot in here and sleep a few hours. Unless you got two bucks to spare you're welcome to stretch out behind the seat if you want. Got an old blanket or two there. Be pullin' out by 10 if ya wanna go on with me." ·

"Sure, Sill," she mumbled, "Looks like it'll fit me fine. I'm awful sleepy."

She was ready, perky, and curious when Sill revved up for the next 200 miles into Philadelphia. She was sure he wasn't a bad sort—even treated her to the biggest breakfast she had ever seen. "Eat up kid, that's a trucker's breakfast. Won't eat again 'til we're in Philly." Anna hid away several napkins filled with sausages, scrambled eggs and fresh rolls. Hunger was one thing she couldn't handle very well.

The idyllic partnership ended just outside the turn-off to Valley Forge. Some of her long, golden hair had slipped out of the miner's cap, and she had taken off the tight breast binder while stretched out in the cramped cab behind the seat. Sill's big hand pulled off her cap, and none too gently. "Well I'll be damned, look at you! Nothin' but a little girl! Oh, Christ, I'll be arrested for carrying you."

Sill slowed to the speed limit and scanned the road for cops before giving Anna a chance to pour out her embellished tale of rape and mistreatment. He soon became incensed, angry, and then protective.

By the time the big rig crossed the frozen Schuylkill River into Philadelphia his sympathy gave way to his usual common sense. He pulled up at the slush-covered corner on Vine where the Free Library had a soup kitchen nearby. It was 30 degrees with a terrible wind. Anna shivered and looked around at her dreary surroundings.

"Hate to, but I gotta leave ya, kid. Can't risk taking you across the state lines—*big* trouble with the law for that. Here—a fiver," and he shoved the bill into her jacket pocket. "You call your folks, hear? Wait in the library to keep warm."

They parted friends, and Anna waved Sill on from the phone booth outside the library.

Wow! Over ten dollars now! I can buy a rummage dress and coat, pin up my hair, and get a job.

"Yippee!" she yelled, and smiled broadly at passers-by as she hopscotched down the slippery sidewalk.

For four months Anna lived in a boarding house on the edge of Germantown, bussing it downtown to 12th Street where she worked 5 a.m. to 4 p.m. in a bakery. Most of the time she stirred pie fillings in huge copper pots nested over gas flames. Delicious nibbles throughout the day rounded out her figure even more.

Often she used her lunchbreak to brave the ruthless foot traffic around Wanamakers in time to grab a "leaning spot" under the eagle for the noon organ concert. It was always magnificent. She had never imagined an organ several stories high. It was so loud. But she sang right along with the more popular tunes. Her booming high notes rivaled those of the organist, and the crowds delighted in her enough to throw change into her empty doughnut bag.

Despite hard work her meager savings did not give her courage enough to travel. But, by March Anna knew that with considerable effort and constrained poise she could pass for twenty-one. This allowed her to frequent Smokey Joe's where the college crowd

hung out. They tossed her coins to get her to belt out her reper-
toire of bawdy songs. Not quite so far from work was J. C. Dobbs
where she could dance and sing familiar tunes from country west-
ern to post-war jazz. She wheedled lots of tips there to feed her
piggy bank.

In May the landlady who ran the boarding house found out,
by chance, that Anna was only fifteen, a runaway. She felt it her
duty to locate the Mayers and send Anna home. When Anna found
this out, she emptied her fat piggy bank and simply ran away
again.

Asbury Park on the New Jersey coast! That's where she had
longed to go for months. Stories of the wild, glittering boardwalk
and the carefree servicemen intrigued her. This time on the road
she hitch-hiked as herself with her new, grown-up look, and had
no trouble reaching the famed beaches. Spring was warming the
days and nights, popping open the buds of azaleas, dogwood and
snowballs, all blooming under a mild sun.

She was enchanted. However, the resort was overtaxed trying
to care for the homeless. It's burgeoning popularity "in season"
brought undesirables to fester in the shadows. No jobs for tran-
sients and meager pickings for those living on the beach. Anna was
frightened and she began to doubt her abilities.

Can I make it? Scariest yet. God, Papa, I sure need you. It wasn't
long before her charm and aggressiveness found her a haven with
an affluent family living right on the beach. She earned a small
stipend plus board and room for doing housekeeping and occasional cooking. Anna worked quickly and thoroughly in order to
be free after noon most days. By summer she was solvent, tan,
slimmer, and emotionally tough.

Asbury Park was *the* hot spot for soldiers from Fort Monmouth
and sailors from the USN Depot. Anna strutted the boardwalk
every night, calling the barkers by name, and making friends with
the merchants.

Jimmy was the cutest soldier she had ever met. She soon coaxed
him away from his leering buddies. They would meet on the beach

as often as he got a pass. One rainy night in late July he became
bold enough to sneak her into his barracks.

"You're sure a spunky kid. What makes you tick, anyway?"

"Smarty! Don't you know anything? A girl's got to keep trying
'til she finds the right man. I mean—to settle down with."

"Jesus Christ—you talkin' 'bout *marrying*? Got the wrong boy,
here. I'm *never* gonna get married."

"Why not?"

"Kids, you nut. Kids. Why'd anyone want to be saddled with
a bunch of dirty, whiny kids?"

"Well, I'm going to have lots some day."

"Not with me you're not!" And Jimmy straightened up with a
frightened jerk. Anna reached up and wiggled her little finger in
his ear.

"Okay, okay, Sweetie, come here," she coaxed. "It's all right.
I'm always careful. Don't worry. I don't want my kids 'til I'm married. Truly! I just like some fun with cute guys like you. So don't
go getting up tight—not now."

They settled back into the narrow bunk with a passionate
clinch, working swiftly on each other's clothing with knowing fingers. But quiet love-making was never Anna's way. Her sensuous
body lurched and she cried out with moans leading into an ultimate shriek.

Of course they were caught. A federal offense for both. It took
only two days for the local police to locate the Mayers in Pennsylvania and advise them to come for their daughter. By this time the
charges added to incorrigible were: delinquency, pandering and
felonious presence on a military base. The Mayers were also informed that Anna had a positive Wasserman (later believed to have
been a false reading).

Conrad and Elsie both refused to be responsible for their
daughter. They maintained they could not control her, and that
she would be better off in a reform school. The New Jersey juvenile authorities had no recourse but to incarcerate Anna until she
was eighteen. She was remanded to the Trenton School for Girls.

It was horrible. She was immediately treated with arsenic powders, a specific for syphilis. However, she became violently ill, not only with gastrointestinal disorders, but with painful, cutaneous pustules. The medicine was reduced and then discontinued. Since signs of venereal infection were no longer noted, and a repeat Wasserman was negative, the nurses convinced the institution doctor that Anna could be released into the general population of the reformatory.

The juvenile prison was harsh and exacting of their rules, and insisted their girls learn some trade while serving their sentence. Anna was surprised at the number of activities and courses offered within those drab walls. She was delighted with the healthful, outdoor chores during good weather, and asked for duty in the fields. She soon became a top hand at gardening, even allowed to teach "poor, city runaways" to have pride in the land.

Her second month there she met Miss Lillian Szesze, the music teacher.

"You have an extraordinary voice, child," she marveled. "It needs discipline, training. And you must learn to read music, not rely on your ear."

"I will! Oh, I love to sing." From then on it was arranged for Anna to spend her few hours of free time developing her talent under the tutelage of this gentle woman who was strict but not unreasonable. Miss Szesze had been a permanent staff member of the school for more than thirty years. A tall, thin widow with tiny, gold-rimmed glasses half down her nose, and high-button shoes which were cracked and mottled. A fading virtuosa whose promise of greatness had shriveled long ago during her husband's lingering demise.

"Anna Louise," she announced one day, "I have permission to take you out to my home once a week for proper lessons."

The weeks merged into months, and the interminable scales merged into operatic solos to the accompaniment of Miss Szesze's finely tuned Steinway.

"You've got it!" raved the teacher. "You've got the magic in your voice which can make you immortal." She treated them both to peppermint schnapps in honor of the governor's visit in three weeks.

"You'll sing for him. Such a talent shall be recognized. Anna Louise, some day you will take your place among the famous mezzo-sopranos of all time." And she was not above getting tipsy in front of her pupil.

When Anna related those magical words to the other girls there was a chortling din of ridicule.

"What, you? Don't be a slug," they laughed. "Old lady Sleazy is just playin' you along—hopes to re-ha-bil-i-tate you like she tried with a dozen others she took a shine to."

"You shut up! That's just not so."

"Shit, you're such a dummy. You'll always be an ex-con now. No one will give you the time of day, much less a chance in opera." They laughed for days, hamming up prima donna roles with their screechy voices, and teasing her about at least being chesty enough to be an opera star.

"Sleazy's pet song bird, nya, nya, nya."

Anna struck out in uncontrollable fury; words, fists, feet and broom handles—even a heavy coal bucket. "Don't you laugh at me! I will *so* sing at the Met."

She was released from lock-up the very day the governor came to tour the center, a first for the New Jersey leader. He did hear Anna sing. Miss Szesze had been able to get her out of detention in time to replace her brown uniform with a long, white dress graced with satin roses and a silk sash.

There was glory and greatness in her true, flowing range when Anna sang the beautiful "Italian Street Song."

Hushed silence roared into a stand-up ovation from all the girls and the matrons. The governor held her hand and promised his patronage when she was released. It was a new and awesome feeling for Anna. She felt pride in herself, and eagerness to experience a promising future.

On Anna's eighteenth birthday in 1947 Conrad and Elsie trav-

eled through an especially brutal, winter storm to Trenton to bring
home their daughter. Both mother and daughter wept as they
embraced. There was an awkward exchange of affection.

"Look at you," said Elsie softly. "All grown up. And the matrons assured us you were a model inmate, and they would miss
you. They say you have a great future in music.

"Honey, I know you've changed, and we're proud of you. Maybe
you'll be our daughter again and stay at home until you can fit
into the world without slapping it."

Anna beamed at her mother in amazement, and hugged her
until they reached the car. After the baggage was packed and all
three were settled into the front seat they realized they were shar-
ing a warm, new closeness. Anna prattled on for miles about her
accomplishments and her aspirations. Finally she became silent as
she sensed an uneasiness about her parents.

"Well, sure, I'm proud of you," said Conrad. "But, damn, we
just can't afford to send you to the Conservatory. No way. You
know we just put your two older sisters through nursing school.
Honey, we're strapped for money. Really strapped.

"Look, finish high school before you think about some off-
beat future. Anna Louise, listen, music never made me a good
living. Besides, your mother wants you to settle down." He glanced
at his wife and cleared his throat.

The strain of old tensions among the three surfaced and intensified most of the way back to snow-covered Uniontown. Anna's
immediate future was inevitable. There was to be no voice training
at the Conservatory. No glowing, cheering tributes. No fulfill-
ment of her dreams. It was as if she had simply lost two years out
of her life. And, lost her exciting new self-respect.

So, she dutifully enrolled in the second semester of the 11th
grade, hoping to earn her high school diploma within a year. With
credit from the reformatory she could do it. It wasn't long before
she realized it wouldn't work.

"I don't know, Mary," she told her friend who was then working at Barton's. "I can't get with it. Been away too long. I just don't

seem to fit in at school. Won't matter, anyway, if I can't go on with my singing."

The two young women were inseparable even as their lives diverged.

When Anna willingly played hookey to be maid-of-honor at Mary's elopement she didn't get home for two days. No one believed the truth . . . that four teenagers with questionable reputations had car trouble for two days. So, although Anna and Hammel, the best man, hardly knew each other, their families practically forced them into the proverbial "shotgun" wedding.

The young couple consumated their expected role, and Anna's first child, Noreen, was born in a tiny room at Hammel's folk's home. Money was tight. The boy drank . . . a lot. And drinking made him abusive. He wouldn't even buy milk.

"You and your goddamn baby. Haven't you heard? The whole country is broke! Prices are outta sight. Hell, I don't see you bringing in any money, and your highfaluty folks don't offer any help. They don't give a shit about us. I can't even get a car of my own. Whatta you want from me for Christ's sake? It's gimmie this and gimmie that! God, how I wish we'd never met."

Damn him. Just like always. Everyone blames me. I never should have come back. I'll have to run away from this town; from everyone I know. It's best for Noreen.

CHAPTER 8

June, 1974

Anna sat on the edge of a bench in L.A. County Jail's crowded clinic hall, her hands clamped tightly over her ears. Unending sounds of strife and futility invaded her small corner. Somehow in her clouded mind she was sure the sounds were deranged ravings of society's pitiful rejects who were going to absorb her into their world, contaminate her beyond return and claim her as one of "them" forever.

"Quiet! Quiet! Hospitals must be quiet!" she shouted angrily. *Where are the nurses? Why can't they keep them quiet?*

"Quiet! You must be quiet so we can all think! I've got to remember things. Somebody, please, make them be quiet!"

Her pleas for silence echoed down the long hall and blended in with all the other sounds of anguish. Moments later her escort officer and a psychiatric aide shook her and jolted her into silence. "It's time to see Dr. Richmond now, Anna. Come along with us. It'll be quiet in his office." They finally coaxed her out of her appropriated corner and into the psychiatrist's office.

Anna had liked Dr. Richmond immediately and looked forward to her daily visits with him. He was a tall, solemn man, maybe fifty, whose gaunt features reminded her of a be-whiskered Gregory Peck. She liked the way he rubbed the back of his fingers, ever so gently, up and down his thick, graying beard. It had almost a hypnotic effect on her and she wondered if he consciously used the gesture as a therapeutic method of relaxing his patients. Each time he finished talking he had a habit of pushing his moustache away from his lip with the back of his forefinger. She liked watching him. He always seemed so calm.

As they entered his office he motioned her toward the big recliner across from his desk. "We're going to spend more time together today than usual. Are you up to it—feeling okay?"

"Sure, Doctor, I don't mind. I like it in here. It's quiet and I can think. All the noise and laughing is making me crazy, or should I say crazier?"

"Forget all that now and just relax. Tell you what, Anna, we've already covered your childhood and the years you spent with your parents, so, today I want you to tell me all about the men in your life.

"Oh, God. So many men to remember. Do I have to? I mean, is it really important? Doctor . . . I . . . well, I don't like thinking about all the things I did with men." She turned her head away and began to draw her knees up to her chest, wrapping her arms around them and rocking side to side as low sobs became quiet whimpers.

Dr. Richmond spoke softly, "It's okay, Anna, I know it won't be easy but you can do it. Here's some Kleenex. Once we figure out what led you to this point in your life we can plan what's the best thing to do for you and your future. Can you try to remember for me?" He sat brushing gently at his beard for several minutes before Anna finally began her jumbled account of marriages, affairs, and liaisons.

"Doctor," she started. "The worst part is that none of them really loved me, not the way I wanted them to, you know, like respecting me and appreciating me, and everything." She blew her nose, sucked in her breath and stared at the damp Kleenex as she wadded it again and again into a tight ball.

"Hammel was my first husband." Anna paused and studied a wall-sized painting of pines and streams which she thought looked familiar to her. "Met him when I blind-dated with my best girlfriend, Mary, who was eloping. I sneaked out of the house that night so I could stand up for Mary without Mama knowing. Hammie was the groom's best man. Having to sit on his lap in an old coupe full of luggage for an hour made us friends real quick.

"We drove over the state line into Maryland where there's no waiting for a license. We only went as far as Keysers Ridge, 30 miles, but the roads were so bad with mud and deep ruts that it took lots longer than we had thought. On our way back, the car broke down, honest, the axle broke. But no one would ever believe us. No one!

"Couldn't get home for almost two days. You know Mama was crazy mad and wouldn't let me in?" Anna twisted in her seat and anger replaced the tears. "She called me a whore and said I was too sinful to be around my sisters. Told Hammie he better marry me or there'd be trouble. She said I belonged to him and I couldn't come home. Even Papa wouldn't believe me.

"Poor Hammie was so scared! But he took me across town to his folks' house and they, too, said we'd have to get married if I stayed there. So you see—Hammel didn't really love me. I think he almost hated me after we got married. I stayed with him, though, for two years and had my first baby, a girl."

Anna got lost again in the cool forest painting, and sat cradling her arm.

"Were you glad to have the baby? How did you feel about being a mother, especially under those circumstances?"

"At first I wasn't sure I wanted it, but after she was born, then I knew, for the first time, what it felt like to be loved. For the first time, Doctor! My baby loved *me*. I knew it. I could love and be loved at last with no reservations—no restrictions. It felt so good!"

She cradled her arms close to her bosom and began to sing softly, "Hush, little baby, don't you cry. Mama's gonna love you 'til she dies."

"Anna? Anna! Okay, so you really liked having the baby—what happened then? Was, ah, Hamel proud of his baby?"

"No. He was mad at that too; started drinking a lot and abusing me. Finally I couldn't stand it any longer so I got a quickie divorce, took Noreen, and went home to Mama. She wouldn't let us stay . . . I knew that before I asked.

"But dear Papa sneaked me some money that I used for train

fare out of the state. I just packed a small bag, bundled up Noreen, and walked into the train station to buy a ticket— didn't know where—just anywhere away from Uniontown. The man ahead of me at the window bought a ticket to Houston, Texas, and said he was 'goin' back to God's country.' So, that's what I did. What a long ride! I thought it would never end.

"Anyway, I met Sue in Dallas where we were both waiting to transfer to the Sam Houston Rocket. She sure was a friendly woman—worked part-time at a meat packing plant on the Houston Ship Channel docks, and on weekends at Eperson's Drug Store as a waitress in the luncheon section. She took to Noreen right away.

"She said, 'You stick with me, kid, and I'll get you settled in Houston.' She did get me a job at the meat packing plant. It was pretty awful, but paid well. And we double-dated a lot. Nothing serious. One boy I met was crazy fun and I wanted to see more of him. So, I changed jobs to where he worked at Speck's, a huge liquor barn."

"Were you intimate with him?."

"No, just good friends." She paused. "Well, a little bit, maybe."

"Go on."

"It's just that Speck's was such fun I want to tell you about it."

"Okay, that's fine."

"Anyway, for a few months I was a really great clerk at Speck's where the owner liked to roller skate through the miles of wine and liquor racks. I had more fun! Once while the boss was away I came to work prepared for a really great prank. With a pair of Sue's boyfriend's shoes and thick socks to hold them on my small feet, I strapped on Mr. Speck's roller skates and put on a whale of a show for the help and the customers.

"'Hey! Get a load of Anna Careena,' they cheered."

"Great story, Anna. Let's get on with your men."

"I'm trying to." Anna was put out by the doctor's constant interruptions, so with deliberate procrastination she rearranged her jail uniform in her best, irritating manner. But, her delight in having someone actually listen to her with compassion urged her on.

"Anyway, I got tired of that job and let Sue get me into Eperson's. Boy, working there I served lunch to lots of millionaires buying or selling oil in some form. The deals made at Eperson's made headlines, I tell you!"

Anna sighed and glanced at the tape recorder.

"Does the recorder make you nervous?"

"No"

"You're doing fine. Can you go on?"

"Well, I was awful restless, and Sue worried about me. She was a gold mine of life, love and the pursuit of happiness. So, when Houston's big Valentine's Ball came around she went to a lot of trouble to introduce me to Reuben Lorenz, the studious son of her mother's boss.

"'Anna Louise,' she said firmly. 'This is a good man—and you need a good, steady man who'll marry you.'

"'Oh, yeah?'" I answered. "'And how is a "good, steady man" going to react to a jaded twenty-one-year old with a ready-made child?'"

"'You'll see,' twinkled Sue. 'Trust me.'

"So, I went out on the town with this stiff, awkward foreign guy whom everyone called Ben. He was sort of Jewish-Italian with some Latin in there somewhere. Boy, was he easy to seduce! I mean that man was unbelievable—a virgin at that, and all of 28. We only had two dates before we had sex in a big, cushioned swing, right on the front porch of my apartment house."

With a devilish grin Anna looked the doctor straight in the eyes and proudly announced, "That's where Garey, my second child, was conceived." Her smile curved crookedly into a wry remembrance as she described the birth of Reuben's first-born.

Dr. Richmond's body blended into his swivel chair as he let his tape recorder absorb the joys, frustrations, and willful self-centeredness of his patient during her child-bearing years. It was all there: delight with each new baby; disappointments with her husband; open recklessness with her marriage vows; and ultimate neglect of her children as they shed their dependence upon her. All there . . . years of having everything, and knowing it not.

Anna easily retreated into her dream bubble with a hypnotic focus on the folds in the office draperies. She stared beyond them, years beyond, into a narrow, Texas moonbeam seeping through her homemade curtains in the bedroom. Reuben's snoring next to her was especially irritating tonight. Their baby was due, and he still insinuated that it might not be his. Anna knew it was his, and the distrust hurt. Her inability to soften his aloofness was a constant, puzzling worry.

She stiffened with a moderate contraction, relaxed, and idly watched the moonbeam slant upward and sideways on its journey. Noreen whimpered in the adjacent room, calling, "Mama."

Anna shuffled her cumbersome body toward her child, still an insecure baby at almost three years old. She held out her arms, and cuddled Noreen against her swollen breasts.

"Hush, honey, Mama's here."

"Da-Da?"

"No, he's asleep." Reuben's reluctance to show even minimal interest in the fair-haired Noreen made Anna wonder whether he would or even could be different with his own child. And if he did accept their baby as his own, and showed it love and attention—what would that do to Noreen? Her troublesome thoughts were interrupted by a jolting pain which made her squeeze Noreen too tightly.

The child's cries woke Reuben who grumbled, "Quiet." Anna ignored him as she snapped on an overhead light and started timing her moderate contractions. A few minutes later she half-heartedly nudged her husband, not sure whether she really needed him yet, or whether she was angry at the sounds of his peaceful sleeping. "Go to sleep," he grunted as he turned over to face the wall. Anna sighed and dialed her brother-in-law.

"We're ready, Ferris. Thanks for the car to take me to the hospital. We need it right away. Hurry."

One pain followed another until she was sure of four-minute intervals. She flew around the apartment calling out to Reuben to get up. She stuffed half a donut into Noreen's mouth before tucking her back into bed with a stern, "Nighty, night."

"Ben, wake up! Hurry! Get up—I'm in labor. Come on, Ben, I've got to get to the hospital *now*."

"Hell, are you sure? What time is it?" He rubbed his eyes and grabbed for his shoes. "Did you call Ferris yet?"

"It's 1:30. And yes, I've called Ferris. He should have been here already. I'm sure the baby's coming any minute. Can't we call a taxi?" Her clipped words and pressed lips showed her irritation with Ben's brother who was the most outspoken in his family about this baby not being Reuben's.

"For Christ's sake, don't start on Ferris again. We're damn lucky he offered his car for this, and volunteered to stay here with your kid when the time came."

"Please hurry. Call him again if you want, but a taxi will be quicker. I mean it. I can't wait." Anna cried out in pain and yelled at her husband, "My water's broke! Quick, throw me that bunch of towels and some sheets."

"God, honey, I don't know what to do." Reuben stared at this usually poised, well-groomed woman with her hair mussed, her nightgown soaked, and her face molded into pained squints as she lay down on the floor with towels between her legs.

"For crying out loud, Ben, get moving. I think it's coming before we can get to the hospital."

With sounds of panting, puffing, blowing and intermittent screams echoing inside his head, Reuben managed to telephone Ferris again, who was apparently on the way, before collapsing onto the living room sofa. He could only groan in disbelief at the sight of his wife sprawled on the floor with her gown drawn up to her breasts, legs bent wide open to expose the imminent birth.

"My God, Anna, what are you doing?" he moaned. "Please wait. Not here, honey. Wait!"

"Ben," she gurgled. "Our baby's coming—I can't stop it. No

one can stop it. It's okay, hon. Just listen to me. Agah! Agah!" She was thrashing and pushing as she gasped quick instructions to Reuben. "Listen . . . need help . . . you have to deliver it . . . Ben, come closer. Grab the head . . . good. Now, pull gently when I tell you."

With a last, great effort Anna pushed with all her strength and screamed, "Now . . . pull it out."

"Got it! Anna, I have it. Wow! It's a boy, dark like me. Jesus, he's all slippery and bloody."

She laughed delightedly. "Here, hon, hand him to me. I know what to do." She worked swiftly to start her son breathing on his own. Suddenly the room filled with the thin, staccato cries of a newborn.

Reuben finally heard Ferris yelling at him through the transom. "Made it as fast as I could. Let me in. Boy, are you going to shit your pants when you see what I got for Anna to ride in. Lucky to get it after my own car wouldn't start. Damn battery. Come *on*, Ben, let me in!"

The door slowly opened and Ferris faced his sweating brother whom he saw was in an obvious state of shock.

"What's the matter?" asked Ferris. "God, you look awful. Is it Anna? Is she all right? Did she have the baby?" Reuben nodded. "Hot damn, let me see." They hurried over to the "happening" smack in the middle of the living room. Reuben held out a shaking hand with the string and scissors Anna had asked for.

"He's here, honey. Ferris. Now what'll we do?"

"Just get me to the hospital so they can take care of our baby and sew me up. I think I'm torn pretty bad. Hi, Ferris. What do you think of your nephew?"

"Yeah, look at him," Reuben beamed. "Isn't he terrific? Look . . . he's dark, and all that black hair. Matter of fact, he looks a lot like you, Ferris. He's *mine*. I know it! Has all of our features— even Dad will agree to that.

"Ben, will you get this baby off my stomach," yelled Anna. "He just wee-weed right in my face."

The brothers roared when Ferris quipped, "Guess he just christened you, Anna." But he had the grace to look a bit sheepish as he cradled the infant and even cooed at it. "Yup, you really have a son there." And he slapped his brother hard on the shoulder.

Reuben laughed delightedly. "Definitely mine. I don't mind saying it's a hell of a relief . . . you all telling me it might not even be mine!"

"Sorry, Ben, guess we were plenty wrong. Can you forgive me, little sister? Sometimes I'm a real ass."

"Well, let's just forget it. Now, will someone *please* get me to the hospital?"

"Yes, ma'am!" They half-carried Anna and the baby out to the curb while she squeezed a clean towel between her legs.

Anna's misery gave way to hysterical laughter. "For God's sake, Ferris, this is a hearse. You really came for me in a *hearse?*"

"Don't knock it, sweetheart. Got it on really short notice. It's luxury throughout: air-conditioning, velvet seats with extra 'plump,' r-e-e-e-ally roomy. And you'll get the right of way through traffic!"

Anna couldn't stop laughing. "This is some weird baby, I'm telling you: conceived in a swing (Reuben blushed), born on the floor, immediately christens his mother with a wee-wee right in my face, and now—now gets a ride to the hospital in a hearse!"

Reuben sped along the bumpy road trying to avoid ruts. He spoke huskily over his shoulder, "Honey, you've made me so proud and happy. You've given me a son, my very own son, and I do love you."

"And did you feel that he really did love you?"

"Yes, Doctor; it was the first time in my life I felt true love from a person sexually close to me. Oh, that first year of our son's life was heaven. Ben made the advances. That shy, aloof man whom I was used to coaxing, constantly, that wonderful husband finally became my lover. I mean he couldn't get enough of me!"

"So you were happy during your years with Reuben."

"Well, don't get me wrong. It wasn't all roses. You know that old saying, 'the honeymoon is over'? When he started ignoring me again I simply allowed myself to get pregnant again. It sure worked before."

"So you had another baby and the honeymoon went on."

"Exactly. Until our third child. He had red hair! God, Ben was upset about that. All his old doubts came back and the great lover went back in the closet, so to speak."

"Is that when you turned to other men?"

"Not yet. He gave me some rough times, but I had the kids and friends. I guess I always supposed Ben married me because I got pregnant. Despite his family's early doubts about me I figured Ben would learn to love me. And he did. As long as I gave him babies who were dark like the rest of his kin." Anna laughed self-consciously. "But I'm getting ahead of myself.

"So, anyway, I understood Ben. He was a proud Latin-American enrolled in prestigious Rice University where his fairly light skin allowed him to pass as Anglo. In the '50s Rice was giving good ol' boys, you know, white boys, free tuition grants. We had to be kinda sneaky, but it was the only way Ben could make it financially. Boy, I tell you, he sure stayed out of the sun!"

"Didn't the cultural clash affect your marriage?"

"You bet. But I'm pretty strong-willed, and I had my ways of getting around him, but he was deeply opinionated about how I must run *his* home. And I told you from the very beginning he resented Noreen—didn't want me to keep her because she wasn't his. It was a blow to his religion which dictated that a man must marry only a virgin.

"Listen, he really was a good man, and he tried hard to be a good father. I think he really did love Noreen, maybe, after awhile, from a distance." Haltingly she told about her four children with Reuben and their often stormy family life.

Dr. Richmond put in a new tape and targeted Anna's words as she wandered around the office remembering Reuben's sporatic passionate devotion and describing intimate scenes as if no one else was around. He remained silent as he listened to a full, promising life move inexorably toward self-destruction.

"Like I told you, those next months after Garey were so wonderful," mused Anna. "Gosh Ben was loving and attentive. He was mad about the boy—took him everywhere including the university grounds where he'd spread out a blanket and play with him for hours. Even took along a bottle so he wouldn't have to bring him home for a breast feeding.

"But he ignored Noreen even worse. Poor little thing. I planned special outings while Ben was at school so that Noreen would get lots of attention. She sure needed me those days— and for a long time." Her gaze into the past mellowed for a moment.

"He could be a bastard, sometimes—Ben. Stayed away at the university most of his last year; spending his time at home with Garey then crashing into exhausted sleep while I lay awake. At least he was starting to get job offers, so every now and then he needed me to get all dressed up for an evening function. He was loving at those times and proud to have me on his arm around all the bigwigs. But his growing aloofness made me mad.

"I fixed him!" Anna laughed. "That's when I got pregnant for the third time; his second. Boy was *he* the mad one then. I ignored his pacing and grumbling. Finally he stormed out of the house with his briefcase and an overnight bag. I didn't see him for four days.

"By that time I had my old job back at Eperson's Drug Store. When the time came my plan for a home delivery was in readiness. I knew it would be successful this time. It was during Reuben's finals for his degree in physics that I went into labor. Things began normal enough but rapidly got out of control. I couldn't understand it. Hours passed in hard labor but no delivery. I remember yelling out at him.

"'Oh, God, Ben, the pain is so bad! I should have already had this baby. Something's wrong. God, I just can't do it. No strength left. The pain! I can't stand it much longer. Tell me if you can see the head yet.'

"He was trembling as he said, 'No, honey. I think I see something but it's not the baby's head I'm sure. I'm scared, Anna. What can I do? Damn, how I hate this.'

"'You've got to call a doctor,' I yelled at him. 'Any doctor who will come. Please! Hurry! One or even both of us might die. Oh, my God, hurry, Ben!' And I almost passed out.

"I guess only minutes passed before a doctor arrived, but it seemed like hours to me. I learned later I was experiencing the painful futility of labor with a breech baby.

"The unfamiliar doctor was wonderful, and so kind to me. He worked expertly with a quick incision and forceps. 'It's a beautiful little girl with dark hair, Mrs. Lorenz,' he assured me. 'She seems to be fine. Just got a backwards start on life, you might say. The long incision was the only way of getting her out fast by the time I arrived.'

"'It's okay, Doctor,' I told him. 'I'm just glad it's over and the baby is normal, and everything. Will it be all right with you if we make payments monthly?'"

"'Fine with me. Not much of a fee anyhow. But, I'd advise you *not* to try another do it yourself birth. Having babies is risky business . . . best do it the proper way . . . in a hospital with your own doctor.'"

Anna turned to face Dr. Richmond. "Sandra was dark with many of Ben's features so he took to her just like he did Garey. But Noreen was rejected more and more, and I tried every way I could think of to make it up to her."

Methodically she circled her finger repeatedly around the pleats in her gray dress as she remembered those trying times after Sandra's birth.

It was summer, warm and sultry in Houston. Anna jabbed at the numbers on the telephone dial, her chubby fingers riding on top of the small holes as she fought back tears.

"Hello, Sue? God, I'm glad you answered instead of the old man. Listen, I'm not coming in today. Can you tell him I'm sick . . . throwing up or something?"

"Again, Anna? Christ, this must be the third or fourth time this month. His wife bitches like hell when she has to come in and wait tables. What's goin' on with you? Is it you and Ben?"

"No, well, not exactly. It's just the same old thing. Before he left for another interview this morning he hurt Noreen really bad. She won't even eat, just cries and won't stop."

"You mean the bastard hit her?"

"God, no. Nothing like that. He hurt her the worst way possible. He made a big loving fuss over the baby and Garey, but sent her out of the room when she tried to join in. I'm telling you I just don't have the heart to drop her off at the Ripley House and go on to work. Not with her sobbing so pitifully.

"I thought I'd take all three of the kids out to Lake Houston and make a special, big fuss over Noreen. Can you understand that? I mean how important that is to me, Sue?"

"Yeah, sure, honey. I'll think up some good story for the boss."

The soft white sand around the lake was hot; it filtered into Anna's shoes as she picked and plodded her way through sprawled, oily bodies, colorful beach towels and picnic baskets.

"Here, Noreen. This is a good spot. Make Garey sit here a minute. I'll get the umbrella set up and you can stay here with the little ones while I go to the car for the ice chest."

Anna turned to her son with a stern warning. "I'll be able to see you all the way to the car and back, young man, so you'd better stay right here with your sister and behave yourself or I'll bust your bottom. Do you understand?"

Garey nodded, whined and pleaded, "But, I gotta go pee-pee now . . . real bad. Can't I go with you, Mama?"

"Oh, for God's sake. You have your bathing suit on. Go on down and pee in the lake, but come straight back."

With those explicit instructions Garey ran to the water's edge, pulled down his little trunks and promptly sent a thin, steady arc into the lake. Laughter washed over the beach like the uneven lapping of the water's edge, and suddenly all was well. Anna hugged her girls up close and smiled. "He really is cute, isn't he?" Then she winked at Noreen and added, "But not as cute as you, honey. I sure love you crazy kids. Now, tell you what. We're going to make this Noreen's un-birthday, and on our way home we'll stop at Rettigs ice cream parlor for sodas or sundaes."

"You mean it'll be almost like my real birthday?" squealed Noreen.

"That's right, honey, but instead of presents we'll just have fun all day. Okay?"

"Okay, Mama. Don't worry, I'll take good care of the little ones."

Anna smiled at the memories and relaxed into her chair. It was time for a coffee break so the doctor turned off his recorder and went out for awhile. But, he was reluctant to cut off his patient's easy flow of words. Soon he was back, urging her to continue her reminiscing about the remaining years with Reuben. She continued—with mixed emotions steadily depleting the doctor's supply of Kleenex.

The birth of William three years after Sandra had brought deep, non-healing wounds to the marriage. The new baby was fair with blue eyes and reddish-blond hair. Anna insisted he took after her family, the German heritage: but Reuben accused her of seeing other men and steadfastly refused to fully accept William as his son.

Even though their marriage remained a futile attempt at togetherness, one more child, James, was born—complete with dark, Lorenz features. As usual, the next few months were fairly happy ones for Anna, with Reuben being tender and loving toward mother and baby. By the time James was about eight-months-old the marriage was again dissolving. Harsh words and hurt feelings widened the rift.

"'Lighten up,' Sue would say, and one day, 'Hey, would Ben mind if we take you dancing in the Empire Room at the Rice Hotel?'

"God, would you? I'd adore that. And I can get Ferris to escort me. He's gotten kinda sweet on me, you know."

And so began a pattern of madcap adventures; first with Sue and her husband; many times with Ferris; and then, on her own, the recurrence of her willful, childhood wildness which she now adapted to the risque underworld of nighttime Houston.

CHAPTER 9

April, 1962.

By the time James was five Ben's methodical advancement in the government's aeronautics program had increased the family's income to encompass a larger home, two automobiles and a regular baby-sitter. The stilted truce became a bearable habit.

But Anna's insatiable desires had to find outlets even though her indescretions became a wedge between her and her children. As they gradually grew out of babyhood she spent more and more evenings away from home.

She sought solace at neighborhood saloons and dance halls.

Even though she was fully aware that Houston was rigidly segregated physically as well as politically it never frightened her to consort with minorities. When she pranced far down Lyons Avenue or Jensen Drive she was wooed by black men as if she were a princess. They would escort her to places she never could have gone alone; along Avondale, or the Strip on Westheimer. She felt important.

However, even when Reuben impugned her with bitter accusations of promiscuity, she could soothe him enough so that the family remained intact.

Until she had a hysterectomy.

"You'll die without it," the doctors warned her. "You've got got to have it done—and soon."

"Anna? Look at me, Anna," interrupted Dr. Richmond. "You were telling me about your hysterectomy."

She slurred over the word and began to mumble.

"What's that? Tell me again, Anna. I heard you say you had a hysterectomy. What happened?" The doctor pulled at the left side of his beard for a full minute, waiting.

"Yes," she whispered. Then, stronger. "Yes, I had a complete hysterectomy. My doctor told me I *had* to have it, Maybe I didn't; I don't know anymore. Ben sure didn't want me to. Something in his culture was dead set against a woman having any changes in her reproductive organs.

"God, I wish I hadn't done it. Maybe I would have been okay,and Ben would have stayed with me."

Her hands fidgeted in her lap and then hurriedly covered her mouth as if to prevent something foul from escaping. Her head sagged and she twisted grotesquely in order to avoid facing Dr. Richmond.

"Take your time. Tell me what happened."

Anna gulped her coffee as she tried to tell about coming home after her hysterectomy. "He . . . he . . ." She slumped into a semi-faint, spilling coffee on the shag rug. She could still hear Dr. Hanamoto's testimony.

Thursday, July 11, 1974, 1:30 p.m.

KAZUMI HANAMOTO called as a witness by and on behalf of the People, having been first duly sworn, was examined and testified as follows:

THE CLERK: State and spell your name, please.

THE WITNESS: My name is K-A-Z-U-M-I H-A-N-A-M-O-T-O.

THE CLERK: Thank you, sir. You may be seated.

BY MR. DURBIN:

Q. What is your occupation?

A. I'm an obstetrician-gynecologist with the Metro Municipal Medical Group.

Q. Could you tell us, please, what your qualifications are as an expert witness in the field of gynecology and obstetrics.

A. I'm a Board certified obstetrician-gynecologist, since, I believe, 1968, licensed to practice in California.

Q. Directing your attention to the defendant in this matter, the woman with reddish-blonde hair sitting at the opposite end of counsel table, did you have occasion to observe and talk to her on May 25, 1974?

A. Yes.

Q. And that was pursuant to request by the nurse in charge plus two police officers?

A. Yes.

Q. During your conversation did you examine the defendant in this case?

A. Yes, primarily a pelvic examination.

Q. What did you ask her and what was her response?

A. Well, as I was examining her abdomen, I asked her about her past surgical history, since I had noted a scar on the abdomen. And she told me that she had gallbladder surgery done—I don't remember when, but early—I think she said 1964 or somewhere in that neighborhood, and they also removed her appendix, and that was the extent of her surgery.

I suggested that she be examined more extensively because of the fact that if she had a laceration or a tear, it should be noted.

Q. Now, at that time you were under the impression, were you not, that the defendant was going to be removed from the hospital somewhere by the police?

A. Yes.

Q. So it was your intent, I take it, to determine what her medical condition was?

A. Yes, it was.

Q. At that time did you have any knowledge or information or belief that she had not had a child?

A. I'm not sure what you mean by your statement. Would you restate it for me?

Q. Well, you were operating under the assumption that the

defendant had just given birth to a child?

A. Yes, right.

Q. And I take it you performed a pelvic examination?

A. Yes, I did, to make certain there were no lacerations in the cervix or the vaginal canal and—well, that's in essence that the examination consists of, precise checking to see that the fundus is well contracted.

Q. What did you observe or what were your findings?

A. When I initially did the speculum examination, I was surprised that there wasn't any blood in the vaginal canal for someone who had just recently delivered. And on further inspection I really could not find a cervix, and on my manual examination, which is the pelvic exam, I could not feel the uterus or the fundus or the cervix. And on palpitation of the abdomen there was no mass I could feel. There was . . .

(Pause for disruption in the audience.)

THE COURT: There will be no histrionics in my court! The bailiff is instructed to remove any person so inclined as to disrupt the proceedings of this preliminary hearing.

You may proceed, Mr. District Attorney.

MR. DURBIN: Thank you, your Honor.

BY MR. DURBIN:

Please continue, Doctor.

A. Since she was rather heavy with a thick abdominal wall, I was concerned that I might be—or might miss viewing it. So I re-examined her and also did a rectal examination, and on my examination I felt quite certain that she had had a hysterectomy prior to admission to the hospital.

Q. Did the defendant tell you that she had given birth to the baby?

A. Yes.

Q. Did the defendant say anything to you about her breasts or breast-feeding or anything of that nature?

A. She said nothing about that. I didn't ask her.

I just read the nurses' notes stating that she was taken to breast-feed the baby earlier that morning and then refused because she said she had no milk in her breasts.

Q. Did the defendant say anything else to you, other than what you have testified to, during the course of the examination?

A. She said that they were trying to "take my baby away."

Q. After you determined in your own mind that the defendant had had a hysterectomy prior to admission into the hospital, did you make that knowledge known to her?

A. Yes. I stated to her—after I had examined her and was quite certain, I said—and these are the words I remember—-
"Anna, you didn't tell me you had a hysterectomy."

Q. And what, if anything, did she respond?

A. She said to me, "You are trying to take my baby away from me, too."

(Pause for counsel to confer.)

CROSS-EXAMINATION
BY MR. WINGATE:

Q. Dr. Hanamoto, on the 25th of May when you walked into Mrs. Anderson's room, you didn't know her, is that correct?

A. No—I did—I was acquainted with her, yes.

Q. How were you acquainted with her?

A. Working in the delivery room.

Q. Sir?

A. Working in the delivery room.

Q. Oh, you mean she was employed in the hospital, as a registered nurse working in the labor and delivery room. So, you had talked to her on prior occasions?

A. Only concerning matters—yes, concerning patients.

Q. Professional matters?

A. Right.

Q. There was no personal relationship?

A. No, none.

Q. No social relationship?

A. None.

Q. Now, when you entered Mrs. Anderson's room what was

the first thing you said to her and what did she say to you in response thereto?

Mr. DURBIN: Objection, your Honor. What he said is hearsay.

Mr. WINGATE: Not at all. He's a party to the conversation, your Honor.

THE COURT: That will be overruled.

THE WITNESS: Would you repeat the question, please?

BY MR. WINGATE:

Q. What did you say to Mrs. Anderson and what did she say to you?

A. I don't remember the exact wording, but the essence of my conversation with her was that she needed to have an examination done for her own sake in case she did have some tears or lacerations, and that was essentially it.

Q. You didn't tell her that you talked to the nurse and had gotten information about two detectives and her being transferred?

A. No. I didn't—I didn't tell her she was—about the conversation with the . . .

Q. Yes sir, I understand. But Mrs. Anderson had not called for you, had she?

A. No, sir, she did not call me.

Q. So, if the two detectives and the chief of nursing had not asked you, you would *not* have examined Mrs. Anderson, would you, Doctor?

MR. DURBIN: Objection, your Honor. That calls for speculation.

THE COURT: It will be sustained.

Q. It was after you talked to the chief of nurses, the two detectives, and the captain that you examined Mrs. Anderson; is that correct?

MR. DURBIN: *Objection*, your Honor; asked and answered.

THE COURT: I hear you. Sustained.

BY MR. WINGATE:

Q. Well, did you ask Mrs. Anderson's permission to examine her?

A. Yes.

Q. Did you walk in and suggest to Mrs. Anderson that she be examined by *you*?

THE COURT: Just a minute. That issue has been covered and answered, I believe, a number of times.

MR. WINGATE: On direct but not on cross, your Honor.

THE COURT: I believe it has.

MR. WINGATE: All right, your Honor.

BY MR. WINGATE:

Q. Doctor, was it after you performed the examinations that you discovered the alleged prior hysterectomy?

A. Yes.

Q. When Mrs. Anderson said to you, "You are trying to take my baby away, too," what did you say?

A. Nothing.

Q. You made no response?

A. I just patted her on the shoulder.

Anna cried unashamedly until Dr. Richmond shook her and knelt beside her with a reassuring hug. "Here," he offered. "Take some sips of water and rest a minute."

"It's hard to tell anyone how Ben reacted."

"I know."

"That first night was awful! Ben didn't bring me home, Ferris did. He was so kind that I felt closer to him than to Ben the whole day. Oh, Ben came to bed with me . . . and almost every night for weeks. But in our bed he always lay with his back to me. Otherwise he slept on the couch in the sewing room. I couldn't stand it! Doctor, I tried, oh, how I tried. I gave him at least two months to come around. Finally, one night I reached out for him, pleading."

She choked as she remembered.

"Dammit, Ben, we need to talk, at least. I can't go on like this."

"Nothing to say," he grumbled, rolling his body even closer to the edge of the bed.

"Ben! *Please* turn over and look at me. I'm still the same. Look, honey, I didn't even put on a gown tonight. I don't even want clothes to come between us because of how sexy I am. *Very* sexy. I'm all soft and warm and wanting you."

She reached under the covers sliding her hand over his hip until she felt the hardening bulge just inside his fly—and she knew he wanted her too. The old confidence about his reactions to her body returned and she strained to press herself against him.

"Don't touch me!" he thundered as he jerked her hand away.

"Don't you ever touch me again. You repulse me, you, you— thing. I told you how I'd feel about you if you had that done. Shit, you're not a whole woman anymore. Why couldn't you under-stand that before you had the operation?"

"What the hell are you talking about, that I repulse you? What does the goddamn hysterectomy have to do with love-making? I'm exactly the same, fully-functioning woman I've always been, I mean, except for making babies . . . and I think I've done my share of that by now." Tears flowed as she leaned on one elbow yelling at Reuben's sheeted back.

"Ben, please believe me! It's not going to feel any different for either of us."

Reuben remained stiffly silent.

"They said I would have died. Is that what you wanted? To have me bleed to death to be rid of me? I bet you think it was my duty to die intact. Humph! You would have given me a gorgeous funeral and a big headstone reading 'here lies a whole woman.' And your precious family pride would have been kept pure and macho." By that time Reuben was moving his things into the other room.

"Damn, Ben, how can you be so ignorant when you're so in-telligent? Well, to hell with you." So Anna wept for days as they started to work out an amicable divorce.

She used wads of Kleenex as she told Dr. Richmond about her deepening depression.

"I tried to endure the strain we all felt. But I had my old feelings of shame and rejection."

"I can understand all that, Anna. Please go on."

"But it gets so much worse from here on, Doctor. I just gave up on Ben *and* myself, and everything. Tried to kill myself! That sadist watched me swallow a whole bottle of pills; stood in the doorway watching with the strangest look on his face. Then he calmly gathered up all the kids and said they were going for a ride. Be gone for supper.

"I guess he either thought I was all show; or else he really thought I'd be dead when they got back. After two hours the older kids came bursting into my room to show me a stray puppy they had found near Hermann Park. I was comatose by then. Noreen was the cool-headed one who called an ambulance and rode in it with me to the hospital.

"They pulled me through, of course, and then, by law they sent me to a mental institution for an undetermined length of confinement. By the time I was released two months later I had promised the psychiatric board that I would leave Ben immediately. That was the main condition of my early release, that our divorce become final.

"So, it did—uncontested. It was over."

Doctor and patient were glad to be interrupted by one of the matrons who announced lunch. Anna had to face another lonely night of solitude and memories until their session the next day.

When she settled into her swivel chair in the morning she was eager to resume her story which was commanding so much attention from this important man.

"I'm remembering how I suddenly had my hands full with Noreen and had to quit dating altogether. She was fifteen then, a looker, pretty sexy, and everything. You know.

"Well, I tried being strict with her. It was hard without Ben. I just couldn't control her anymore. Took me awhile to notice her growing vulnerability and how it was clashing with her immaturity. My baby was growing up . . . and yet she still needed me. *Needed* me. Boy, that was a real shocker."

URE

Anna got up, walked around her chair and stood mumbling as Dr. Richmond slid his microphone across the desk for a better position, rubbed his fingers against his beard, and watched as he encouraged her to go back in time again. It was fascinating to him how she could relive her past with changing voices, mannerisms and gestures: acting out mirrored incidents of her troubled life.

"Noreen, where do you think you're going? It's nine o'clock and you have school tomorrow. Just hang your coat up and get ready for bed, young lady. Did you do any homework? It's no wonder your grades are so bad. All you think about is boys."

"See, there you go, Mama. How can you possibly know what I'm thinking about or what I'm doing? You never ask. As for school, you never have time to help me when I need it. All you ever want to do is be with the little ones, that is if you're ever home. So don't blame me for wanting to get out of here. I like to be with my friends. They have time for *me*."

"I bet they do! The gang you hang around with . . . they strike me as a lazy bunch of drop-outs . . . probably into LSD. Honey, I know school is hard for you, but life is hard. If only you would study more, everything would seem better to you.

"Oh, Nory! My baby! I'm really sorry I haven't spent more time with you; but working full time doesn't leave me many minutes for you kids. And I have to pay more attention to the little ones because they can't take care of themselves. Can't help it if they need me more than you do."

"How do you know how much I need you, Mama? What about right now? Do you have time for me right now, Mama? I know Dad doesn't. I've phoned him a dozen times. But do you? I really need you now." Noreen turned away, yanked the ribbon from her long, blonde pony tail, letting it fall around her shoulders as if to shield her from the expected wrath of her mother. She paced and punched at the furniture.

"You might as well know right now, I'm not even going to school anymore. Haven't gone for weeks. I'm never going back. Never!"

"What are you saying? You *have* to go to school. My God, Noreen, you're only fifteen. What have you been doing all day if you haven't been in school?"

"Most of the time I just go out walking and crying. I go to Hermann Park and sit a lot and cry. I even thought of running away, you know, like you said you used to do. But I didn't know where to go. I was too scared. Maybe I should leave now . . .

Oh, Mama, what can I do? Everyone's gonna hate me. But please, not you, too."

"Of course not! Don't talk like that. It's not the end of the world. You can go back to school. I'll get a tutor, or something, to help you catch up. I can teach you myself, enough for you to graduate. It's going to be all right, you'll see." And she swept her daughter into her arms.

"No, Mama, it won't ever be all right," sobbed the distraught girl. "I didn't tell you all of it. But I have to. Oh, promise you won't hate me?" The choking sobs couldn't be held back any longer, and she broke into loud, uncontrollable wailing.

"What! Tell me about what, Noreen? Tell me! Nothing can be that bad. Tell me what's wrong. I'm your mother. Haven't you always known you can tell me anything?"

Noreen wiped frantically at her wet face as she muffled her startling revelations against her mother's neck. She finally managed to blurt out, "I'm going to have a baby, and, and, I'm so scared, Mama!"

"Dear God!" whispered Anna.

"See there—I knew you'd hate me."

"No, no, honey. Oh, no, I could never hate you."

Dr. Richmond sat forward in his seat, watching intently as Anna's head drooped, tears rolled untouched, and her own voice softened to a childlike whimper as she answered her own "accusing mother" voice. She stood transfixed, facing the big recliner, then slowly walked around it. Her arms circled its back as she hugged it close to her body and stroked the vinyl lovingly.

She continued on from her dream bubble as if she were there again, with her firstborn, her baby. As she caressed the big chair she started crooning her lullaby. "Hush, little baby, don't you cry . . . Mama's gonna love you. . . ."

The doctor hurriedly changed his tape and urged her to go on with her acting out of Noreen's problems. Anna kept her arms cradled, and her head bowed over them.

"Pregnant? You're pregnant? And only a baby yourself. Oh, my dearest, my little Nory, don't be afraid. I'll always love you and be there for you and take care of you. A baby. A beautiful little baby. Oh, honey, are you sure?"

"Yes, Mama, I'm sure. You mean you aren't mad? You're not gonna send me away?"

"Of course not, sweetheart, I'm going to take care of you and the baby too. It'll be all right. You'll see. After it's born you'll be able to go back to school while I watch my grandchild. Wowie! And I'll work nights while you're home.

"By the way, who's the father, and what does he plan to do about it? I might as well know right now."

"Nope, can't tell you that. He's older, a big wheel downtown. Mama, he turned nasty—told me that if I cause any trouble he'll deny everything. Claims he's got a lot of friends who'll swear they were with me too . . . you know, that way. That's why it hurts so much !" She started crying again. "I really thought he loved me. That's why I let him do it whenever we were together, 'cause he said it was a way of proving our love to each other. Now he can't stand the sight me." She wept a long, long time while her mother hugged and rocked her.

"Hush, now, my baby, don't you worry about that S.O.B. We don't need him. I'll take care of this new baby like it's my very own. And everything will be just great, you'll see."

Dr. Richmond guided Anna around into the chair while calling to her and gently shaking her back to the present. "Listen to me, Anna. Up to that time in your life you were probably a better mother than your *own* mother was. Don't you feel that?" She nodded gratefully.

"Tell me, did you like having Noreen's baby with you as much as you did your own? And did you mind being a grandmother so young?"

"Damn, I sure didn't feel like a grandmother. It was like *I* had that baby . . . like it was mine. Eventually I even taught him to call me Nana—sounded almost as good as Mama."

"And Noreen? Did she go back to school like you planned?"

"No. She got a 'nothing' job and started running around again until she found a boy who wanted to marry her. And that really hurt because they moved to Colorado. I lost my baby."

The doctor appraised her as she started pacing again. "Anyway, after the divorce I went back to school, nursing school at Memorial Baptist Hospital. Got my R.N. certificate too. Boy, I worked hard for that; had to keep my part-time hours at Eperson's. Can't say that I fooled around much then! Still, I guess I continued to neglect my children something awful. But, at the time nothing was more important than that R.N., and everything. It was all for Mama, to make her proud of me."

"And what happened? Was your mother happy about that?"

"No." Anna used more tissues for a moment. "No, Mama disowned me for good, I think because she heard I was going out with black men. Don't know how she could have found that out.

"I guess she just couldn't love me, not ever." Anna stared at her lap for a full minute while the doctor watched her. He prodded softly.

"Can you tell me more about that period in your life?"

She thought about Garey. How well she remembered his quick, bubbling leap into his teens.

God, wish I could go back . . . my Garey, so good, so clever. Why didn't I pay attention?

Anna frowned, thinking of the day her son grabbed her around the waist and boomed out a song which startled her and intruded into her schemes for the day.

"Mama, listen: 'Sweetheart, sweetheart, sweetheart—will you love me—ever?' It's from Maytime, you know that one. It's made for me! 'Cept I have to kiss the heroine; and then I get killed in the duel. Boy, do I die great!

"It's the lead. Me! The *lead*, Mama, in our spring musical. And I'm not even a senior yet. Do you realize they chose a *musical* play just to star *me*? Jesus, think of . . ."

"Don't swear, Garey."

"Are you listening? About the musical?"

"I'm listening—through one ear."

"Well, here, tickets for the first row. They gave me my choice of seats for you and three others. Gosh, my very own 'big-time' show!"

"That's nice, hon, but calm down. Hand me that bowl over there—on top of the breadbox."

"Mama, pay attention. This is big!"

"Okay, okay, so when is this 'really big show'?"

"It's May eleventh and twelfth. May. Get it? Starts at 8:30 p.m. All you need is a baby sitter for Bill and James, and a fancy dress for yourself. Boy, are you gonna be proud of me!"

"Sure, honey, I'll check on the dates."

"*Mama*. Nothin's more important than this. Whadda you mean 'check'? Of course you'll be there!"

"We'll see. Don't forget I have commitments of my own. I just can't drop everything for you kids the minute you think I should."

Garey looked hard at his mother, gave her a hesitant kiss, and slowly left the kitchen.

Anna slumped in her seat and continued shredding damp Kleenex. Oh, yes, she remembered. Remembered that very week-end of the school musical. *She* spent it on the Strip. Away from home. Away from her children. Playing her game of 'love me?' while her son's play and his brilliant performance were forgotten.

She remembered Garey's hurt recriminations, his withdrawal further into the street scene, his disinterest in any further school activities. Why had she done it? Why had she missed his big event?

And later, with Bill. She had ignored him too. Sweet Bill with his sunny disposition. Dear Bill.

Bill was almost eight when he could finally read some of the worn pages in the old Spot primers she had never turned back in to her first grade teacher.

"Look, Mama," bragged Sandra. "Look what Bill can do. A whole page."

"Not now, dear, can't you see I'm dressing for a party?"

"But, Mama, he wants to read to you."

"Sandra, not now. I mean, that's good—even terrific. But I'll listen some other time. Now go play. I've got to get a move on." She hugged both before rushing off to the Satin Doll.

What had happened after that? She couldn't remember hearing Bill read. Not ever. *Didn't I ever know it? That he had learned to read?* "Oh, Bill!"

Little James was bright. Maybe brighter than all of them.

Anna loved to kiss his smooth, round face framed by dark curls. What a loving baby. He hugged everyone, but especially his mother. Her last one. How quickly he had grown past elementary school. What kind of a student had he been? She couldn't remember. She did recall some of his childhood, how all the neighborhood kids rang the doorbell incessantly. "Can Jimmy play?" Since she discouraged whole bunches of children in her apartment James usually played at his friends'."

So soon he left me.

"They all left—all my babies. Why can't I remember where they all went?"

Anna's thoughts wrestled with conflicting emotions. Her babies had grown up so fast! There were blank years. What happened to her children during those years? They were around, somewhere, living with her, eating at her kitchen table, wearing clothes she bought them for birthdays and Christmas. Yes, and piling up school reports for her to see. But . . . she couldn't remember any of the school papers.

I lost them . . . the children, the years, the plays, the grades, the hobbies.

"I want to go back," she sobbed. "I want to grab onto them, hold them. I want to tell them I *do* love them. If only I could go back and pay attention to them. What have I done?" She cried silently, her emotions laboring to control overt sobbing.

Dr. Richmond quickly broke in before more tears started.

"Okay, let's take a break, and then I want you to recall all about nursing school."

Anna enthusiastically remembered her good times while in nursing school. It was 1967, and she, Anna Louise Mayer Lorenz, at almost 38 years of age, was getting a diploma from the much-honored school connected with Memorial Baptist Hospital. The entire complex was a stately, revered institution, set way back from traffic on Lamar Street.

It had been somewhat of a struggle for her to finally get her high school credentials and commit herself to the three years necessary to earn a diploma in bedside nursing. A wonderful, rewarding struggle!

She felt as if she had grabbed the brass ring when the director announced, "Anna Louise Lorenz will now sing the school hymn."

She stood by the curtain, carefully smoothing her new starched uniform; then stepped onto the podium with regal bearing. She smiled into the proud faces of her children and her one grandson beaming up at her.

"Anna Louise," whispered Mrs. Boomer, "you're our prize student. You have made us very proud—you—at your age—such a *good* nurse."

But will Mama be proud? She wished her short legs weren't so rubbery. And that stupid mascara, smudging and streaking. Should have left it off today. *Lord! I didn't change my shoelaces.* After she sang the six-stanza hymn Anna squirmed through endless speeches while alternately winking and smiling at her children.

During the last cheer for the last award she dashed out through the arched doorway at near Olympic speed. Her padded nurses' shoes stumbled over themselves, and her crisp uniform skirt blew straight out behind her. One hand held onto her graduate cap, creasing it slightly on one side. The other gripped her rolled diploma so tightly that her fingers were numb.

She headed for the public telephone booth on Lamar, waving her children back to wait for her. Such a pretty day! Too many blossoms to identify were showing off in the spring warmth. All of Houston's flora and fauna were blooming as fast as they could before the sun could singe them permanently.

"It's like me! Blooming for all their worth before withering." She laughed delightedly along the well-groomed pathway. Her happy senses nudged at her crowded thoughts and squeezed into her mind all the messages of beauty that any one human could absorb.

She grabbed a clover with two fingers freed from around her diploma, raised it to her nose, then impulsively kissed the parchment. Her skipping and whirling amused sedate faculty who momentarily recalled their own days of glory. She burst out again with the full force of her splendid mezzo-soprano. Pedro, her staunch confidant paused and laid down his shears as she passed.

"Okay, senorita, okay. You do it!"

Anna waved her cap and stumbled into the phone booth. She impatiently juggled her cap, diploma, and change purse. Dimes were scarce in the crocheted handbag her mother had made for her in the fifth grade. It also held two handkerchiefs, bandage scissors, a Kelly clamp, and a crumpled tintype of Elsie and Conrad. Her fingers fumbled so that she had to dial twice just to get the operator.

"Collect from Anna Louise," she screamed into the mouthpiece. Her body trembled. Through the crackling of the phone Anna heard the operator repeat, "Will you accept the charge?"

And then a pause, a pause which lengthened into a lifetime of silence. Anna could barely hear the thin voice of her mother:

"I know no one . . . named Anna Louise."

CHAPTER 10

Two hours later, Graduation Day, 1967.

Anna found herself miles away from the telephone booth before she could concentrate on her surroundings. People passing her were staring at her. She realized how absurd she appeared in her starched uniform, holding her cap and diploma with clenched fists. She noted the street signs and walked over a block to catch a bus going to her neighborhood.

Her apartment was silent. No children. No friends. She felt as if she was a damaged survivor of a modern holocaust; to be shunned as a mutant, an undesirable. She clamped her head to block out the emptyness. It all seemed so futile. Suddenly her door opened with a familiar bang against the wall. Squeals of hilarity and smothering hugs tipped over her rocker.

"Hey, what's . . ."

"Mama, Mama, we're so proud of you," said Noreen. They were all there—her beautiful children, her classmates, and even her teachers. Neighbors crowded into the living room, all jabbering at once.

"Surprise!" they were yelling.

For me? All this for me? The horrid words were gone; replaced with sounds of joy and celebration. Even shy, cynical Ferris was there. She looked through the crowd, searching, but Ferris shook his head.

"Live it up," he cried as he kissed her.

There was music and dancing and food and champagne. Her children had planned it all weeks before graduation. She toasted her future with warm pride in herself.

I do have it . . . the brass ring!

July was hot and humid. Anna enjoyed her new job on the maternity ward of Houston General. But something was nagging at her. Her children were hardly ever at home when she was off duty except James and Noreen's baby. One Friday evening everyone was nearby, and Anna had shopped and cooked all afternoon for a big, family supper.

"Garey," she called. "Get the other kids in if you can find them. Dinner's ready."

"Okay, Mama, but I'm not eating here . . . got plans. A bunch of us guys are going to Galveston to the beach for the weekend."

"You never stay home anymore, dammit. All you kids are always running off somewhere, God knows where. What's happening to us? Look here, I've made a big, fried chicken dinner with all the fixings for us, and you're not even interested."

"Take it easy. I'll see if I can round up the other kids for you, Mama, before I go. Just don't expect me to be around all the time."

She sighed good naturedly. "Just like your father. Well, good luck finding the others. I have no idea where they are. Been at work most of the day." She sighed again. "Everybody goes their own way. None of you need me anymore. You're all too big."

"Oh, come on now, Mama, you have to cut those old apron strings . . . can't keep us babies forever, you know. We had a lot of fun times with you. Listen, there was little league, the scouts, fishin' at Hermann park, and all the camping we did in that big ol' droopy tent. Remember? We really had fun growing up, Mama, but, well, we're older now and things change. I know Bill and James are still here most of the time. Why don't you do something with them tonight? Like taking them to the roller rink maybe. You could always skate circles around all us kids. Come on, loosen up. How about a smile?"

"Yeah, sure. Well, maybe I won't miss you so much once I get some money in the bank. Then I'll be stepping out myself, and there won't be time to feel lonely, and everything. You're right, son. Maybe I *will* take the boys skating. Sounds like fun. Might even stop at Rettigs on the way home. See what you'll be missing, Garey?"

"Gee," he teased. "Guess I'll just have to suffer since I've already got these beach plans. Not much to do there but watch beautiful girls in skimpy bikinis—and, of course, show off my gorgeous, bronze bod."

"Go on with you! Have a good time, but be careful how you pee in the ocean." Anna laughed at the family joke on Garey.

Dr. Richmond's office, third interview.

"You were telling me about your fifteen years with Ben. I gather you believed those were mostly happy times, Anna? So after Noreen and the baby left you still had your other children, and a good job. And you told me Rueben helped you out with finances. Why wasn't all that enough for you?"

"God, I don't know, doctor. Seems like I have some kind of addiction for men and babies. It all adds up to love. I think I would do just about anything for love." She glanced up quickly. "Guess I have, haven't I?"

Dr. Richmond shuffled some notes.

"I can tell you that after I started nursing school I definitely realized that Ben and I had parted for good—the marriage would never be resumed. With what little free time I had I started right in searching, as usual, for a man who could love me. Crazy, huh?"

"Where were the children?"

"Ben let me have them—he was really generous about that. I told you we stayed at home until I could find a suitable apartment for all of us. Then he helped pay the rent, and extra stuff for the kids. He never saw me again, never called. Just sent money. Ferris kept in touch with me and would let me know how Ben was doing. I suppose he kept Ben posted on me and the kids as well."

"I guess you went without a man then for several years?"

"Oh, I wouldn't say *that*. Lord no."

"You said you were too busy to date."

"Umm, some. Ben had done a number on me those last months

together. Always preaching at me about 'dirty sex' with other men and how that's what made me sick enough to need the hysterectomy. But I needed a man, any man. I started hanging around the black bars down on Dallas Street—when I wasn't studying, that is."

"Your children?"

"They were okay—Noreen watched the two youngest while I wasn't at home." She glanced at Dr. Richmond.

"Okay, Anna, what next?"

"So, I knew black men would fall over themselves to have me, just because I'm white. You know—be proud of me—I had always heard that." She winked. "And I can tell you first hand it's true. Some black guys will actually fight over an attractive white woman. It's a hell of a status trip for them."

She paused and sighed enough to hyperventilate.

"Take it easy, Anna," soothed the docter. "So, I take it the black men did a lot to boost your sagging ego as well. Okay, let's get into some of those various affairs."

"Good Lord, do you want a blow by blow description of my one-night stands? Or can I just hit the highlights?"

"However you want to tell me is okay. Remember, we're trying to analyze what led you to commit murder."

Anna blanched as she remembered why she was in this office and in a drab uniform. She set her mind on Houston, and the hectic, promiscuous escapades which pushed her toward and into a period of sick insanity.

"Doctor," she began. "I was too young to shrivel up and sew or rock away my vibrant years. You remember that hit, 'What Kind of Fool am I?' It bugged me. I felt there had to be something more for me.

"As luck would have it the first man I got serious with was 'Mannie' Manning, a con man, a player."

"Wait a minute. What's a player?"

"Oh, that's a guy who lives off women, and everything. Sort of like a kept woman only a kept man."

"Okay, I see. Go on."

"I rented a cheap motel room on the Strip, off Westheimer. Black people could come and go around there without too much trouble. I insisted on keeping my life with Mannie separate from that with my children. I had them with me most of the time, over on the east side of town in a fairly nice apartment complex. Anyhow, it only lasted a few months with me and Mannie.

"He was into drugs and criminal activities of all sorts.

I was sure he was involved, somehow, when I got shot at several times after I witnessed the murder of a black drug dealer.

"I was so scared for myself and my kids that I packed up, rented a U-Haul trailer and left Texas. I drove all the way to the state of Colorado and parked the four kids with Noreen, who had two children by then, and a pretty good marriage.

"I sure had fun with those little ones!" Anna acted out some hugs and mouthed endearments and baby-talk. Dr. Richmond took hold of her hands and encouraged her to go on.

"I was 40 by then and, damn, I was so lonely. Even tried to vamp Ferris, but he just laughed at me and began ignoring my calls. I soon started hanging around the bars, again, down in the Montrose section. It's a mixed up, wild part of town to say the least. That's where I met Skeeter Maxwell. Ummm—I think that was in 1969. Yes '69 because that's the year we got married. A grand wedding at Antioch Baptist Church, the oldest one in Houston."

"Was he black, Anna?"

"Yes; you see I only had black men after I left Ben. I loved them—I thought—and I was so sure they loved me.

"Skeeter was an ex-con, in for seven years although I didn't know that for months. Jumped parole in the '50s. He sure could sweet talk, and I needed that. He was a real smoothie—a moocher—never worked after we were married.

"And *that* worried me. What was even worse, he bothered me about money where *I* worked, often yelling and stomping around so much that I was actually forced to resign before they fired me.

"Well, after a stormy year with him I began to pressure Skeeter to let me bring my kids back. At first he agreed, but, I don't know, he just kept putting it off. Got mad at me one night about my nagging him for my kids, and beat me so badly he broke a rib. Then, he actually *raped* me. That really did it.

"After I notified the local police Skeeter hid out for weeks. I finally heard he left Houston and went to Amarillo. I don't know how, not to this day, but he persuaded me to join him there. So, we tried again. I know, stupid. Anyway, I sent for the kids, and I made a good home for all of us in Amarillo. But it was the same old story all over. He wouldn't work. He just wouldn't ever work. And he started a regular habit of abuse against me and my children.

"It was about 1970—no, '71, I think, when I left him for good. Packed up everything and took the kids to California to my oldest sister. I didn't have any trouble getting a job. Nothing to it if a person has an R.N. diploma. There's always a shortage of nurses. Heck, as long as you look alive any hospital will hire you."

"Wait a minute . . . how long had you been with Skeeter at that time-uh-before you left him?"

"Close to two years."

Dr. Richmond wrote half a page before motioning, "Go on."

"That fool followed me to California! First he threatened me, and I told him I would report him to the authorities if he ever bothered me or the kids. Well, he promised me he never would. I told you he could always sweet-talk me. So, I took him back, *again.*" She shrugged and looked down at the mess of shredded tissue in her lap.

"Why do you think you did that? Did you love him?"

"No, Dr. Richmond. I don't think I ever loved any of the men after Ben—not until Luther. Like I said, I guess I just needed to at least *think* I could love and be loved."

"I understand. Continue. What happened with you and Skeeter?"

"Well, he started abusing the kids while I was at work. It was then that I shot a 22 revolver at him to scare him, and threatened to kill him if he didn't leave us alone. You better believe he took off then! I never saw him again. Got a divorce in absentia.

"About June or July in '71 I changed jobs to work at L.A. County Hospital as a surgical nurse. There I met a white prisoner, younger than me, *very* handsome; made passes at me every time I got close. I really fell for him. What really got me was a photo of his baby. Cute baby!

"So, when he wrote to me from New Orleans I wrote back and promised I'd go see him and help with the baby. Damned if I didn't leave my own kids alone in our Hollywood apartment with only enough money for two weeks. Headed straight for Texas on a share-expense plan with a hippie acquaintance of mine."

Dr. Richmond shook his head.

"Well, you asked me—I'm only telling you *some* of my affairs," Anna sniffed as the doctor appologized.

"Anyway," she continued, "this woman had promised me I could use her car to go on to New Orleans for a week. But, when we got to Dallas and she met her husband, she just laughed at me and drove off. God, I was mad! *Laughed* at me! There I was, stranded in Texas with very little money and no transportation. *They laughed!* I could have killed them!"

"Anna, how could you get yourself into such situations?"

"Heck, aren't *you* supposed to explain it? I don't know. Anyway, I phoned my prisoner 'friend' in New Orleans to see if he or his people could help me but they couldn't. Then I tried a black priest I know here in California. About a month later he was able to send me a bus ticket.

"That was a very costly fling. While I was gone my kids were evicted, the furniture confiscated and I had lost my new job. She sat forward, cocked her head sideways, glanced morosely at Dr. Richmond and asked, "Do you think I was a mental case even then, Doctor?"

"I can't say, Anna. Your good judgement was off, that's pretty obvious. We're trying now to understand why you made such bad decisions. You had five healthy children, a good career—your R.N. diploma. That gave you respect and an above average income."

"But, Doctor, I've told you! I was desperate to have a man. One that might need me—that if he needed me he maybe would love me, and everything. It just never worked out that way. It was babies, only my babies who ever really loved me."

The doctor stopped her to ask, "About your lovers, how many more were there before Luther Anderson?"

Anna laughed delightedly and bragged, "I remember them all, Doc., but I'm not telling all! Let's see, there was Quinton P. Dollard, maybe his name attracted me to him. Everyone called him 'Cupie Doll.' He was a black hustler I met in a bar on Sunset Boulevard. He was a sexual gold mine. I had never known such ecstasy before. I was very happy and content with him.

"Things were going good until he asked me to go to Nebraska with him to get his three-year-old daughter. She was with his ailing mother, whom I gathered was alcoholic; and he wanted to bring up the child here with us in California. I was thrilled—another little one!

"So, off I went—leaving my kids again."

She sighed and wadded up another Kleenex. "Anyway, I thought it was all right because we were only going to be gone a couple of days. We flew to Nebraska where he was immediately *arrested* on an old robbery charge. Can you believe it? He was sent to prison. Of course, he had all our money and wouldn't give any of it back to me. Just laughed at me as he was led away saying, 'That's the breaks, sweet Mama.'

"His dotty mother had the return tickets and wouldn't give them to me. So, there I was—no money and no way to get home. After five months I had enough to return to Callifornia. Just like before, the kids had been evicted and scattered around with friends: my youngest went back to Ben in Houston. The furniture was taken back, my car repossessed, and personal items missing."

Dr. Richmond got up and walked around the room, then turned to face Anna.

"You left your children often. Can you explain to me why you did that? I mean, apparently you just risked everything you ever attained in life, over and over. Was it all to get more babies? Yet, you readily left the ones you already had. Do you know why?"

"Don't you understand, Doctor? Why doesn't anyone try to understand? I love the babies—they love me back. But when babies get big, it's . . . different, and everything. They want to do their own thing and they don't need me anymore. My babies were almost grown before I started running around.

"I didn't neglect my babies, not when they were little. I *never* neglected or hurt a baby. I did keep my children with me for years. Guess I didn't realize it wasn't good or happy for them anymore. They never liked the men I picked—except maybe Luther.

"It wasn't ever again like when they were babies, and when everything I did for them felt good."

There were wracking sobs again as she tried to explain and tried to excuse the years of misery endured by her children.

"My babies, my little, loving babies. I did so love them. But something happened. Where did they go? *All* gone now. They're all gone."

Dr. Richmond lit his pipe and leaned back appraising her through the aromatic wisps of smoke. He noted the spasmodic facial contortions as his patient relived the inception of her own destruction.

"Anyway," she mumbled defiantly, "I did get another baby, Nancy, didn't I? Yes! And I was brilliant. Nancy . . . our baby . . . mine and Luther's."

The doctor slid his notes into a folder and called in the escort stationed by his door.

"Come on, Anna. Lunch time. Meet here about 1:30 and tell me all about it, about Luther, and how you got Nancy."

How it all began. Yes, she would tell Dr. Richmond what fun it was the night she met Luther; the night she vowed to keep him loving her . . . no matter what.

CHAPTER 11

Sunday, October 31, 1971, 5 p.m.

Halloween . . . what a marvelous time for parties! I can stay out all night, too—this dumb back injury's giving me a lot of excuses for not working.

But I'm all for partying—I'm not that crippled. She didn't worry about the kids. With street-wise Sandra and young Bill the only one still living with her, Anna felt free to do as she pleased, every night including weekends.

Their mother was pleased that Sandra took good care of her younger brother, often tutoring him with patience and love, in case, some day, he might be able to promote into high school. Tonight Sandra was taking him to a young people's party right inside the apartment complex. Of course, everyone knew and liked Bill.

"'Bye, dears," called Anna. "Have fun. I'll be gone when you get back." Deep in her heart was an ache, a void, a fleeting remorse at her loss of James who was now living permanently with his father in Texas. She wondered, only for a moment, what her youngest was doing on his 12th Halloween.

She continued adding green eye shadow in bold swaths to her heavily rouged cheeks. Another moment to press a purple beauty spot into one side of her chin. There. With the headdress, the black wig, and a silver cape she had made herself, the effect was much like the evil but exotic queen in "Snow White."

That'll wow them at the Ham-It-Up. Bet Melly'll be jealous.

She smirked. "You temptress, you," she addressed her mirror. "So? Why couldn't the mean queen have been short and plump?" Impatient honking below her apartment spurred her on.

Right on time. She reflected upon what a good friend Melessa was. They had met at the Ham-It-Up where Melessa was a bartender. Almost immediately they became inseparable, calling each other "sister." It was great to have a confidant, a woman who understood another woman's needs and hopes.

Anna grabbed her purse and swept out onto the curb in regal splendor. The cab driver ogled her with exaggerated gallantry, and handed her into the back seat where Melessa was wrestling with her pumpkin costume.

"Good grief, Melly, whatever have you got on?"

"Don't you dare make fun of me," scolded Melessa. "Boss wants me in the 'spirit' if you get my drift. 'Though how I'm going to mix drinks and serve in this damn, orange globe I don't know. At least he'll see that it'll take me ten minutes just to sit down. Shit, no break all evening!"

"That's probably the very reason he gave you that costume in the first place."

"Humph. But, 'ha, ha' to him. Once I'm inside, well, I've figured out how to solve my problem."

"Oh, really. What's the brilliant plan? Going to materialize the fairy godmother and have her turn you into a skinny Phyllis Diller?"   ·

"Cute, Anna, just keep it up. But, really, I'll fix this thing and the boss too. See these metal stays that are sewn into the material to make it round out? I'm gonna pull out all the ones that are in the back: then I can sit down easily whenever I want."

"Clev-er. Then everyone can see that you're a mushy, *rotten-assed* pumpkin. I love it, Melly! God, it's going to be fun tonight. I can feel it already."

The driver chortled all the way to the Ham-It-Up bar, bowed low, and blew them a kiss for the hefty tip. "Happy Halloween!" They both had to help Miss Pumpkin stand upright on the sidewalk.

"You're waddling," giggled her friend.

"Am not, you green-eyed bitch."

"Better get on with your 'spoiled butt' plan, or, I'm telling you—you'll never be able to handle it with that funny waddle."

Melessa flounced into the bar with odd, dumpy movements needed to avoid customers and furniture. There were plenty of witches and Draculas and ghosts sopping it up: but no lumpy pumpkins.

And no wicked, green-eyed queens. Anna alternately strutted and glided through the admiring crowd before squeezing herself in between two men at the piano bar.

"Hey, look, look," whispered Melessa as she tried to lean over the bar to grab Anna's cape, "there's that handsome, black bastard I been tellin' you about. Got a mask on, but I know his silver-streaked hair and smooth walk. Ain't them some *great* buns?"

Anna turned and smiled at this debonair gentleman who seemed to know most of the revelers. Melessa had raved about him for weeks. "He's what you've been lookin' for. Black as aces and twice as sweet. Honey, he's it, I tell you. Money in his jeans too."

"Come here," she yelled across the tables. "Come here you 'mother' and meet my best friend, Anna Louise."

"Sure, Melly, I'm with ya."

"An' she's free. I mean, not working right now so she has nothing to hold her. Oh, shit. Just come over here!"

The meeting was wary. Not only were they two, self- assured pros and seductive rascals; each had the other pegged. But the night itself was charismatic. The festive, light- hearted mood encouraged risque bantering between them.

By midnight they were dancing, with Anna crooning oldies requested from the willing combo. "You're quite a prize, Lu- Lu," marveled Luther. "You know, I've never known another woman who didn't drink. Sure has saved me some bread tonight. Hmm, Lu-Lu and Luther. Sounds prophetic."

From the moment they met Anna knew she had her man for the night. Maybe, if she was ever going to really prostitute and try taking instead of giving all the time—maybe this one would be as good as any to start with. Why, a successful businessman like him ought to be good for at least half of her monthly rent. She brushed aside the inference from Melessa that this one should become a regular. No more of that, she thought, no more moochers or bums to break her heart and then laugh at her.

They stumbled into her quiet apartment about 3 a.m. Tepid lovemaking between the two, weary merrymakers started slowly. Each performed as sort of a duty to one another, and their moves were mechanical attempts at adept pretense.

When Luther finally focused enough to appraise the white perfection of Anna's skin, and the sensual curves of her plump body, his startled arousal was quick, powerful and demanding.

"Sweet Jesus, Lu-Lu," he groaned. "You're somethin' different. Lemmie see it *all*. Ohhh, yeah. You're somethin' I wanna keep, baby. Come here!"

Luther told her that her perfect, china-white body fit his as if molded by God's own artistry. "Hey, baby, this Sunday has brought us closer together than a black and white ice cream sundae with all the trimmings. I mean, we've got some crazy, mixed-nut topping—giant size—and the melt-down is gonna take a lifetime."

To Anna's delight her tired emotions crescendoed two, three and four times. This remarkable, ebony sculpture of flesh and explosive passions was more, oh, so much more than a one-night stand. She pressed his hand between her legs and cradled his head into her bosom.

They slept. Luther was up, showered and dressed by 7:30 a.m. His small business thrived because he paid attention to it. He was boss, accountant, driver and principal worker for his home-based maintenance monopoly of apartments covering six blocks in west Van Nuys. He buttoned up the overalls he had carried upstairs last night in an old, battered briefcase; and was hanging his blue trousers in the closet when Anna awoke. She saw him putting several bills on the dresser.

"No you don't! Oh, but, no. This one's on me. Don't you dare pay me for that trip to heaven."

"Lu-Lu, doll, take it. I'll be back—count on it. Just call it doodad change to prepare for our next Sunday. Pick you up 'bout 7? Okay? I'm not losing you, no siree. Get dolled up, doll, 'cause you and me are now an item."

The idyllic liaison blossomed into passionate lunch breaks, an intimate hour after supper, then one to three late evenings a week. Luther's clothes crowded her closet. His large shoes jutted out of a corner beside her laundry hamper. Shaving lotion, his special cologne, and a toothbrush nudged her space in the bathroom: and intimate items nested close to hers.

He told her about Mattie and their children on their second date.

"Can't leave them, doll. Can't. I'm a sentimental family man; a fierce husband and father. Besides, she don't care much what I do long's she gets most of my pay. Funny, but I think I might just love you. It's different with you. You could be a lasting love—I know it. And you must know it."

He wrapped his strong arms around her and pressed her against his pulsating groin. "Love ya, Lu-Lu. I *do*. And I promise I'll never, ever have another woman again besides my wife and you."

Anna believed that. Living was fun: winter, spring and into summer. She called herself Mrs. Anderson, took out credit cards in their names as husband and wife. Always bragging about her man.

Melessa chided her in a sisterly way. "Headin' for a fall, girl. The fact is, he's not your husband, and you'll have trouble explaining that someday."

"Bal-der-dash. Mattie doesn't know about me. There's not a reason in the world anything can take Luther away from me. I'm keeping him forever."

Melessa knew better than to laugh at her friend for her foolish outlook on life. She glimpsed a strange wildness about Anna whenever she was questioned too closely about Luther, and she worried about the all-consuming affair. After much thought she came up with a plan that might cool it. Friends. More friends might dissipate the available time spent alone by the enamoured pair.

Melessa arranged for her pals to meet another mixed couple

she had known for some time, for an old-fashioned double-date at the Fourth of July dance on the Long Beach pier. It was a good idea, and it worked. And it lasted. Usually the four had more fun than either pair could alone when out on the town.

Her new friend, Rosalind Delgato, was a pretty, carefree, particular temptress who turned a few tricks only when really desperate for money. Rosalind's steady boyfriend, Oscar Banks, had initially endeared himself to her with his wild, Haitian expertise at love-making.

Despite Oscar's obvious good health he regularly drew a disability check. However, although a generous escort for his white woman, he would never spend his money on any of her three, fair and freckled children. Rosalind soon told Anna what a constant irritation that was between them. But, Oscar was kind to her kids and certainly handy around the apartment. Apparently every six months or so she tried to get rid of him. It just never worked. He always came back with a thoughtful gift to perpetuate his charm.

Anna recognized Rosalind's sincere congeniality right away and responded in kind. Her new friend loved meeting different and interesting persons. She had a knack for giving her undivided attention to whomever was sitting next to her.

She reared her youngsters with alternate attack-slaps and maudlin, smothering kisses. On sunny days she forbade them to bare their fair skin to the Santa Monica beaches: in rain or smog she pushed them out into cluttered Reseda Park, "for their health." Her faith in people was child-like in its simple philosophy: "Do unto others. . . ."

Rosalind's erratic personality invited an immediate, kindred attraction between Anna and herself. Her lovely black hair, always immaculate, framed a bright, pixie face which laughed at the world. Anna envied the optimism but delighted in the closeness of purpose.

"Ya know—we're a lot alike," bantered Rosalind. "Lookin' for love, and what do we get? A couple of m-f darkies who use our bodies and get away with no commitments."

"You laugh at Oscar if you want to," countered Anna rather testily, "but I've got me a *real* man."

The foursome met weekly, usually frequenting the Ham-It-Up where Anna often sang for tips. Melessa joined them briefly at their table during slack hours. Sometimes Anna filled in behind the bar when Melessa wanted off. They were fun dates.

Oscar always wisecracked when Anna had her usual Pepsi while the others downed beer all evening. It didn't matter how many kicks he received under the table; he liked teasing Luther's uppity woman. She and Oscar barely tolerated each other from the first meeting. The chemistry was bland to abrasive. However, the others merely grimaced at the discord and ignored what might become sour notes between them.

But Anna's disdain of Oscar was close to loathing. She was even suspicious of why Rosalind kept him around. Why would such an attractive woman bother with a loser? Didn't make sense. To her Oscar was an undesirable bum.

She marveled at his ability to fall asleep in the middle of a noisy crowd. His perpetual toothpick would stick out of his slack mouth with nary a droop as he dozed. Sometimes the tip of his tongue protruded at the height of a snore. Rosalind would kick him and pull up his head. Didn't help much. He'd just doze off again, his misshapen belly swelling at each long intake of breath. Definitely an unlovely man.

But Art: now he was something else. Tall and quiet and absolutely devoted to Rosalind. He would appear only when Oscar was in a drunken stupor or wasn't around at all. In his sober way he would coax Rosalind out on the tiny dance space and hold her close, bending low to press his pale cheek against hers.

"That's a damn good-looking man, Rosa," said Anna when she first saw him. "Why don't you encourage him?"

"I *did*. Oh, boy, I did! You bet we were close. . . ." explained Rosalind. "Almost three years we went steady. Of course he's married. But, separated. The oldest story in history. Children! Has two kids he adores—feels divorce will `scar' them. Aint that a bitch?

I know I'd be good for him, but he's dead set against divorce. That's what broke us up. I knew there could never be anything in it for me.

"Maybe his job bothered me too. You know he's a captain in the Van Nuys Police Department?"

"You're kidding!"

"Nope. He's a genuine policeman. Me with the fuzz. Sure did dig that po-lice. Funny, huh? But let me tell you that Captain Freeley could have been the best thing in my life. Why didn't he know that? We *should* have gotten married. But, well, you know . . . kids, mine and his . . . no chance of a divorce. I got mad. Really mad."

"Girl, he still loves you. It's so obvious!"

"I know."

Anna's forties intensified her emotional insecurities.

After a year with Luther she began to doubt his love. Old fears of rejection warped her perceptions. She could see he had genuine affection for her children, but it bothered her terribly that he constantly fussed about not yet having a child from their common-law union.

"Come on, doll, let's do it," he insisted. "Let's have a little Lu-Lu of our own."

But I can't. Now he'll leave me like all the rest.

She talked incessantly to Melessa about having a baby. "I could do it! I could steal a baby, Melly, and I could get away with it."

"You crazy broad," warned her friend. "Of course you can't do that. No way. Kidnappers are always caught, unless they skip. You can't run away with someone else's baby! And what good would that do for you and Luther? He'd find out."

"No, I could do it—I know. I've got a plan."

"Maybe you *are* getting funky like Rosa said. Hey, just try harder with Luther. Go to a specialist. So you're forty-two. No big thing, hon, you can still have a healthy baby. Lots of women do. Try it."

Anna kept quiet after that. But the inference that her supposed friend, Rosalind, thought her funky—well, that angered
her.

In June of '73 she went back to work, this time at Metro Municipal Hospital, to implement her great plan.

First she established her credibility with nurses and staff physicians. Her efficiency was obvious. The doctors relied upon her
for many of their own responsibilities, much to the disgust of
Carlotta, her head nurse.

"**Mrs.** Anderson," Carlotta advised. "You'd best do your own
duties and not interfere with the obstetricians. They can do their
job a hell of a lot better than you can."

Anna ignored Carlotta. She wasn't important to her plan. But
her next step was. She began to comment, often, that she was
pregnant, stating vaguely that she thought she was due sometime
before Thanksgiving. Carlotta took a dim view of it all—Anna and
her condition.

The night shift was essential to Anna's plan. August was not
too soon to start. The nursing office was delighted that she requested permanent duty on that shift. To Anna its loneliness and
secrecy of darkness would be perfect.

The night of August 30th was black with sultry smog. Nothing could waver her elation when the evening nurses described a
pitiful stillborn delivered minutes before the change of shifts.

"About five pounds, Anna. Of course we won't know what
happened until they do the PM tomorrow. The parents are mourn-
ing, in a private room, 'til they decide upon a time for a traditional
Catholic burial."

"Okay. I'll be able to give them special attention," murmured
Anna.

Tonight! My God, it'll start tonight. "Leave it to me."

It took forever for the three nurses to tidy up and get off duty.
Anna flew around her wing ahead of schedule, then helped Doris
with the census sheet.

"Lord, Anna, what's the matter with you? I know you said you were expecting soon, but your hormones must be doing double duty." Doris appraised her. "Sure everything's okay?"

"Of course," snapped Anna. "I'm just nervous waiting." *What if I'm caught?*

She delayed until almost 6 a.m. to dash down to the basement. There was no problem for her in slipping into the morgue. With her flashlight poised it took hardly any time for her to find the tiny form, still in its baby shroud, and remove it from the near freezing slot.

She realized that any staff could recognize a hospital shroud, so she couldn't risk carrying her bundle like it was. She began searching frantically through drawers and closets until she found a used, brown paper bag.

Whew. This'll do. Thump!

Anna stood petrified, watching the double doors fly open. She gripped the brown bag, as every overhead fluorescent light shuddered on in unison.

"Hi, Annie Lu, whatcha doin' in the dark?" asked B.G., the night orderly. A suspended heart beat did not allow for an immediate answer. Anna flashed her best smile.

"Boy," B.G. grumbled good-naturedly, "whatsa matter? Afraid you'll wake the dead, or are you a stickler for saving electricity? Why the hell are you stumbling around in the dark? Jeez, you'd think this energy crunch was your own, personal crusade." He chuckled and delivered his sheeted corpse into an empty cubicle.

She gave him a hurried, lame excuse about needing supplies for the delivery room.

"In here? Jeez, the job's gettin' to you. You're lost. Come on, nurse. Let's get out of here—too cold. If ya want more bags I can get you plenty from Central Supply, next door. Just shoot me a requisition before you go off duty."

"Okay, B.G., I'm coming. Thanks." She managed to move one foot after another while grabbing at tables on the way out.

"So long. See ya later." He pressed the elevator for her and went on around the corner with his gurney.

Anna slipped back into the morgue, grabbed her gruesome bundle and stuffed it into the brown, paper bag. It took only moments to guide the noisy stapler around the edges. She thought of it as sealing a cocoon around the lifeless mass until it could become useful in creating her chance for a living child of her own. For her and Luther. The package would remain sealed in her home meat tender until just the right time for her to use it.

She was glad the elevator was still there and empty.

Anna gave report and hurried off duty clutching her bulging knitting bag. No one looked at her twice.

CHAPTER 12

Tuesday, July 16, 1974, 3 p.m.

THE COURT: I think at this time we will take our afternoon recess to 3:15.

(Afternoon recess taken from 3:00 p.m. to 3:20 p.m.)

THE COURT: Counsel, you may call your next witness.

MR. DURBIN: People call Melessa Birdsong.

(Duly sworn and called as the next state witness.)

DIRECT EXAMINATION

BY MR. DURBIN:

Q. Is it Miss or Mrs.?

A. Mrs.

Q. Mrs. Birdsong, I want to talk to you about Rosalind Delgato. Did you know Rosalind?

A. Yes, I did.

Melessa glanced at Captain Freeley, pale and slumped with his hair blown to one side. Spoils his gray sideburns, she mused. And she wondered how he had time off to be in the courtroom every day. Her head snapped around toward the persistent voice of Mr. Durbin.

Q. How long had you known Rosalind?

A. Three, three and a half years.

Q. And is this the same Rosalind Delgato that lived on Victory Boulevard, Van Nuys?

A. Yes.

Q. To your knowledge, did the defendant know Rosalind?

A. Yes.

Q. Do you know how they met?

A. Through me. About two years ago.

Q. How many times have the three of you been in each other's company over the past several years? By "the three of you" I mean the defendant, yourself and Rosalind.

A. A number of times.

Q. Would you say more than a dozen?

A. I would think dozens.

Q. Had you ever been in Rosalind's apartment there on Victory with the defendant?

A. No.

Q. To your knowledge, had the defendant ever been at Rosalind's apartment?

A. I really don't know.

Q. How many children does the defendant have?

A. Five that I know of.

Q. Could you tell us their names, please.

A. Yes, Noreen, Garey, Sandra, Bill, and James.

Q. Did you know of a child that was called Nancy?

A. Yes, I did.

Q. And did that child live with the defendant within the last year or so?

A. Yes, she did.

Q. Did the defendant ever tell you where she got Nancy from?

A. She told me she had Nancy, that it was her child.

Q. Now, when you just listed the children, you didn't mention Nancy, is that correct?

A. No, I didn't.

Q. Are there any other children that perhaps the defendant claimed that she had that you have not mentioned?

A. No.

MR. WINGATE: Your Honor, that would—well, the answer is in.

BY MR. DURBIN:

Q. Do you recall when the defendant had Nancy?

A. I believe it was August, or maybe later last year.

Q. Were you present with her at that time.

A. Yes.

Q. Do you recall whether or not the defendant ever told you that she was pregnant at anytime prior to your finding out that she had this child Nancy?

A. Yes she did.

Q. Did she tell you she was pregnant over an extended period of time?

MR. WINGATE: Your Honor, that's irrelevant to the issue of this case. Nancy is not an issue in this case in any way whatsoever.

MR. DURBIN: Well, your Honor, I think that the existence of other children that the defendant may have attained by means that were illegal, unethical or immoral tend to go to intent to commit murder and the state of mind of the defendant.

MR. WINGATE: There's no showing this witness has any such knowledge.

THE COURT: I'll overrule the objection, subject to a motion to strike.

MR. WINGATE: Thank you, your Honor.

MR. DURBIN: Your Honor, could we have the reporter read back the question, please?

THE COURT: Yes.

Please read the question.

(Pending question read by the reporter.)

THE WITNESS: Yes.

BY MR. DURBIN:

Q. So, as she was going through her pregnancy with Nancy, did she discuss it with you as time went on?

A. Yes, she did.

Q. So when she produced a child, Nancy, you thought nothing unusual about it; is that correct?

A. No.

Q. When you say, "No," that means you—

A. I did not think anything unusual.

Q. Now, up until—well, let's take the seven months or eight

months immediately prior to the death of Rosalind Delgato. Did Anna ever tell you that she was pregnant during that period of time?

A. Yes.

Q. When did she first tell you that she was pregnant?

A. She had told me for the past—about seven months.

Q. And did you ever question that, whether or not she was pregnant?

A. Well, she looked like she was pregnant.

Q. Has the defendant had any significant weight changes, to your knowledge, over the past several years? Does her weight go up and down quite a bit?

A. Definitely.

Q. Could you describe some of those significant weight changes, if you can.

A. Well, she's gained quite a bit of weight over the last period of years. She was—until the last four, maybe five years, she only weighed about 130 pounds.

Q. Well, she had, as you described it, *two* pregnancies within the last year or so; is that correct?

A. Right.

Q. Did the defendant ever tell you that she had had a hysterectomy back in the early '60s?

A. Yes, she did.

Q. When you found out about these pregnancies that the defendant told you that she had during the last year or so, did you ever question her about reconciling the pregnancies with the hysterectomy?

A. Yes, I did. She said she had a partial hysterectomy, not a complete.

Q. Incidentally, what was the defendant's occupation?

A. Rosalind's?

Q. No, Anna's.

A. A registered nurse.

Q. What specialty, if any, did she have?

A. She was working in OB and delivery.

Q. At or about the time that Anna had the baby Nancy, did she ever make any statements to you about swapping a dead fetus with a newborn?

MR. WINGATE: Object, you Honor; beyond the course of this preliminary hearing. That's an accusation of murder.

THE COURT: Counsel?

MR. DURBIN: May we approach the bench?

THE COURT: All right.

(Whereupon, the following proceedings were had at the bench:)

MR. DURBIN: Your Honor, as is quite evident, this is a rather bizarre incident, and one of the theories, one of the many that the prosecution is working under, is that the defendant has over a period of time created pregnancies and obtained children when she was in fact not pregnant.

The fact that she had a prior pregnancy and obtained a child—how she obtained each and the course of each pregnancy are really inextricably intertwined to show intent, knowledge and sanity, and I think it's all relevant.

MR. WINGATE: Your Honor, these are serious charges that Mr. Durbin is talking about. To just casually throw them in as window dressing in this case I think is prejudicial to the rights of the defendant.

She's charged with murder and kidnaping in this one case. Now, to try to inject the dead fetus of another baby, I think that is inflammatory and not within the bounds of this witness' testimony—for that reason.

This is like accusing a person of murder and then saying, "By the way, did she tell you she committed any other murder while she was on the subject?" It's the same thing, your Honor. It's beyond the scope of this preliminary hearing.

MR. DURBIN: I think intent is always an issue in a murder.

I submit the matter, your Honor.

THE COURT: I'm going to overrule the objection. I believe that the prosecution has the right to show the intent, motive and so on.

In reference to your objection, the record will show that I have weighed the probability of the prejudice to the defendant against the relevancy of the evidence, and I believe that it is relevant and should be admitted.

MR. WINGATE: Your Honor, so my record is complete, may I say also that I am objecting under the provisions of 352 of the Penal Code, where the probative value of this offered evidence is far outweighed by its inflammatory nature.

I accept the Court's ruling as long as my record is complete. Thank you.

THE COURT: I find the probative value outweighs the prejudice to the defendant.

MR. DURBIN: Thank you.

MR. WINGATE: Thank you.

(Whereupon, the following proceedings were had in open court:)

THE COURT: All right. The objection has been overruled.

The reporter will read the question back to the witness.

(Pending question read by the reporter.)

THE WITNESS: Yes, she did.

BY MR. DURBIN:

Q. Would you tell us—first of all, where did that conversation take place?

A. In my home.

Q. Who was present?

A. I don't think there was anyone there except me.

Q. What did she tell you?

A. She told me that she thought she could get a child through a hospital where she would be working by placing a fetus—a dead fetus in the place of a newborn baby.

Q. Did she ever tell you that she had in fact done such a thing?

A. No, she didn't. She called me later, after she was working, again, at Metro Hospital and told me she was glad that I had talked to her and asked her not to do it, that she had found out that she was pregnant.

Q. I see. So when she told you about the feasibility of doing something like this, you tried to talk her out of it; is that it?

A. Yes, I did.

MR. WINGATE: Your Honor, that's a misstatement of the evidence. The evidence is clear that the witness thought that she could get a baby by replacing it with a dead fetus and that she's glad she didn't do it. That's the testimony, not what Mr. Durbin stated.

MR. DURBIN: Whatever the record states—

THE COURT: Just a minute. I'll sustain the objection.

You can reask the question and rephrase the question so the witness understands it.

MR. DURBIN: I'll withdraw the question.

Cross-examination did not elicit any further facts to counteract the impact of this part of Melessa Birdsong's testimony.

The next witness was called.

WILLIAM VICTOR LORENZ called as a witness by and on behalf of the People, having been duly sworn, was examined and testified as follows:

THE CLERK: State your name for the record, please.

THE WITNESS: William Victor Lorenz.

THE CLERK: Thank you.

DIRECT EXAMINATION

BY MR. DURBIN:

Q. Mr. Lorenz, do you know the defendant in this case, Anna Louise Anderson?

A. Yes, I do.

Q. What relationship is she to you?

A. She's my mother.

Q. How many brothers and sisters do you have?

A. Let's see. Four.

Q. Four?

A. Uh-huh. That I know of.

Q. Could you please tell me, are they all, to the best of your knowledge, children of the defendant, Anna?

A. Yes.

Q. What are the names and ages of those four people?

A. Noreen Rancon—she's around, well, middle 20s; Garey Peter Lorenz, 24; Sandra Belle Lorenz, 21; and James Granville Lorenz, 14—he was just 14.

Q. That's it? Is that correct? Mr. Lorenz, would you please answer audibly. She's taking it down on this funny machine here. Now, you, yourself, are about 17? Is that correct?

A. Yes.

Q. Mr. Lorenz, I want you to think back very carefully to the early morning hours of May 25th, 1974. It was still dark. Were you with your sister on that day?

A. I've been informed not to answer on the grounds that it might in . . . in . . . *incriminate* me.

(Pause for discussion with the Court)

MR. DURBIN: May the record reflect, your Honor, that I am handing the Public Defender for the witness a photocopy of a handwritten statement of Mr. Lorenz's statement; having been written by Investigator Walters.

THE COURT: Yes. The record will so reflect.

Based upon Jefferson's Benchbook on page 768, which describes the claim of privilege, I am going to rule that Mr. Lorenz does have the claim of self-incrimination to that question. Previous testimony has indicated that his sister, Sandra, drove the defendant, her mother, to the hospital. The Court will find that the answer to this question might tend to incriminate him, and will sustain the claim and privilege to that question.

PUBLIC DEFENDER: Thank you, your Honor.

MR. DURBIN: Thank you.

BY MR. DURBIN:

Q. Mr. Lorenz, sometime in the early morning hours of May 25th, 1974, were you instrumental in disposing of some bags that your mother had given to you?

A. I wish not to answer the question because it may (pause) incriminate me.

Q. Sometime prior to May 25th, 1974, did your mother tell you that she was pregnant—the months immediately preceding May 25?

A. Before or after? What does "prior" mean?

Q. Oh, before.

A. Before? Yes.

Q. Does your mother—or, did your mother have a child by the name of Nancy?

A. To my knowledge, yes.

Q. When did your mother have this child, Nancy?

A. Sometime in September. I do not know the exact date.

Q. September of 1973?

A. Yes.

Q. Where did she have this child?

A. Metro Municipal Hospital.

Q. Were you present?

MR. WINGATE: I'm going to object to this line of questioning, your Honor. It's irrelevant to the issues of this preliminary hearing.

THE COURT: I'll overrule that objection.

You may answer, if you were present.

THE WITNESS: I've been told by my lawyer that I shouldn't answer the question because it might intimidate me—or . . . incriminate me. Sorry.

BY MR. DURBIN:

Q. I have been called intimidating before.

(Pause for distraction in the audience.)

Did you remove or cause to be removed a child from Metro Hospital in September of 1973?

A. I must not answer the question because it might incriminate me.

Q. Specifically, did you ever take home a baby in a suitcase from Metro Hospital in September of 1973?   •

A. I must not answer the question. It might incriminate me.

MR. DURBIN: I have nothing further.

THE COURT: Any cross?
MR. WINGATE: No questions, you Honor.
THE COURT: All right, you may be excused.

Anna stared at her son and then at Melessa. Haltingly her thoughts took her back to that Sunday night in September—back to the greatest, most thrilling hours of her life.

What the defense attorneys would not allow into the transcript she remembered in detail. Her Nancy! So . . . they wanted to charge her with that crime, also? Well, it didn't matter now. But what a grand plot that had been! What a clever, exciting feat. She smiled proudly as the memory behind her stoical facade relived the thrill of Nancy—sweet, dark, vibrant Nancy.

CHAPTER 13

Sunday, September 9, 1973 . . . 10:45 p.m.

Gusty winds swirled the autumn leaves into dusty circles before pushing them against the north wall of Metro Municipal Hospital. Scores of bright lights above the hospital entrances blazed like beckoning beacons to all who might be seeking refuge and comfort. Two of the automatic doors leading into an impressive main lobby parted with the usual "whoosh" backlash as Jane and Martin Fields entered and walked hurriedly toward the reception desk.

"Hi. Brought my wife in 'cause she's in labor," panted Martin. "I've already talked to some nurse in maternity. She told me to bring her on into the hospital."

"Fine," answered the clerk in a noncommittal tone. She glanced at the patient to see whether she must hurry. "Relax now and we'll get everything started. I'm Roberta Hall, the night receptionist. Now, I'll need your name and your wife's name, please. Is *she* a member of our HMO plan here?" Her tone, sounding like an impersonal recording, irked Martin.

"Yeah, of course she is. Me, too. Her name's Jane—Jane Fields, and I'm Martin Fields, her husband. Say, can't you do something for her right away? She's hurting real bad."

"Sure. We'll do that soon. I'm calling for a nurse from OB to take your wife right up to the maternity floor. But you'll have to stay here awhile to fill out some forms for me."

As she wedged the telephone between her neck and shoulder and punched three buttons, Roberta systematically began gathering different colored papers which she stacked neatly in front of her. The telephone clicked and she spun around in her chair away from the nervous couple.

"Hi, Anna, it's Roberta. Patient here at the front desk. I need you . . . yep, in labor . . . okay." She cradled the telephone and turned back to the anxious pair.

"Let's see . . . do you have your medical card with you?"

"Yeah, yeah, here," Martin grumbled as he tossed the card at her. He didn't mind showing his exasperation at her calm efficiency and unhurried movements.

"For Christ's sake, get going. You people already have all the information on us. Jane's been coming here ever since her second month."

"Well, I'm sure we do," soothed Roberta. "But you know how these new computers are. Always needing constant feed-in." She pushed a lot of keys, starting over four times until she finally got a print-out on Jane Fields. By the time she returned Martin's card he was scowling and sweating. "Here, if you'll just answer a few questions for me I'll try to get the paper work finished so you can join your wife. She'll be pretty busy with the OB nurse for awhile, anyway."

Martin turned to check on Jane just in time to see her bend over and circle her large belly in both arms. "Another pain, honey?"

"Jeez, yes. Strong one. Please, Martin, can't you get them to give me a room—or something? I feel awful having to stand around in the lobby like this."

Abruptly the elevator doors opened and they saw a smiling, rather short and heavy, white-uniformed woman coming toward them pushing a wheelchair. Her ash blond hair was piled high on top of her head, highlighting the natural Belleek beauty of her complexion. The only discordant note, aside from the too- short skirt, was the dark, thick mascara and silvery-blue eye shadow ringing her eyes. Nevertheless, she was a nurse, and Martin was grateful. He held out his hand in welcome, and presented his wife.

"Hi, honey," greeted Anna. "You must be my patient. I'm Anna Louise, one of the night nurses in OB. Why don't you sit down in this royal chariot and I'll get you right on up to maternity."

Roberta leaned over the counter and said belatedly, "Anna, this is Jane Fields and her husband, Martin. They spoke with someone in OB about an hour ago, so I guess you've been expecting her."

"Yes, I took the call. We'll go on up and get Jane settled in, and everything."

Roberta sighed with relief. "Great. I'll be sending her husband up soon."

Anna tucked the small suitcase under her arm and deftly steered the wheelchair into the elevator. She started with the usual small talk. "So, this isn't your first baby is it, Jane?"

"Nope, but I'll tell you one thing . . . it's sure as hell gonna be my last. I really didn't plan this one. I mean, sure, I like kids, but we already have three, and you know how that goes. Oh, damn, another pain. Christ, why did I ever let myself get pregnant again? Should have been more careful. I feel terrible!"

Anna's brow furrowed as she looked down at this pretty, dark-haired woman who appeared unhappy at the prospect of becoming a mother again.

Maybe, just maybe . . . this can be the one. Maybe this is the night I've been waiting for.

She snapped back from her thoughts as the elevator jerked and stopped at the third floor. She glanced down at Jane as she pushed her out into the quiet hallway. Her patient's face was contorted with both pain and anger now as she arched her body hard against the back of the wheelchair.

"Oh, God, I hope this'll be a quick birth. Can't stand this for very long."

"Easy now, honey. Since you've had others you should know what to expect."

"That's just it! I know it's gonna get a whole lot worse before it gets better. Wish I knew why women have to be the ones who do all the suffering. If men ever had to go through all this they'd be damn sure it didn't happen again."

"No doubt you're right about that," soothed Anna. Her

thoughts returned once again to her great plan. She wondered about this mother not really wanting another baby while she, herself, yearned for one so acutely. More and more the crazy exhilaration of her plan took hold of her senses. She wheeled the chair along side of the nurses' station and reached down, carefully locking the wheels before going behind the counter.

"Jane, this is Doris, the other night nurse. Say, Doris, how about fixing an I.D. bracelet for her while I pull her chart? Name is Jane Fields. I'm putting her in 332B."

"Sure, no problem. Is that F-I-E-L-D-S?"

Jane leaned heavily on the arms of her wheelchair and answered testily, "Yes. And let's get it over with, huh? I've got to lie down. Please!"

Anna grabbed the chart and winked at Doris. "Thanks a lot. Here, I'll take the I.D." She secured it on Jane's wrist and called back to Doris, "I'll probably be taking her into the labor room pretty quick. She says her pains are getting harder and lasting longer. Let you know when."

"Okay. Meanwhile I'll notify the front desk of her room number, and then wake Dr. Pauley and brief him. Be in to help you after awhile."

Anna's thoughts were racing as she quickly answered, "No! Oh, well, I mean—I'm pretty sure I won't need your help. I know I'm getting near term, myself, but it doesn't bother me. Thanks, anyway." Her heart thumped erratically. "But I would appreciate it if you would make all the rounds and answer call lights while I devote my time to Mrs. Fields. I think she's going to need all my support. And, besides, I know you prefer anything to the labor room."

"Great. That's fine with me. Things are quiet and no one else expecting right now."

There . . . that's another good reason why tonight is the night. It's perfect. I know it! Got to keep Doris away.

They wheeled into 332B where Anna tossed the usual skimpy hospital gown on the bed with routine instructions to Jane. "Can you manage? Just lay your clothes here and put on this 'Paris original' while I put away your things."

Jane grumbled and swore as she undressed and thrust her arms into the muslin gown. "Oh, no! It's another contraction. *Please*, give me something for the pain. Can't you?"

Anna held her hand on Jane's abdomen. "Gosh," she agreed.

"It's pretty strong. But I can't give you anything this minute. Got to check your vitals, ask a few questions, and everything, and let the doctor check you. Can't mask any signs with medication, you know. He'll be right in. But I am timing your contractions, so be sure to tell me every time one starts. Okay?"

"You needn't worry about that. You're gonna know about every time I'm having one 'cause I'm not one of those idiots who suffer in silence. No siree. You better believe I let everyone know when I'm hurting."

Anna just smiled and asked, "When was the last time you had something to eat or drink?"

Jane thought for a minute. "I think I ate dinner about six o'clock. And, yes, I had a glass of iced tea around eight. That's when I had my first contraction. Haven't had anything since then."

"Good. Let's see. It's after eleven now. You haven't had any kind of medication, have you?"

"Hell, no! I keep asking you for some. What kind of a dumb question is that? Come on, give a little, will you? How much longer do I have to wait for a shot?"

"Now, Jane, you must understand. I can't give you a thing, not even water—until a doctor orders it. Can't you try to relax between pains and think about how happy you're going to be, and everything?" She puttered about the room emptying Jane's suitcase and lovingly arranging the baby clothes.

Suddenly a twist of envy tugged downward at the corners of her mouth. *I'm sure she doesn't want the baby. Who does she think she is? I'll show her.* She pushed the receiving blanket angrily into a drawer and slammed it shut so violently that Jane flinched.

"What . . . ?"

"'Scuse me. I must be nervous, too," laughed Anna with a quick transformation into the kindly, motherly nurse.

"Babies are so wonderful," she mused. "It's the only time of life when we can give and receive love without question. Do you realize that? Our looks, our intellect, our abilities; all mean nothing to babies. We don't have to prove anything to them to earn their love. Isn't that something? Of course they have to grow up, and everything."

She hesitated, and stood transfixed for a moment; an odd, cold look replacing the wonderment in her eyes. Just as quickly her mood changed again.

"Anyhow, I love them to pieces when they're little. See? Look at me. I'm expecting my sixth most any time now." Her heartbeat quickened as she uttered the lie. Still, she smiled at Jane as she rubbed her big abdomen in a circular motion and went on. "My Luther is thrilled to death that I'm having his baby. I guess, for me, it's a way of showing him how much I love him, you know . . . having his baby, and everything. Isn't your husband happy about yours?"

"Are you kidding?" moaned Jane. "He's like most men: wants lots of lovin' but only a couple of kids. Personally I can think of a lot better ways to keep a man. You must be crazy, having six kids and working too. How can you ever have any fun for yourself?

"Oh, God, here comes another pain. Hey, please call the doctor. I know he'll order something right away. It's getting much worse now."

Anna stared intently at the minute hand on her watch as she held one hand on the bulging abdomen stiffening into a hard, painful contraction. "Hang on, honey," she encouraged. It'll ease off in a minute. Oh, great, here's Dr. Pauley. Now we'll get some orders."

"Well, how's our patient doing? She'll be Dr. McHugh's patient. He's the attending physician on call tonight and will be doing the delivery."

"Right. Here's her chart. She's progressing quite normally."

Dr. Pauley listened with his stethoscope, trying to look wise and efficient while stifling deep yawns. "Well, Mrs. Fields, I'm the doctor on duty all night, so whenever you're ready, we're ready. Until Dr. McHugh gets here the nurse will be with you."

"Dr. Pauley, is it?"

"Yes, that's right."

"Well, will you please tell her—the nurse—to give me something for this pain? I really need it! Can't stand much pain. I'm telling you!"

He nodded absently, finished his examination, and, while peeling off his plastic gloves, remarked. "Everything looks real good. You should have no trouble. From the looks of things you're going to have a big one.

"Now, as for the pain, I can help you a little, but you know the pains are inevitable and we can't stop them with drugs. Dr. McHugh might order something different for you when he gets here, depending on your progress."

Turning his head toward Anna he spoke softly near her ear. "I've already ordered something. You'll know when to give it."

Anna walked out with the exhausted intern who was finishing his 48 hours on call. "Doctor, she seems emotionally agitated at having this baby. I hope it'll be okay, but I think it's going to be quite awhile before she delivers."

"You may be right." He shrugged and leaned heavily against the wall. "Tell you what. I'm really bushed, so I'm going to lie down again and catch a nap. Call me when I'm needed, okay?"

"Oh, sure, doctor. No problem. I'll let you know in plenty of time. Besides, I'll be notifying Dr. McHugh and he'll probably be here soon."

"Then you call me for sure when he gets here."

"You bet."

"Fine. See you later, then," he mumbled as he turned toward the darkened hallway leading to the OB doctors' quarters.

Anna shivered. *Are things really going my way? He's plenty sharp, but he's also plenty sleepy. Will he stay asleep?*

She ordered Jane to empty her bladder, check herself for bleeding, and try not to strain.

Should I do it? May never have another opportunity this good.

"I'll be right back," she called. "Going to get you that pain shot."

This is it—got to be the chance I've hoped for. She's perfect! Doesn't want her baby. I know it. But I sure do. I need it. Hmm, dark hair and eyes. Both dark skinned—maybe a little Spanish blood? Luther will believe it's his. Damn, it's a wild and crazy scheme.

She shivered again while preparing the morphine injection. *Will I get caught? Melessa says it's impossible. It has never been done before, I'm sure.*

"First, let's give you that shot, and get you down to the labor room. Then I'll check on him for you."

Jane quickly turned over to get her pain injection.

"Say, was there any vaginal bleeding when you urinated?"

"No. I don't think so. Is that good or bad?"

"Well, doesn't matter too much. It tells me it'll be a little while before you're ready. There, ought to feel comfortable and lots more relaxed in about 15 minutes."

Martin was at the nurses' station when they approached on the way to the labor room. Seeing him standing there Anna was able to pay special attention to his features. He was a nice looking man, probably in his mid-thirties, she thought. Slight paunch—receding hair line. It should be a healthy, cute baby.

"It's about time you got here," said Jane. "Nurse, can he stay with me?"

"Sure, for a time. I need to do some charting, anyhow, so he can keep an eye on you." She smiled at Martin.

"Uh, wait, I'm not very good at this sort of thing."

"I understand. Relax. I won't be long, and you should leave soon, anyway." Anna nudged her patient into a cold, plastic-sheeted bed in the stark, sterile-looking labor room, cranked up the head and foot, and tucked two incontinent pads under Jane's buttocks. "Uh-oh, another contraction. Let me in there to time it."

Martin positioned himself across from Anna, lowering his head to look directly into her eyes. "Is she all right, nurse? I mean, she sounds so terrible. Is she about to have it?"

"No, no, of course not. She's fine! Don't worry so. Why don't you go home and get some sleep?"

God, why doesn't he leave?

Anna patted her patient's hand as her mouth tensed into her best, motherly smile. "And don't you worry, either. I'm going to be with you all night. I'll be back in a moment."

The sack in the tender. Must use it soon . . . got to think. Can't keep putting it off. It's now or never.

A public telephone was in the visitors' lounge. She hurried in, practically threw a dime into the slot, and quickly punched out the digits to her home telephone. It rang a long time.

"Hello? Sandra? Listen, go wake Bill for me. I need to talk to him." She tapped the side of the cubicle.

"What do you want him for, Mama?"

"No questions. I'm in a terrible hurry. Just do it."

"Okay, okay, gee whiz. ... ."

Anna looked around toward the doorway, half expecting some-one would enter and put a stop to her madness. But she was very much alone. She resumed tapping.

"Mama?"

"Yes? Oh, hello, honey. Bill, I need you to do me a favor— only you. Listen . . ."

"Mama," he interrupted, "It's real late and I'm sleepy. Can't Sandra help with whatever you want?"

"No, Bill. I need *you* to do it. Now listen carefully. I want you to do exactly as I say." She knew this gentle, quiet son would not understand, but he would always do as she directed.

"But I'm awful tired; can't you just ask Sandra to help?" "No! Bill, honey, I know you're sleepy, but this is very important. You're the only one I need. Pay attention. Are you listening?"

"Yes, Mama."

"You must do exactly what I tell you. There's a brown paper

bag way in the back of the meat-keeper drawer, you know, in the bottom of the freezer side of the refrigerator. The top is stapled together. You'll recognize it because it's the only brown package in there. I wrote 'do not touch' on it.

"Got that? Now, I want you to take out that bag, just as it is, and put it in my small suitcase. *Don't open the bag!* Remember the nylon case in my bedroom? The one I have the baby clothes in for when the baby comes? Put the paper sack in there.

"Bill?"

"Yeah, I got it, Mama."

"Okay. Now pay close attention. After you put the brown bag in the suitcase drive down here with it. Can you do that?"

"I know what you want me to do, but why? Are you 'bout to have the baby tonight? Is that it, Mama?"

"Yes, yes, that's it! I think I might have the baby before I get off duty, so I really need those things. I'm counting on you, so don't let me down. Okay, son?"

"I guess so. But I still don't see why Sandra can't do it."

"Because I'm telling *you* to do it, and to do it exactly like I said. Bye, bye, hurry now.

"Oh, by the way, I'll meet you by the staff door. You know, where I go in to work? Just sit there in the car until I come out. Be sure to wait for me. *Don't Leave.* I'll be out for sure, and you must be there. Bye."

Anna sighed with relief. The palms of her hands were sweating, so she rubbed them briskly against the sides of her white uniform. With quiet, nervous steps she ducked into the linen supply room, selected two, soft flannel blankets and placed them in the warming oven.

God help me—I've done it. No turning back.

Doris was back at her post charting. "How's she doing?" she asked without looking up.

"Oh, slow but sure. Hey, you might as well take a coffee break for a half hour or so. I'll watch the floor while you're gone."

"Gee, thanks. Sounds good to me. Shouldn't get busy 'til five or six. Don't let me fall asleep."

And don't I wish she would. Anna's fingers raced down the list of GYN doctors that was taped near the telephone until she found the one listed on Janes chart. She dialed and listened for Dr. McHugh's raspy voice.

"Doctor? It's Mrs. Anderson on OB. . . . Yes, it's about your patient, Jane Fields. Sorry to call so late, but I wanted to report that we've checked her and don't expect her to deliver until morning. . . . Right . . . yes, fine, except an unusual amount of apprehension. . . . Okay, I'll watch for it. We'll call if anything changes . . . goodnight."

Can I fool him? The great Dr. McHugh?

She was breathing in great gulps of air, trying to still her shaking and stabilize her thinking as her bizarre thoughts threatened to race out of control.

"Oh, my God," she whispered. "What the hell am I doing? I must be crazy. God, planning it was one thing—like dreaming—but really doing it? No . . . I can't let myself do this. I've got to put a stop to this madness. But, it's working—just like I planned. Lord, can I carry out the whole scheme without messing up, or worse, falling apart? . . .Got to, now; it's all set in motion.

". . .If I can just get her husband to leave *right now.*

Wait, first, better get all the medication I'll need before Doris gets back. Easier that way. God, so many details.

"It's working so beautifully, everything right on schedule. Couldn't be better . . . stay calm . . . let it happen. Easy does it all the way. Can't quit now."

The key to the medicine cabinet shook as Anna struggled to fit it into the small slot. She filled two syringes with morphine and carefully replaced the vial: she would doctor the dosage sheet later to cover the shortage. Next, buccal pitocin, to hasten labor. That would put the birth at the time *she* wanted it. She slipped a couple of empty syringes and three vials of sodium pentathol into her pocket.

Quick. Lock the cabinet and get back to Jane. "How you doing,

Martin? Ready to leave?" Anna tried to sound calm. Her wide smile was comforting to the Fields.

"Well, guess I may as well go on home for awhile. Check on the kids and make a few phone calls. Honey, the nurse'll stay with you, so I'll be back in the morning unless they call me sooner."

Anna walked to the elevator with Martin, but scarcely heard what he was saying. Her elation acted like speed in her veins. The fixed smile became genuine, and she visioned herself with the baby.

I can do it! I can. I know it. I feel it's right. But what if I'm wrong—if I get caught it'll mean the end of everything. I don't want to think about that now. It's already happening. I'm going to have a baby! But . . . can I really fool everyone? Can't worry about that now . . . just get on with it . . . quit wasting time.

Back in the labor room Jane was now so sedated that she didn't question anything. She readily held the pitocin pill under her slack tongue; and nestled heavily into her pillow.

Suddenly she jumped as she felt another injection. "What the . . . ?"

"Shh," whispered Anna. She dropped the empty vial of pentathol into her pocket to be disposed of later; then glanced out into the hallway toward the exit sign over the back stairwell. Doris was rounding the corner from her break.

"Hey," she called. "Everything okay? You need me to help attach the fetal monitor?"

"Oh, no. She's not ready yet. I'm just checking the halls for call lights, and everything. Looks like we'll have an easy night. My patient's resting better—slow progress though. Since you're back maybe I'll take a few minutes to go down to the candy machine. Being pregnant always makes my sweet tooth ravenous." Anna giggled.

"Go ahead," said Doris. "I'll watch, so take your time."

"Okay. Just don't bother my patient. She needs an hour or so of rest."

"Right."

Anna fidgeted in her pocket, as if sorting the correct change, until Doris was out of sight. She then turned sharply left down the service stairs and out the back door. She was still wheezing when she spotted her car pulling in slowly, and she was opening the door even before it stopped.

"Thanks, Bill, oh, thanks, son," she sighed as she took the soft suitcase from him. "Now, listen very carefully, son. I want to be sure you understand what you are to do now."

"What now, Mama? You look funny. Are you sure you're gonna have the baby tonight? Shouldn't you be in bed or somethin'? I just want to go on back home."

"No, Bill, for God's sake will you do as I say! You must stay right here until I come back. It may be two or three hours, *but you must not leave.*"

Anna slammed the palm of her hand hard against the car door as she spoke softly, yet with a threatening tone. Her eyes snapped as she told Bill what she expected of him.

"Now, listen to me. You can sleep in the car if you want, but no loud music. Nothing to attract attention. I'll bring the baby out to you when it's born and I want you to take it home and stay with it until I get there. That's the way it has to be—so just do as I say. Do you understand me, son?"

"Yea, I'll wait like you want, Mama, but I don't think any of this makes any sense. I'll just lay back and sleep 'til you tell me different, I guess."

"That's fine. You're a good son, honey. See you as soon as I can. Bye."

Anna tried to rush back up the stairs but had to stop twice to catch her breath. She looked cautiously toward the nurses' station before slipping into the linen room. There she took out one of the flannel blankets from the warming oven and spread it open on the shelf. Hurriedly she struggled to remove staples and tape from the limp, brown package. With one impatient wrench she tore open the damp paper and exposed the bag's grizzly contents tightly encased in the sweating plastic of the tiny shroud.

Lovingly, now, she gently unwrapped the cold, wrinkled fetus and bundled it up in the warm blanket. "Soon, little one, soon," she whispered. It took another quick moment to push everything out of sight behind a stack of draw sheets.

"Whew!" she sighed. "There, should be safe now until I'm ready for it." She grabbed the other blanket from the oven, smoothed her skirt, and reached for the light switch.

Another hand closed over hers!

Anna yelled out in panic and clutched at the doorjamb. Her throat tightened and her face drained of color.

"Hey, easy. It's only me," cried Doris. "Gosh what a reaction. Sorry I frightened you. Boy, you look awful! Better sit down for awhile." She chatted on, unaware that her colleague was close to collapse. "I just came down for a blanket to curl up in . . . but I'll be glad to take over for you. Maybe you should go lie down in the lounge for awhile."

"No! No, I'm okay." Anna forced a smile. "Guess I'm getting to term, myself. Wow! Been edgy for days. I just didn't expect anyone to be around, that's all." She let go of the wall next to the door and laughed reassuringly.

"You know how I am; worried about money, the kids, when my baby will be born, and everything. No, indeed, I don't need any help. Nothing to do right now."

Her eyes were too bright, her speech too fast, and her words too shaky; but Doris shrugged, patted her arm, and started back toward the nurses' station with her blanket.

Anna called after her, "Be down in about an hour, okay?"

Her pulse slowed and she let her mind concentrate on the next step in her plan.

Have to complete the delivery while she's still out. Pitocin should be working. Probably dilated enough so a hard contraction can move the baby down. Have I enough time?

She found Jane moaning softly with her knees drawn up to her abdomen. Anna shook her, but got only incoherent babblings in response. She forced her trembling hand into a sterile glove, pulled up the sheet, and visually as well as manually evaluated Jane's progress. The drugged woman offered no resistance. Anna estimated the probable amount of time for labor to reach the point of delivery. The cervix was dilated nine centimeters; enough for the baby to be at its lowest point in the birth canal. Almost ready.

Once again she checked the hallway. All clear: Doris was napping; supervisor not due for two hours yet.

She hummed excitedly while lathering on Phisohex and scrubbing up to her elbows. Her instruments were arranged precisely on a Mayo stand nearby. She noted Jane's eyes were partly open, but evincing no comprehension. Instead, she was mumbling crazily as if in a private twilight zone of distorted lenses and drowning sounds. Anna smiled as she donned a sterile gown and snapped on fresh gloves.

"Jane," she hissed close to her patient's ear. "Jane!"

Anna shook her again, fingers pitting the swollen flesh of Jane's limp body.

No response.

"Jane, your baby's coming! Your water broke already. Push, Jane, push."

The dazed woman writhed and moaned as contractions vied with breathing. However, she did push at the voice's insistence. Anna grabbed a spreader and deftly stretched the vaginal opening. One hand pressed on the distended abdomen while the other held the legs apart.

"Push, honey—I see it! Almost over. The head . . . I have it. Just one more hard push and you can sleep. Got to help me a little longer. Now, Jane! Now!" The exhausted woman responded subconsciously to the urgency of Anna's voice. She reacted to the overpowering demands with a forceful enough push to expel the source of her unbearable pain. With one, deep, agonizing effort the baby was born . . . and Anna had it.

She worked feverishly to clear the baby's air passages; then rubbed the tiny form vigorously with the warm, soft blanket. It took only another moment to clamp and cut the cord. She then gave the struggling little newborn a mild sedative by injection.

Not until she was wrapping it in the blanket did she realize it was a girl.

Elapsing time was now her most pressing worry. *Hurry!*

A glance at Jane proved that she was still unconscious.

Once again she checked the empty hallway and then ran with her precious bundle back to the linen closet. Within seconds she had laid the two babies side by side: the one, cold and lifeless for nine days; the other, pink and warm and new and beautiful. For a moment—only a moment—she stared down at them, searchingly. This was her last chance . . . the final decision as to whether to complete her devious plan . . . or abort it now.

She shook her head and whispered softly as she stroked the forehead of the tiny corpse, "My poor, dear one. You've been cold for so long. But today you will serve a purpose. Soon you can rest peacefully. I do love you, my poor, wee one."

Turning her attention toward the newborn, she began to pick at the still visible, telltale signs of recent birth clinging to its body. She spoke tenderly, "Oh, I love you, too, my own little one. I need you and I want you."

It squirmed sleepily as Anna lifted it into her arms.

Hesitating a last, crucial second, she impulsively zipped open the soft, nylon suitcase, emptied it of clothing, quickly pinched a couple of creases on both sides, and cut four two inch slits with her bandage scissors.

"There," she cooed as she wrapped her baby in a clean blanket and carefully placed it in the suitcase. "You're mine, now—mine and Luther's. Sleep, little one. Sleep."

She returned the case to its hiding place, stuffed the baby clothes into her knitting bag, and immediately directed her attention to the gruesome task of preparing the tiny fetus to be discovered in Jane's bed. She would describe it to the doctors as a precipitous stillborn. The plan was working perfectly. She wrapped the now warm body in the stained delivery blanket, grabbed another blanket to hide her bundle, and headed back to the labor room.

Doris saw her this time and asked, "How's it going? She must not be getting any closer to delivering; she's too quiet."

"Yeah, right. But she's cold. Needs more blankets."

Damn Doris—why can't she nod off again?

Anna paused just inside the labor room to regain her composure. It was almost over.

She busied herself with morbid details that would be essential to convince a doctor that Mrs. Fields had, indeed, given birth to this undersized, stillborn baby. The many traces of birth had to be smeared over the tiny body: amniotic fluid, meconium and blood. She worked a piece of the new umbilical cord over the old shriveled one, still stuck to the fetus. The body must look, feel, and smell like a newborn. She went over the scene again and again.

Yes, it was all she could do. Her stage was set. The rest would depend on her acting talents and some slight of hand in front of the doctors to finalize the imminent, distressful situation for them and the patient.

The last minute details were mechanical: clean and rid the tray of her instruments; leave the placenta in the bed to coincide with the position of the fetus; and wash down the Mayo stand, the sideboard, and the floor. With a trembling sigh she placed the pathetic fetus between her patient's legs and covered it with the stained sheet.

For the last time Anna busied herself inside the linen closet. Feelings of fear, happiness, desperation, excitement and incredible exhilaration were all like giant waves flooding her mind. There were still self-incriminations . . . and that terrible fear of being caught. She knew it wasn't over yet.

Must keep calm. Can't quit now. The hardest part is still to come.

If only the doctors would accept just what she wanted them to see and not ask for an autopsy. Everything depended on her convincing all parties that this was like any other stillborn. She *must* do it right.

It was almost five o'clock. She'd have to get the baby down to Bill and on its way home. Luck was still with her; no one was around. Only two flights of stairs to safety. Bill was waiting. She pushed on the heavy door . . . and gasped.

The security patrol was edging past her car with its spotlight scanning the windows.

Oh, God, is the radio on? Bill must be stretched out asleep. What if somebody checks on Mrs. Fields before I get back?

The spotlight lingered on her employee sticker, then moved over to light up the car trunk. Anna barely had time to pull shut the iron door. She came close to panic during the fleeting moment it took for the patrol to move on, knowing those few seconds could have been the fatal moment which had threatened her all night. She cracked her door enough to watch the red taillights fade into the mist.

"Bill! Wake up, honey. Here's our new baby. She's sleeping inside the suitcase. I've got to get back inside right away; you take her straight home and stay with her until I get there—couple of hours at the most."

"Oh, Mama—gee whiz—what am I gonna do with it for that long? I don't know what to do. Can't I just give it to Sandra when I get home?"

"No, Bill! Please listen to me. You don't need to know anything. Just leave her in the suitcase with the top open so she has plenty of air. You can stay in my bedroom. She'll probably sleep until I get home. Go on now, straight home. No need to even wake Sandra. I'll explain everything to her later. 'Bye, son."

Anna raced upstairs to complete the nightmarish plot she had set in motion. Back to the labor room where a quick check told her no one had been in to discover the "tragedy." She stood silently staring down at the pathetic scene she had created. The last act had started.

She pressed Jane's call button, keeping her finger on it until Doris came running in.

"God, Doris, it's so terrible!"

"What?"

"Well, look! Mrs. Fields had her baby all by herself. It's dead!

Stillborn, I'm sure. God, I feel so bad. Don't know how it could have happened so fast. Doris! I was only gone long enough to stretch my legs a bit. When I got back I found her like this." She wailed into a tissue while Doris put an arm around her shoulders.

"Now, now, hon. You know these things happen. Pull yourself together. Look at the little thing—you know it was born dead. Nothing you or anyone else could have done for it."

"But . . ."

"Listen. It's pretty macerated. Obviously it didn't have a chance of making it through labor. Now you *know* that. Remember I had a patient do that last year? It does happen. Come on, now. You stay here while I notify everyone. The patient seems okay. Better let her sleep until the doctor is ready to tell her. All right?"

"All right. Thanks. I feel terribly inadequate. Sure, I know babies can be born dead, and everything, but it's too hard for me to accept when my own time is so near."

Doris shook her head sympathetically and said, "I'll be right back with Dr. Pauley."

The minute she left Anna wrapped the fetus in the blanket stained with amniotic fluid and placed it on the Mayo stand. Jane never stirred.

Dr. Pauley rushed in; his eyes bloodshot, eyelids puffy, one cheek imprinted with three small, button-shaped marks. His hair stood up from his scalp in four different directions, and his shirt-tail was hanging out on the left side.

"How the hell did this happen?" he croaked. "Why wasn't I called? Damn it, Anderson, what happened?"

"I don't know! God, I don't know. I was *sure* she wasn't ready. Her water hadn't broke and she wasn't even five centimeters dilated, so I hadn't even put on the fetal monitor. I just don't know!"

"Christ. Why did you leave her alone in the first place? That's what I want to know!"

"I know I'm responsible," Anna sobbed, crying real tears now. "I did leave for about fifteen or twenty minutes. I had given her another shot, like you ordered for pain, because she kept begging for it. Guess I thought she would be able to rest for awhile and I could take a short break. Being pregnant myself I have to go to the bathroom more often than I should. I'm so sorry, Doctor. God, I'm sorry."

"Hey, take it easy. I know it wasn't your fault but I get so damn angry when these things happen. I keep thinking maybe something could have been done to prevent it. The patient seems all right—probably overly sensitive to the pain medication since she's so totally out of it."

"I know, Doctor, she was asleep like that when I came back from my break and found the stillborn. She never even roused when Doris and I were running around taking care of things in here."

Dr. Pauley wiped at his brow with his surgical mask and motioned to Anna. "First, where's the baby? I'll take a look at it now. When I checked Mrs. Fields at eleven that baby was alive! I swear there was a strong fetal heartbeat. Does it appear to be deformed in any way? Did it have the cord around its neck? Could you see any reason why it was stillborn?"

"No, Doctor, it isn't deformed—except it *is* very small and *so* frail. I think it simply was too weak to survive a long, hard labor. That's my professional opinion after checking it over pretty thoroughly. I've wrapped it and put it over here," she explained as she walked toward the Mayo stand. "I knew you wouldn't want the patient to see it. It's not a pretty sight. However, I did save the placenta so you could examine it . . . if you want to. I thought I should take the baby directly to the morgue. Mr. Fields will probably want to make arrangements as quickly as possible. It's usually better for the parents when that's taken care of right away."

She picked up the obviously soiled blanket and opened it enough for Dr. Pauley to see the emaciated body inside. As he stared down at it the wrinkles in his brow deepened. He finally turned away in disgust.

"Damn it! How could I have missed a problem like that? I still can't believe she could have such a small, weak baby. I was certain it was going to be at least seven pounds. But— seeing is believing, I guess. How the hell could I have been so wrong, though?"

"Well, Doctor, she did have an unusually large amount of water. We're all fooled some times on the size of babies because of the full sac. I'm afraid this one just wasn't strong enough, because of his size, to make it through the labor. It seems the logical answer."

Dr. McHugh thundered into the room and walked heavily over to the patient's bed, glancing only momentarily at Dr. Pauley and Anna. "For Christ's sake, can either of you explain how the hell this sort of thing could happen? I want some answers and they better be good. First of all . . . why was she left alone when she was obviously in advanced labor?

"And can you explain . . ." Before he could go on Dr. Pauley broke in.

"Please, sir, let's step outside to discuss this. I'll give you a report as best I can. Listen, we all feel bad about what's happened here, but I'm fairly certain that it couldn't have been avoided . . . I mean the stillbirth probably would have been the same even if we had been here. I've seen the baby and it didn't have a chance." ·

Dr. McHugh stepped back into the room, somewhat placated but he did glower across at Anna who was still holding the wrapped fetus. He motioned to her abruptly.

"Bring that over here. I want to have a look at it. I'm going to have to get some answers for the Fields."

Anna's heart halted momentarily as she realized this moment was the crisis for her. This was her "moment of truth." If she was going to be found out, what would happen to her? She suddenly realized the gravity of her crime.

I'm going to be sent to prison or a mental hospital for sure—my children lost to me. And Luther? He'll leave me, of course. Why did I ever think I could do such a crazy thing and expect to get away with it?

Stark fear of exposure mesmerized her and she stood immobile, staring down at the faceless blanket in her arms.

"Mrs. Anderson! I'm in rather a hurry, if you don't mind," he snapped. "You should get Mrs. Fields into a private room as soon as possible. And, I want to examine the baby right now before it's taken to the morgue."

"Of course, Doctor. Sorry. I've been trying to finish up here and get it out of here before the patient wakes up. Dr. Pauley and I both feel it will be better if she doesn't see it."

Clutching the tiny bundle tightly against her side she folded back one corner of the blanket for his scrutiny of her work. He peered down at the tiny, four and a half pound fetus, quickly scanned it without touching it, then, with a pained, puzzled look Dr. McHugh turned away from the fetus shaking his head and cursorily examined his patient. Eventually he stripped off his gloves and addressed the room in general. "I see it, but I simply do not understand it. There's nothing in her chart that indicates she would have any problems with this delivery."

"Dr. McHugh," Anna stammered, "I feel somewhat responsible . . . I mean . . . maybe things would have been different if I had been right with her when it happened. I don't know. Maybe I should have realized something wasn't right because her labor was so slow. Maybe the baby was already dead . . . or just too weak, . . . and everything. I just don't know. I . . . ." And she started to weep, all the time squeezing the gruesome contents of the blanket, and swaying side to side.

"Lord, Anna," he said testily, "don't you add to my problems. Get the baby down to the morgue and I'll finish the paperwork you started. Take care of Mrs. Fields. I've ordered sedatives *if* she needs any. How the hell she can sleep through all this is beyond me. But, guess we should be glad about that—gives us time to get her husband in here before we break the news to her.

"Well, that's about all I can do for now. Damn, how I hate these times. Come on, Pauley, let's get some coffee. I need it."

The day nurses came in for report just as Anna was returning from the morgue. She went over the tragedy rather briefly. "Mrs. Fields hasn't fully awakened yet. To tell you the truth, I don't want to be here when she does." She fidgeted about, avoiding the head nurse's eyes. "I'm about off duty, anyway, so if it's okay with you,

Carlotta, I'll go on home. Not feeling too great. My time is very near, now, and this has been a terrible, emotional strain on me."

"Yes, I can imagine. However, don't just disappear like you usually do. I don't want to be blamed for any of your mistakes. Before you go I have to be sure you filled out all the necessary forms and actually put the fetus in the morgue. You surely remember one was lost from there, somehow, only a week or so ago. I always thought it might have happened on your shift. Remember all the lectures we had to go through because of that?"

"I sure do. But, I can assure you that all the forms have been filed and the poor little thing is in the morgue—took it there myself. See you tomorrow."

She left, dragging her feet and holding on to her obese abdomen while looking sad and weepy. Her progress was slow into the elevator and down the long corridor to the staff entrance. Slow . . . until she reached the parking lot. There her stride quickened, and she ran across the pitted macadam with her smile widening into exalted laughter. She could no longer suppress her need to vocalize her triumph.

"Dear God, I did it, I did it! I have Luther's baby!"

She rushed past her usual bus stop and frantically waved down a cab. No way could she sit patiently today and wait for a crowded bus.

No . . . no . . . not this day.

CHAPTER 14

Monday, September 10, 1973, 8 a.m.

At home Anna immediately set in motion the rest of her plan to insure that her precious baby would remain hers, hers and Luther's. A hurried check assured her that Sandra and Bill were asleep. No explanations were necessary yet. The proud mother wrapped her baby in the same, stained blanket she had used around the fetus, and hurried back out to her car. She drove all the way to Children's Community Hospital south of L.A. Rushing inside their emergency entrance she pushed her baby at the first nurse she saw.

"Please, help me. I had my baby all by myself, out on one of the canyon roads. Took me two hours to get here soon as I felt strong enough. Is she all right?"

There was no waiting: a young intern quickly took the baby and checked it.

"Fine, fine, we'll send her up to the nursery. They'll clean her up, treat her eyes, and do a thorough work-up. Now, how about you? Got to get you adm . . ."

Anna interrupted and backed away from the slight hold he had on her arm. "Oh, no. We're not staying. I just need her checked and the birth recorded, and everything. I'm fine, really! I should know—have five other children, and I've got to be getting back to them."

"But Mrs., uh, what was your name?"

"Anderson. Mrs. Luther Anderson. Our daughter is to be registered as Nancy Lu-Lu Anderson. Here's my driver's license and a Master Charge card."

The puzzled intern stammered through memorized rules and

formalities which had to be followed, and sent for some forms.

"You should have an exam. And I'd like to see the placenta. Also, I'll need your prenatal doctor's name."

"Will you hurry!" urged Anna. "Just give me the forms.

I'll pay for the certificate, and for the care we received, not a cent more. Humph, prenatal my eye. We don't have money for nonsense. I didn't have a doctor, and, no, I don't have the placenta—left it beside the roadway."

"Don't get so upset," urged the intern. "I guess we can do everything now at very little cost. But you must sign a form releasing this hospital from all responsibility for you and your baby. Understand?"

"Yes, yes, I know all that."

An hour later Anna clutched her baby and its birth certificate to her breast. Sounds of triumph filled her car.

"I did it! I did it. God Almighty, I did it. She's ours forever . . . legally ours."

Anna watched all speed limits despite her haste to get home and call Luther. She'd let him know she had a tremendous surprise, and he must hurry over—take off from work, it was that important. She imagined all the loving things he would say to her as he cuddled their daughter.

Have all the risks been worth it? She would be in a sexy gown, hair perfect, a smidgeon of makeup—enough to cover the signs of aging beginning to show in her mirror.

"What shall we call you, my little love baby?" she mused as she guided the car into her apartment cubicle. "Well, let's not worry about that. Your daddy can decide upon a suitable nickname. He has to have *something* to do with this miracle. Hey, maybe we should dub you 'Mira' for miracle." Her laughter echoed off the carport walls and roof.

All expectations were fulfilled when Luther came to Anna almost every day to hold his baby and brag about it. "She is so beautiful! No nicknames for her. She'll always be our Nancy. Just like the song—'Nancy, with the Laughing Face.'"

Anna knew he couldn't wait to make love to her. But she held him off, claiming soreness from the birth. However, she couldn't keep up the pretense for more than two weeks.

"Come here, you big hunk," she urged. "I'm ready for you tonight."

"Damn, Lu-Lu, I been ready for days! My big ol' love stick is going crazy waiting for you. Let's get down, Baby."

"Easy, you sexy old geezer. Are you sweet-talking me into bed with the children not asleep yet?"

"Hell, they know more about us than we do."

"God, Luther, I do need you!"

"Lu-Lu, our baby is beautiful, that's for sure, but she's no match for her mother. You're a temptress, and I just love being tempted. Now I'm gonna show you how much I love it."

Anna trembled as he unbuttoned her blouse and slipped it down slowly, to let his mouth find and savor her protruding nipples.

"Nectar of the Gods," he murmured. "Umm, your whole body tastes good, every little nook and cranny."

Anna tore at his clothing with frantic fingers. "Ohhh, Luther, you *do* still love me! God, how I need you inside me."

She slid down his chest, nibbling at the short, wiry hairs until she reached the peak of his passion, gently brushing it with her warm moist lips.

"Down Lu-Lu, here, now . . . on the floor. Damn, I can't wait." And there, without music or candle light or incense, there beside the crib, they made love for hours. Anna felt complete again. She had Luther's baby and she had his love.

From then on making love on the floor between their bed and Nancy's crib became a ritual for Anna. She convinced Luther that her passion was always greater there because of the symbol of their love above them. It always worked. No matter how or when it began, they would end up thrashing wildly on the floor by the crib.

"Say, doll, you know we gotta cool it when Nancy gets a little older."

"Sure, honey, sure," giggled Anna. "Then we'll just start over with *another* baby!" It was heaven for her for almost four months.

"You bet, doll, more kids mean more fun." But she was already worrying about his ardor fading as time intruded.

Four months later.

Rosalind telephoned in a terrible snit, asking Anna to join her at the Ham-It-Up right away.

"Rosa, it's only 2 o'clock. I don't even think it's open."

"Well, the coffee shop then. I've got to talk to you!"

The two women huddled over coffee while Anna slowly rocked Nancy's stroller.

"Hell, I don't want it at all," said Rosalind. "It's going to be black; and Mom's comin' out for the birth; and, well, it's just one too many for lots of reasons." She dunked her bearclaw with such vehemence that coffee sprayed onto Nancy's cheek.

"Watch out!"

"Sorry. Now listen, Anna, the truth is, Mom doesn't know it's gonna be black. Isn't there something you can do? I *can't* have this baby. You can help me. I mean, get me something so I can miscarry."

"Oh, God, no! I wouldn't even if I could. How far along are you?"

"About four months. Haven't been to a doctor yet. I'm scared to go to Mexico for an abor . . ."

Anna broke in. "Don't do that! I don't think you can have one now, anyway. Too risky."

"Jesus Christ, aren't there some pills you could give me?"

"Too late! Besides, I told you I couldn't do that. My God, Rosa, it's a real, live baby already."

"Then what am I gonna do? Mom'll disown me!"

"What about Oscar? I assume he's the father—why can't he keep the baby? Doesn't he want it?"

Rosalind hesitated and looked over her shoulder. "Hell, no. He won't help support it, either. I'm sure of that. In fact I'm thinkin' about kickin' his ass out for good. See what I mean? I just can't have this baby.

"Hey, wait a minute. Anna, you could deliver it in secret and take it home with you. Anna, you could! You're always talkin' about babies. You'd love having another one to raise with Nancy. How about that?"

"Sure, I can deliver babies with my eyes closed. But you're asking me to risk my license. Lord, just so your Mom won't know you had a black baby? That's heavy, Rosa. I could lose my job—even go to jail."

Anna's mind conceived, studied and interchanged the troublesome possibilities of her delivering Rosalind's child in secret, without a midwifery license. Her baby slept through the genesis of a scheme which immediately appealed to her pseudo mother's monomania—babies. A mad scheme? Sure, but not as risky as getting Nancy. Dangerous? Yes, it could be. There was always the possibility of something going wrong during delivery like breech birth . . . hemorrhaging, but she knew she would take a chance for that thrilling reward of getting the baby for her own. That would be her price.

"You say it's due in May?"

"Right, I'm about four months along."

"And you say I can have it?"

"Ya, I guess so. Can't think of what else to do . . . at least not yet. Sure can't show it to Mom."

"But what would you tell everybody?"

"Hell, I'll just tell 'em it was born dead down in Mexico, and I left it there. I . . . fell, or somethin', and lost it."

"Hmm, yes, that might work."

"I know it'll work. Whatta ya say? Everyone knows I go to Mexico every two months."

"So, why didn't you have an abortion before, while you were down there last month?"

Rosalind vigorously piled jam on the rest of her pastry.

"Anna," she explained, "I thought of it. Seriously. I'm still thinking of it, but you say I can't now."

"That's right. All you can do now is let it be born."

"Then you'll do it? Damn, I know, you got to think about it. Hey, how about gettin' together tonight? I'm going to explode if I can't figure this out soon. Let's get the guys to splurge for a change."

"Sure," said Anna, "okay, let's go out on the town. Maybe I'll have an answer for you by tonight."

"Thank God! It'll be a great night, and we can iron out any details you think of. I'm desperate!. Listen, come prepared to liven up the joint. A little song and dance should cheer me up. You and Oscar can outdo each other on the stage."

"You bet. If Hank's on at the Ham-It-Up I'll give you a real concert. That man plays a mean piano. Luther loves it when I sing along with Hank; says he likes to show me off. My Papa used to do that at home. Wish he could be here now to see Nancy." Anna leaned over to kiss her baby.

"Okay, okay, see you 'bout 6." Rosalind was impatient.

"Listen, I'm so excited about our plan. *Do* think about it good."

Anna thought about nothing else all afternoon. A chance for another baby. A sure thing for keeping her man. *Two* children from their union would cinch his attachment to her. She knew it.

Her thoughts started arranging the scheme in sequence. If she was to convince everyone that she was again pregnant, she'd have to forge a prenatal chart at Metro Hospital and get a few doctors' orders written in it. Nurses often stopped a favorite doctor in the hallway, asking for prescriptions or advice. It would be fairly simple to get orders for vitamins, for instance, and have her chart ready for them to sign. She could fill in other routine information herself.

But, only eight months from Nancy's birth? That would be tricky. Somebody would surely question that. Especially that skeptic, Carlotta. If she took time off when Rosa was due, it could work. She'd explain her baby was premature.

How can I pass it up? Will Rosa really want to give it to me? She said so.

Anna thought on about the need for careful planning. She could start collecting her needed drugs and equipment from the delivery room. A little bit at a time wouldn't be missed. Besides, she did most of the supply check and the necessary ordering on her night shift.

The other nurses? Will they believe me?

She had gained weight lately, and she could always get a couple more maternity uniforms. She would start right away telling people at work that she was expecting again—maybe as soon as June. It could work, she thought.

The bar was dimly lit and musty with the stink of beer and cigarettes from last night. Weekends had more patrons than other nights, with those willing being encouraged to perform, to "ham-it-up," on the tiny stage angling across one corner opposite the bar. The trash, obnoxious by 2 a.m. Sunday, was always left until Monday noon, so Melessa was still busy cleaning when her girl-friends arrived.

"Look at that," scolded Melessa. "I remember when that Baby Grand was new. Now look at it. Scored all around with nasty cigarette burns."

Rosalind calmly lit a cigarette and laid out several quarters for the juke box. She was wearing her prized rabbit- fur cape over a flowing, hot pink dress. Sparkling flakes high-lighted her dark hair, immaculately groomed in pompadour swirls. Rings glittered on every other finger. She really did look at least five years younger than her admitted 27 years.

Anna was glad she had decided to show off her new, black leather mini skirt with high, black boots and a loose, flowered overblouse. Because of the young styles she chose to wear, few knew she was 44. She sat down close to Rosalind.

"I'll do it," she whispered. "Your mother will never know you've had a *black* baby—that is, if the timing is right. I can only do it if you're at term before your mother gets here. Remember, you said I could have it." Her palms were sweating and her pupils dilated.

Rosalind squeezed her friend's hand. "God! What a relief to hear that."

"What?" called Melessa from behind the piano.

"Nothin'. Just gettin' ready to burn a quarter."

"Well, please, not another one of those old-lady tear- jerkers like Luther is always playing for Anna. Shit, might as well tune in Lawrence Welk on the TV. Damn, business is bad enough already."

"Keep your shirt on." Rosalind countered and quickly punched in a Mills Brothers' favorite. "Just for you, my dear friend," she said, and ordered a beer from the disgusted Melessa, and turned back to Anna.

"You're a peach. It'll mean everything to me to keep Mom happy. You know, she's so proud of me and the children. Sends me money even though she thinks I'm makin' it on my own out here. Christ, if she ever found out about Oscar—I think it would kill her!

"I never told you, but she's as racist as they come. Daddy was a Clanner. After I married Tommy he got him into the Clan. Oh, I didn't like it. I hated all that white supremacy stuff, but a southern white man is boss of his home and his family. Poor Tommy— victim of a bunch of bullshit.

"It was a pretty good marriage except for that. I'm not cryin' about it. But Tommy was wild; I never could change that. He was killed by a neighbor while trying to steal a valuable coin collection. I felt I had to leave town. Hell, doesn't every girl dream of Hollywood? So here I am."

She laughed and slapped Anna on the thigh. "More beer, Melly. This is a great day!"

"Hey, boys!" yelled Melessa. "Get in here and take care of your women. So far I've sold two beers, both to Rosa."

Oscar had on his fancy, camel-colored leather jacket and a royal blue turtleneck sweater. He was the perfect dandy despite his flabby belly and balding dome. Anna was relieved to see Luther in a tweed sport jacket. She thought him quite distinguished with his graying sideburns and natty motoring cap.

"Gimmie five, Melly, and set up a coke for my girl."

"An' I'll have a beer, too," mumbled Oscar as he made a great show of searching his pockets.

"Okay, pal, me and Melly can figure out the bill later."

The men whooped it up with shuffleboard while their women huddled over the table once more.

"Listen, Anna, I haven't told Oscar I'm pregnant. Maybe I should; he'd move out on his own if he thought he might have to pay child support. Hey, you're always braggin' about how great and generous Luther is. Think he'd stake me for the pay I'm gonna miss the last month?" Rosalind seemed to regard that thought as hilarious. "He . . . he could . . ." And she doubled up with laughter.

"What's so dammed funny?" asked Oscar peevishly. "I don't see no comic on stage."

Rosalind continued to giggle as Luther ambled over. "Say, Oscar," he jested. "These two broads look fairly good. Think we should give them the pleasure of our company tonight?"

"What? You talkin' 'bout *white* broads?"

"Don't knock it. Look at you. Livin' with a white woman is turning you white yourself." Luther loved to tease Oscar about the large, pale blotches over most of his body. They were scars from near-fatal burns suffered years ago, but Oscar remained sensitive about losing so much of his dark skin.

"Come on," he growled. "Let's eat. And I mean a ritzy place this time. I'll go ya half."

"We-e-ll," said Luther. "That's an invitation we can't ignore, huh, Lu-Lu?"

"You bet. Let's go."

The following months Anna built her illusion of pregnancy. She kept a chart on herself in the prenatal file. Every now and then she gave some unsuspecting doctor a progress report and asked for a diet plan or a prescription. She carefully filed any authentic orders in her chart.

Fooling Carlotta wasn't as easy. When Rosalind's time neared, Anna had to start complaining about cramps or spotting. But the head nurse was dubious.

"Look at her," marvelled Carlotta in her sarcastic manner.

"Another baby in only nine months? I don't believe it. I still think there's something phony about her. Didn't I always say she was too good to be true?"

Anna knew about Carlotta's remarks and tried to be very sweet to her, especially in front of others. They usually met only briefly during report, but Anna knew this nurse could be a threat.

Humph. She's jealous. Dried up old bag who never had any children. Why should I worry about her?

Carlotta complained to Dr. McHugh, "Has anyone really examined her? I'm telling you, something's fishy. It's her clever way of getting more time off. I just don't buy it—that she's pregnant again already. She's up to something."

The next time they met Dr. McHugh questioned Anna. "Who is your doctor? I mean, the one who's following your pregnancy? Where are your lab tests? The amniocentesis? Surely you've had one?"

Anna stammered, "Doctor, you know how it is. I've not been to anyone special. They all watch out for me."

"Just the same, your pregnancy this soon after the last could give you problems. You're no 'spring chicken' and I'm making you an appointment with *me*. Let's see. It's Sunday. How about a week from next Tuesday, the 28th?"

Anna's pulse skipped. "Sure, Doctor," she answered. Thanks a lot for taking an interest. See you early after I get off duty?"

"Good. About 9."

Damn that Carlotta!

She had just entered her apartment about 7 a.m. when Rosalind telephoned. She told Anna that her baby was due in about two weeks, a few days before her Mom was arriving. Anna assured her everything was ready. They made a tentative date for Friday. She then telephoned her supervisor that she might have to start her maternity leave as early as Friday morning, May 24th.

Here we go! To Hell with Carlotta. I'll be in the clear by the time I'm supposed to see Dr. McHugh.

Anna swung Nancy around and around, singing and laughing

with the joy of imminent success. *Another baby for me, for me and you and Luther!*

On that same Sunday, back in Uniontown, the Mayers felt a final spit of winter—a coating of freezing rain on the hills. It slicked Idaho Street and juiced icicles on their spruces and on red, maverick oak leaves which hadn't let go in the fall. Winter's coiled blasts had finished storing their frozen waters in the high places for Spring release. A late, sluggish thaw had started its flow to become the life's blood of farmlands below the mountains.

Conrad half-slid down the hill, digging in his pointed cane to steady himself. He limped into Barton's blowing warmth into his bent fingers swollen with Heberden's nodes. Not for 20 years had he been able to loosen their former, nimble talent for the reeds. His frame was as bent as his fingers.

"There ya go, Con," offered Jerry. "Delivery only an hour ago 'cause of road delays from the river flooding south of Brier Hill. Trucks got through about six this morning." He carefully spread open the Sunday paper for Conrad to scan the entertainment section.

"No one left *we* care about, Con."

"Nope. Shame. It isn't real music today. Just a mix of screaming and jumping around. Well, thank God for 8-track. I can listen to the Big ones same as if they were all in the room with me.

"I set the recorder on top of the piano . . . you know Elsie doesn't play anymore? . . . and I turn up the volume and pretend it's all of us in the living room, singing and playing like we used to."

Jerry poured some coffee. "Tough. All your daughters gone. Must be hard on ya. Say, anything from Anna Louise?"

"Oh, sometimes. She's doing nursing in a big, Hollywood hospital. Writes about singing in some neighborhood nightclub on her days off. Still a wild streak in her.

"I don't know, Jerry, all my daughters couldn't get out of this town fast enough. Maybe it was my fault." He sighed.

"Remember `go west, young man'? Well, my girls took that cry to heart during all that women's lib junk. They're *all* out west now, bossing their families around and fighting for equal rights. Learned that from Elsie, yesiree.

"Well, take it easy, Jerry. Gotta get back home 'fore Elsie gets there from church. I don't want her fussin' at me today. Feel too . . . too tired to try and fight back. And, say, don't mention I hear from Anna Louise to her, will ya?"

"'Course not. See ya later."

Conrad folded his newspaper into his overcoat against his chest so his hands were free to dig in his cane and grab at poles and fence slats as he pulled himself up the hill. The door seemed harder to pull open. The living room was darker, sort of foggy in the corners. The house was colder. He stoked the furnace, poured a beer, and slowly stretched out in his new rocker-recliner.

Then began his Sunday ritual of scanning every page of the thick, Pittsburgh paper.

He had a gentle smile on his face, with a gnarled finger resting on an article about Hollywood when Elsie found him, cold and lifeless. It was shortly after noon.

In Hollywood it was a little after 8 a.m., and Anna had no time for reading her paper. There were things to do. After Rosa hung up Anna knew she wasn't going to get any sleep for awhile. She made sure Nancy was dry and fed before securing her in the playpen.

She took out the bag of midwifery equipment she had kept hidden in her closet, and sat down to check her list. A sudden chill clutched at her.

"What . . . ?"

She could feel that warm air was flooding her apartment with a certainty of hot days ahead. And yet she was shivering uncontrollably. She snapped on her radio and switched stations until she found the early weather news.

The forecast was for 80s all week. She frowned and shivered

again.

Why am I so cold?

CHAPTER 15

Thursday, July 11, 1974, 11 a.m.

JOYCE NICOLLE CASSADY, called as a witness by and on behalf of the people, having been first duly sworn, was examined and
testified as follows:

    THE CLERK: State your name, please, and spell it.

    THE WITNESS: Joyce Nicolle Cassady, C-A-S-S-A-D-Y.

    THE CLERK: Thank you. Spell your middle name, please.

    THE WITNESS: N-I-C-O-L-L-E.

                  DIRECT EXAMINATION

BY MR. DURBIN:

    Q. Joyce, did you know Rosalind Delgato?

    A. Yes, I did, since about the beginning of February of this
year.

    Q. Was she living in the Victory Palms at that time?

    A. All during the time I knew her, yes.

    Q. Who lived there with her, to the best of your knowledge?

    A. Oscar Banks and her three children.

    Q. What were the circumstances under which you met or knew
Rosalind.

    A. I babysat for her, and I was—I used to reside in those apart-
ments and I was a neighbor.

    Q. How much time do you think you spent in Rosalind's
apartment per week for, let's say, the month of April.

    A. The month of April?

    Q. Right.

    A. Per week?

    Q. Yes.

A. Approximately, oh, between 10 and 12 hours.

Q. Incidentally, were you regularly scheduled as a baby-sitter for her?

A. Yes. Every Monday and Tuesday night.

Q. Between what hours?

A. Between 7:00 and 11:00.

Q. Were you paid to babysit or was this as a friend?

A. Rosa paid me.

Q. Okay, I want to direct your attention to the evening of the 24th of May of this year. When was the first time you had any contact with Rosalind that evening, either in person or telephonically?

A. I telephoned her at approximately 7:00 o'clock that evening, just for general conversation, and to see how she was.

Q. Could you tell us what the conversation was.

A. She said that a friend of hers named Anna was going to be coming over, and that Oscar had called her and wanted her to come over and see him. She said she had told Oscar that she was going to a drive-in with me, because she didn't want him to come over when Anna was there. She also said that Anna was coming over to induce labor. That's about all I can remember right now.

Q. When she said Anna was coming over to induce labor, did that surprise you, or had you known—

MR. WINGATE: I think, your Honor, that calls for a conclusion.

THE COURT: Yes. That will be sustained.

BY MR. DURBIN:

Q. Had you ever had any prior conversation with Rosalind concerning her desire or wish to induce labor?

A. No.

Q. After that telephone conversation, what did you do?

A. I have a friend that lives in the same apartments, so I drove over to the apartments to talk to my friend. And when I arrived, Anna had arrived and my boyfriend had arrived approximately all at the same time.

Q. Please tell me more about that.

A. Just—when I had just been pulling in to the apartment, I saw Anna pulling in at the same time. I was stopped at a red light on the opposite side of Victory. She was turning into the alley road. I followed her. I got out of my car, and Rosa was outside. I spoke to Rosa and I went and found Les, my boyfriend, and started talking to him.

Q. Now, when you use the name "Anna," you are referring to a person; is that correct?

A. Yes.

Q. Is that person in this courtroom?

A. Yes, she is.

Q. Would you point her out, please.

A. The lady sitting there.

THE COURT: The record will reflect that the witness is pointing to the defendant, Anna Louise Anderson, sitting at the end of counsel table.

BY MR. DURBIN:

Q. When you use the term "Rosa," are you referring to Rosalind Delgato who lived in Apt. C?

A. Yes I am.

Q. I take it, then, that you observed Anna when you first arrived at the compound?

A. Yes, I did.

Q. Then at some point in time, you observed Anna and Rosa together; is that correct?

A. Yes.

Q. Did they appear to be talking?

A. Yes.

Q. Could you see whether or not Anna was carrying anything?

A. No, I did not notice.

Q. At that initial time did you have any conversation with either Rosalind or Anna?

A. With Rosalind. Just, "Hello. How are you?" She told me that Les was home. I said, "Okay. I'll talk to you later."

Q. Was there any conversation about inducing labor?

A. No, not at that time.

Q. Had you ever seen Rosalind or the defendant together at anytime before that date?

A. No.

Q. Approximately how many times, to the best of your recollection, did Rosalind mention to you the name Anna?

A. Oh, several times, just mentioning the name Anna.

Q. Did she ever mention to you the fact of knowing someone who was an obstetrics nurse?

A. Yes, she did.

Q. Did yoy ever connect the two together?

A. Yes. She told me that Anna was a nurse.

Q. Did you ever have any conversations with Anna?

A. No.

Q. All right. After your visit with your boyfriend, approximately what time did you arrive back at your apartment?

A. Approximately 8:00 o'clock.

Q. What did you do when you got home?

A. I telephoned Rosa.

Q. How many times did you telephone her?

A. Between 9:00 and 10:30, I tried to call her approximately four times—four or five times.

Q. At any time did you receive an answer?

A. No.

Q. Did you do anything after that?

A. I got worried and I tried to phone Les. He was not at home. Because of what Rosa had told me before, I tried to phone—or I phoned Valley Presbyterian Hospital to see if she had been admitted to the hospital, and she had not.

Q. What else, if anything, did you do?

A. Nothing. She said she would call me back later. So, when I went to bed, I put the phone by my bed so I could answer it right away.

Q. Approximately what time did you go to bed?

A. Approximately 11:00 o'clock.

MR. DURBIN: No further questions, your Honor.

CROSS EXAMINATION

BY MR. WINGATE:

Q. Now, did Rosalind ever tell you she was impatient to have her baby?

A. No.

Q. Well, she told you that Anna was coming over to induce labor, you said, didn't you?

A. Yes, but that was the first time she had ever mentioned it to me.

Q. Did you express any surprise when you heard that Anna was going to induce labor for her?

A. A little.

Q What did you say?

A. I said, "Why?" I asked her why.

Q. What did she say?

A. She said—then she said that she was—wanted to have the baby and she was getting impatient, but that was all.

Q. Did she say she wanted to have the baby so her mother would not know who the father was?

A. No.

Q. Did she tell you she was proud of the father's identity?

A. No.

Q. Did she ever tell you that she was trying to conceal the identity of the baby's father from anyone?

A. No.

Q. To your knowledge, did Rosalind ever tell anyone that the father of the child was someone other than Oscar Banks?

A. Oh, no.

MR. WINGATE: No further cross, your Honor.

He joined Mr. Stokes with a slight movement of his head.

"What can we do?" whispered his junior colleague.

"Nothing."

The noon break was shorter than usual. Ralph Durbin was

exuding confidence. "Hey, Windy," he called respectfully. "It's the breaks, but this time your notorious end run has been blocked at scrimmage."

"Yah, well, got a few surprise calls, yet."

"Well, don't keep them secret too long. The handkerchief has dropped!"

Her preliminary trial was proceeding swiftly, just six weeks after Rosalind's death. The entire week had been a hazy, confusing stage play: cameras scanning her; notebooks fluttering at her; microphones sputtering close to her face; flashbulbs distorting her eyesight with multicolored spots. Prosecutors, her own attorneys, and the judge spewed out legal terminology she could not comprehend.

Adding to her bewilderment was the spectator section with its scores of curious faces staring at her. Jane and Martin Fields were always there, in the courtroom, right behind her.

But why? Why were they there? She knew them, from some-where; their names, their faces . . . but where had she met them? Why did they glare at her? Why couldn't she remember?

Finally the week's ordeal ended and she was again returned to the Los Angeles County Jail; to the tiny cell with the barred win-dow high above her reach, and the oblong slot in the door . . . and the silence. Here, every night, she could think back and piece it all together. Night quieted her mind.

Yes, she *was* starting to remember: blurred pictures and garbled sounds of Victory Boulevard, traffic, a sultry spring evening, an-ticipation. . . . She shivered a little, both at the awakening memo-ries and at the chill of her isolation cell.

Her hands couldn't keep still. She twisted dank strands of hair hanging straight down the sides and back of her head. No curlers or pomades or aerosol sprays allowed here. Not even a comb. Nor a lipstick to soften the tight line of her lips so seldom parted in speech these days.

Anna Louise Anderson, once pretty, imposing, voluble—was now wan, slumped and silent.

The security unit was isolated from everyone except a 24 hour guard and an occasional supervisor. Her room seemed so small, almost a box.

Why am I here? It's some kind of cell.

She stared down into the seatless toilet bowl as if the answer to her question might float up through the water. The clanging of a distant gate jarred her memory back to the day she was brought to this jail with her hands and ankles shackled. And the noise! Oh, the noise, all those women screaming at her, the terrible words. She grabbed at the iron bed and remembered why they brought her to this room.

"Baby killer!" they had yelled at her. Why? "We don't want no baby killers. Get her outta here!" Why had they called her that?

She had called back haltingly, "Don't scream at me. Please! What? *Baby killer?* No! Not me, I love babies. Why do you call me that?" She had turned to her guard. "Matron, what are you telling them? It's all lies. I *saved* my baby. Why do they hate me? I didn't kill my baby."

But the caged inmates continued to curse and yell at her as she passed between the long rows of cells. No one could hear her. Wet toilet paper rolls pummeled her from all directions as the matron hurried her along. Obscenities followed her down the corridor, their vitriolic intent increasing in volume.

"White whorin' bitch! Shit—scum. We don't want no baby killin' bitch in here with us. Kill her! Yeah, get out, you cocksuckin' white trash!"

"No! Somebody make them understand—I never, ever hurt a baby. Where's my baby? I'll show them. Please, help me! I'll show them!" Her voice cracked and weakened, and her head bowed as her body slumped.

It was a painful memory of why she had been placed in an isolation cell. But, there was a measure of peace here. Now she couldn't hear the lies. It was quiet, like Dr. Richmond's office. Now she could concentrate. She frowned and scanned the concrete walls.

Tonight distorted memories confused her further: memories out of context, as if in the endless struggle of a nightmare during the seconds before awakening. Puzzling concentration made her forehead ache. There was something . . . things she had to do. Iron her uniform? Wait, wasn't that Nancy crying? Had to get ready. Why wasn't Luther home yet?

Was that, Papa? *Oh, Papa, I miss you!* Or, was that Papa in the shadow? He would help her. But, not now. Wasn't he dead? Now she must hurry, yes, hurry to go on duty. Someone was crying.

Anna pushed tentatively at one gray wall as if it might open wide and let her exit her bubble of painful thoughts and images— to get on with living. But the cloudy bubble which had enveloped her since the handcuffs first snapped around her wrists seeped ever deeper into her consciousness. Gradually it grew in size, with its opaque lens focusing on a scene far beyond her cell walls.

Was she crazy? No, she could both see and hear the mundane activities of a busy thoroughfare. Something in her memory cleared a little. There was a nagging awareness of heavy traffic and impatient drivers.

Anna shook her head several times. Her eyes fixed absently on the surprisingly good drawings above her bunk. She stared intently at the now familiar drawings; figures which blurred and sharpened and moved until one of them, staring back at her, unexpectedly became a real person . . . Rosalind.

"No!"

Anna thrust up an arm with flat palm outward to hide from the blank, oval eyes . . . and she shivered again. There were other drawings, flat outlines, many Chicano symbols, and lengthy crayon-scrawled soliloquies all intermingled like "pop art" wallpaper. But tonight the blank eyes came alive—living, oval eyes which mocked her and followed her around the walls.

Words and figures jumbled together in a blurry rush to become the wavy outlines of cars and people . . . noise . . . cars . . . speed . . . traffic. . . . And suddenly she remembered that night of May 24th.

"Oh, no, it's going to hit me!"

A near miss. Anna swerved over close to the curb with a mere six inches to spare. A souped-up Chevy sped by, the driver giving her the finger for daring to block "his" lane.

"Damn you!" she yelled after him. "Not tonight!" Dear God, she thought, there just couldn't be any mishaps—not this night-with the new baby almost hers. She slowed to a crawl and stopped behind a rental truck. It was three blocks off the Hollywood freeway on Victory, one of the busiest streets in Van Nuys. She was visibly shaken. This night was too vital for her to jeopardize with a common traffic accident.

Steady. I've done deliveries before. But, what if Rosa's baby has something wrong with it? Will I still want it?

She had to calm down. The birth should be a cinch compared with Nancy's when she was under stress. What a scarey caper that had been! No, Rosa would be alone, and they had all night before them for the labor and birth.

Adjusting the rear view mirror she checked her lipstick and pushed one small strand of hair back in place on top of her head. She liked the ash blond color Melessa had suggested. There— neat. She'd be okay now. Just needed to relax. It would be all right. She felt better; even smiled at the way she was dressed. Blue slacks and beige sweater instead of her usual leather mini skirt and black boots which she had found provocative.

Tonight she had dressed for the work at hand which could be messy to say the least. Carefully shifting into drive she pulled out behind a bus in the slow lane.

Only another mile to my baby.

Anna glanced at the plastic bag she had cautiously packed a week ago at the hospital, and mentally went over its contents for the umpteenth time:

Stethoscope—to monitor fetal heartbeat.

Scalpel—to cut umbilical cord, and, for a possible episiotomy.

Sponges—plenty, to clean cord and mop up in general.

Benadryl, IM—to dilate uterine muscles.

Sodium pentathol, IV—to relax and sedate Rosa.

Buccal pitocin—to induce labor and speed contractions.

And, of course, equipment from the delivery room—surgical adhesive tape, rubber gloves, plastic sheeting, clamps, tourniquet, syringes and needles, plus a clean lab coat.

Yes, her patient would be in good hands. She had thought of everything. After all, she was a damn good OB nurse. What could go wrong?

Suppose the cord is around the neck? What if it's a breech? Hemorrhage? God, maybe I should turn around and go back home and forget the whole thing.

But, I've told everyone I'm pregnant. I need this baby! Again she went over the steps in precise order.

Everything was ready: the plan, the preparation, the secrecy. She was sure she hadn't forgotten anything. It would soon be over and the baby would be okay.

Suppose she wants to keep my baby?

Her baby! Rosa had promised hadn't she? She had said that she didn't want the baby . . . hadn't she? Didn't she promise? Yes, all Anna had to do was initiate labor and deliver the baby, all by herself. Cinch. She didn't need anyone's help.

She shrugged her shoulders, squared herself in the seat, and glanced approvingly in the mirror. Now, where was that corner, anyway? A little music, to steady her nerves. She turned up the volume on the car stereo and sang along to the new hit, "The Way We Were," with her perfect pitch. But her voice began to waver as she neared her destination.

"Something *is* wrong." Anna frowned deeper as she brushed at her cheeks moist with sweat. Her stomach was queasy.

Am I having my baby tonight?

Of course she wasn't pregnant . . . was she? No, that couldn't be right. Tonight? No, it was Rosa who was having the baby tonight.

Papa? Help me do the right thing. But, of course her father couldn't help. She remembered he was dead these past two weeks.

No, tonight was just between Rosa and her. She dabbed at her face with a Kleenex, glanced at the lumpy bag on the seat beside her, and shook off her fears. Everything was in readiness. She didn't need anyone's help.

A new baby to keep Nancy company. Nancy, she mused. Her little Nancy. She'd worried a lot the night she got her, too, but it had all worked out okay then. Precious Nancy who would soon have a baby sister or brother.

Anna broke into song again, following an "oldie" on the radio. "I'm gonna buy a paper doll that I can call my own—a doll that other fellers cannot steal. Ummm . . . ummm . . . flirty, flirty eyes . . . when I come home at night she will be waiting. She'll be the truest baby . . . ummm . . ."

A disk jockey was murmuring something about 15 minutes of the sweetest songs ever written as the strains of "You Made Me Love You" started her smiling. "Yes, you made me love you," she sang softly. Her pulse quickened and she fidgeted as she thought about last night's love-making with Luther. Her body tensed as she pressed her thighs together to ease her throbbing.

Gentle Luther, she thought. This time someone really loved her. Really loved *her*. God, but he was a handsome devil with that sleek ebony body, silver-streaked hair, and flashing eyes. He was everything she had ever wanted and needed in a man, and she would do anything, *anything* to keep him wanting her. Hadn't she proved that by giving him Nancy?

The sweat on her lips and temples was not all from the mild, spring-like warmth lingering under the smog after sundown. No, she was recalling how wonderful it had been last night with Luther's full, warm mouth gently teasing and tasting her entire body before he would give in to her pleas. "Please, now! I need you. Do it now . . . oh, Luther!"

Her pulse was still racing when she spotted the old church and turned sharply left into the adjacent alley. There it was. A long apartment complex of coral-pink stucco trimmed in a fading charcoal gray. The four, two-story structures were rented to mostly low income families.

Someone was just pulling out of the graveled lot behind the apartments and Anna quickly swung into the unexpected opening. She glanced at her watch. Quarter to eight. She locked her wallet in the trunk, gathered up the plastic bag and her knitting, and walked briskly around the corner into a spacious courtyard.

Kids everywhere! Babies, skateboards, even an outdated hoolahoop swirling around a cute, fat muchacha with coal-black bangs and sparkling white teeth. Anna pushed away a slobbering mongrel and deftly skirted his mark on the pathway while also dodging two, racing tricyclists.

"Hi, Rosa," she called out.

Rosalind, lounging outside her apartment doorway, turned and waved to her.

Come on over, Anna. Am I ever glad to see *you*." She lowered her voice. "I was afraid you'd changed your mind and decided not to come after all."

Anna winked and pressed Rosalind's arm. "Well, let me tell you, I'm lucky I got here the way that traffic is out there, and everything. Boy, people drive like maniacs this time of day. There's no such thing as `courtesy of the road' anymore. It's just every man for himself. I'm sure glad to be off the streets. Now all I have to worry about are these pesky mosquitos," she complained as she fanned her arms back and forth above her head.

"Yeah, do I know!" countered Rosalind. "Just look at the size of this welt on my arm. Hope the little sucker who did that died of a bloody overdose."

It was getting dark and Anna began to inch toward the door. Rosalind, putting a hand on her friend's shoulder, ushered her into the living room of the apartment.

Three little figures, in various poses of sprawled abandon, were watching "Chico and the Man" while munching nuts and bickering half-heartedly. Their fair features impressed Anna with how much anxiety Rosalind must have gone through about introducing a black baby into her family.

"Hi, kids. Good show?" Anna asked.

"Yeah, it's okay," mumbled Corinne, the older of the two girls.

Rosalind plunked her ungainly body down on the sofa next to her son. "Come on, Bobby, time for all of you to get to bed. Take your sisters into the bedroom . . . now!"

"But, Mom, tomorrow's not a school day. It's Saturday. You usually let us stay up if we don't have to get up early for school. Mom?"

Rosalind ignored his whining, patted him firmly on the bottom and said, "Don't matter what I *usually* do, Bobby. I'm telling you . . . tonight you're gonna do as I say. No arguments. You can read if you want, *after* you're ready for bed, but you are absolutely to stay in your bedroom, all of you! And be sure you close the door. Anna and I have some private business to take care of and I don't want you kids bothering us. Do you understand me?"

"Okay, okay! But it's not fair. Come on Corinne, you gotta get Katie ready for bed tonight. I had to do it last night."

"Mommy, can we take some cookies in with us to eat while we read?" Corinne pleaded.

Rosalind stood up and put her hands on her hips in a threatening manner. "Yeah, you can each have three cookies, but get going. I want you *all* off to bed right now, so move it!" With that she collapsed awkwardly back onto the sofa, uttering little self-pitying moans.

"C'mon, sit down, Anna," she waved toward a big, vinyl, overstuffed recliner with a bathroom rug pressed tightly over the seat. Anna sat on the chair rubbing her hands over the wooly rug.

"Pretty clever. Putting this here. I always hate to sit on vinyl furniture. It usually makes me sweat; then I stick to it."

"Yeah, well, actually I put that rug on 'cause there's a big rip in the seat. When Luther was over the other day to move the furniture around for me he offered to haul it off but I just couldn't bear to give it up. If you push on the handles it'll tilt back. Damn shame I can't do it anymore since I've gotten so big, but you can probably manage it. How long do you think we'll have to wait 'til I'm ready to have this baby?"

"Shouldn't take too long once we get started. I've brought everything we'll need in this sack. So, whenever you say we can get on with it." Anna began to dig in the bag.

Rosalind squirmed. "No, wait . . . go get us a beer first. We'll need it before we're through, I bet. Oh, shit, for a minute I forgot you don't drink. Pity. Well, pour yourself a cuppa coffee and there's a piece of steak and some salad left from dinner if you're hungry."

She gestured toward the kitchen and smiled wryly as she sprawled out further. One hand patted wearily at her elaborately teased hairdo. Finding a couple of curls out of place, she licked a finger and dabbed at them carefully as they continued to fall loose, and now damp against her forehead.

"Hold it a minute," objected Anna. "No beer or anything else for you 'til this is over. I'm only going to give you what's necessary to deliver this baby. By the way, you didn't eat supper did you? I mean, we sure don't want you getting sick, and everything, right in the middle of things."

"Well, let's see. Haven't had anything since about five or so. I fixed dinner early 'cause I knew you were coming. I ate meat, potatoes and a salad then. Okay? Sure would like somethin' cold to drink right now though."

"I'll get you some water—but not much. We've got to take every precaution to do this right."

After pouring herself a cup of coffee and a glass of water for her patient, Anna sat down beside Rosalind and opened the plastic bag.

"Now tell me again exactly what your doctor said today when you saw him."

"Ain't no big deal, Anna. Like I already told you on the phone, he said it's due any time now. It's in position. It's ready! Shit! How many times do I have to tell you? Now can we get *on* with it?" Her eyes didn't meet Anna's and her fingers twisted the torn fringes of a sofa pillow.

"Well, okay, honey. I'm all ready. Just have to be sure it's time— term, you know. So don't get all huffy, and everything."

"It's time! It's time, I'm tellin' you. Just do it, whatever you gotta do. You know Mom's comin' next week. Gotta have this done and over with and the baby out of the way before she gets here. Shit, I've told you what it would be like around here if my mom found a black baby outa me. Whew! Like I said, all hell'd break loose! No, by God, this baby's gotta be gone."

"Rosa, you know I can induce labor and deliver the baby easy enough, but you still don't realize how serious it is. We can't afford to take chances. It would be too risky if you weren't term."

"Listen, you told me you could do it. You promised! I'm depending on you. If you want it, you better get it and you better get it *now*." Rosalind sank back, exhausted from her tirade.

"Sure, sure, honey, I'll do it for you. Just remember, you said I could have it to call my own. I really do want it, Rosa. I *need* it! Since I told Luther I'm pregnant again with his child he's been marvelously passionate. I've got to have your baby."

Anna's palms were sweating and her eyes searched Rosalind's face as she waited for reassurance that the deal was still as they had planned it.

"Yeah, I know. I did sorta promise," sighed Rosalind. "If that rotten Oscar would of done the right thing by me, I could keep the baby and to hell with Mom. . . . But he was too damned afraid he'd have to work a little and support all of us . . . lazy, black bastard!"

Anna sat thinking how happy she and Luther were going to be with another baby. Poor Rosa . . . her man a no-good welfare bum, always coming around for a handout and a quick piece. All he ever gave Rosa was this new mouth to feed. Well, never mind. Rosa's baby would be fed and loved all right. And sweet Luther would stay with her forever.

"Well, come on, let's get started," urged Anna as she took a bottle of small white pills out of the bag and handed one to Rosalind. "Put this under your tongue and leave it there. Okay?"

"Right, now you're talkin'. Oh, by the way, I meant to tell you, if the phone rings don't answer it. No matter how long it rings. Just don't answer. I don't want Oscar knowin' what's goin' on. He's likely to come over and spoil everything if he finds out I'm home." She willingly poked the buccal pitocin under her tongue as directed. "Can I still talk with this pill in my mouth?"

"Sure, as long as you're careful and keep it under your tongue." Anna noted the time and settled back in the recliner with some knitting. The room was quiet now, except for the television and sporadic small talk.

An hour later Rosalind was as lively as ever. Not a sign of labor. She chatted on irrelevantly; while Anna began to feel uneasy and a bit concerned.

She should be feeling cramps by now.

As she rested her hand on Rosalind's abdomen, hoping to feel a contraction, she noted a snapshot of Oscar holding up a big fish. He and Luther often fished off the Santa Monica pier on weekends, and she wouldn't see her man for days. Those were times which made Anna so jealous that she hated Oscar. He had a way of goading Luther into doing things without her, by teasing him about being hen-pecked by his women.

"Humph," she mused. "Sure hope neither of our men come around tonight. Of course Oscar wouldn't anyhow if he knew I was here. I'm sure glad you said not to answer the phone. I don't want him finding out what we're doing. That'd be almost as bad as Luther finding out!"

She couldn't resist some sarcastic bragging about her man to Rosalind who was keeping quiet for a change.

"My Luther's working tonight, doing some clean-up jobs, at that new apartment complex they're building over on Van Nuys Boulevard. He's hoping to get on there, too, with the maintenance crew when they start renting. That man sure isn't afraid of work. He already spreads his talents around five other apartment complexes right in this area."

Rosalind looked over scornfully, but kept silent.

Anna was beginning to worry now. Over an hour . . . no sign of labor. What could be wrong? . . .something should be happening.

She jumped, suddenly alert as the telephone rang. One, two, seven times.

"I knew it," Rosalind snapped. "That's him. That damn Oscar, callin' to see if I'm home. Hope he doesn't plan on doin' that all night."

Anna laid aside her knitting, got up, and leaned over Rosalind with a stethoscope. Heartbeat okay. But . . . no contractions yet. Why? What could be wrong?

"Here, Rosa, try another pill under your tongue," she ordered. Rosalind blithely took the pill and continued her chatter.

"Be still," snapped Anna. Why wasn't she starting labor?

"What's the matter ?" asked Rosalind.

"Quiet, I've got to listen some more. Maybe I better try benadryl. It'll dilate the muscle around your uterus so your baby can start moving down. Don't worry. This is just part of the procedure." She unwrapped a sterile syringe and needle, drew up 1cc of fluid from a half empty vial, and turned to Rosalind.

"Hey!" yelled Rosalind, pulling back into a guarded position. "Do you have to stick that in me? I hate needles."

She tried not to cringe, and laughed nervously.

"Aw, come on, be serious. This goes right into your butt just that easy, won't hurt a bit. Come on. Let's go into the bedroom where you can relax, and so I can do a pelvic and get things ready for the big event."

Rosalind lifted her cumbersome body off the sofa and shuffled one foot after the other with protesting effort. She began talking a blue streak, still confident, and willing to follow Anna's orders.

But Anna wasn't so sure. Things were not going by the book. Why were there still no contractions? *What was* the problem?

She arranged her instruments and medicines on a small table close to the bed. While Rosalind went to the bathroom, Anna laid out a stack of terry towels and an extra sheet from the hall closet.

Her patient came plodding back and collapsed awkwardly onto the bright pink, satin sheets of her king-sized bed. "Boy, am I huffin'," she sighed. Whew, that's better."

"Hey, wait," cautioned Anna, "get up a minute. First, take off those britches. Then you've got to lie on this plastic sheet so you won't soil your bedding, and everything."

"What? I'm not ready to get undressed yet. I'll keep my clothes on, thank you, 'til I'm actually in labor. Shit, I haven't felt any labor pains yet. A plastic sheet? What a bummer. I hate plastic. Sticks and crackles and makes you sweat. How do you expect me to relax on that? Can't you put somethin' over it? Damn!" Rosalind continued to grumble and squirm. "Can't even watch TV in here. Damn it's hot! Would you *please* turn on the fan?"

Anna sighed, disgusted with Rosalind's constant bitching.

But, she complied; snapped on a small table fan, turned off the overhead light, and settled back uneasily. Her thoughts faded in and out of her dream bubble. She turned toward Rosalind.

"Listen, Rosa, did your doctor say for sure the baby's due anytime now? I mean, did he say exactly—or approximately?"

Rosalind glanced up at her. "Good grief," she wailed. "How many times do I hafta tell you? It's due! I oughta know. Why don't you just get on with it?"

She frowned nervously and again avoided Anna's eyes. "Why do you keep asking me what the doctor said? What difference does it make? You can do it can't you? I mean, even if the date's a little off, you can start the labor anyway, can't you?"

"Rosa!" cried Anna. "Dammit! I've warned you over and over about the time . . . we have to do this thing when the baby's due— not just when *you* want to do it. Now, what are you saying?" She could feel an ache in her throat, and a squeezing pain around her heart. Rosalind's peculiar uneasiness alarmed her.

The younger woman turned away, her own nervousness intensifying into doubts. She stared at the wall, tiny droplets of sweat streaking her carefully etched make-up.

Anna was up again, ignoring her fallen knitting, now tangled and pulling loose from the long needles. Once again she tried to feel some movement, some sign of normal labor. Just then a hard, cramping pain twisted Rosalind's body; and the palms of her hands pushed hard against the mattress.

"All right," she gasped in relief. "It's startin'—it's startin'."
Turning to Anna she laughed delightedly, "See, you ol' worry wart.
Didn't I tell you? Everything's gonna be okay!"

Anna smiled. Her face brightened and her mind pushed away
the gloom. Both women, their fears lulled, clasped hands, relaxed,
and started chatting with the exhilaration of imminent success.

"Say," mused Anna as she rocked and repaired her knitting,
"You know, after this baby's born, and your mother goes home,
and everything, you should find yourself a good man and settle
down. A good, loving man like my Luther. One who'd stay with
you and take care of you and the kids."

Rosalind squirmed but said nothing.

"Why, I bet with your good looks you wouldn't have any
trouble at all attracting a decent, hard-working guy. All you need
to do is quit hanging around with dead beats like Oscar and start
thinking about making a real home for you and the kids."

Rosalind giggled sarcastically. "Jeez, you really think I could
attract a *good* man like Luther, huh? Well, let me tell you, men are
all alike. They take whatever they think they can get from a woman
and then start lookin' around at other women to see what they can
get from them, too. Believe me, I know! That includes *your*
Luther. . . . Oh, look out . . . here comes another pain."

Anna reacted instantly, pulling at Rosalind's pants while hurriedly trying to time the contraction. But, it was a short, weak
one: and fear again welled up inside her. She crammed her right
hand into a sterile glove and tugged again at the bothersome jeans.

"Rosa, raise up some," she urged. "I've got to do a pelvic exam.
You should be dilating now. Darn these clothes. *Why* won't you
get undressed?" Her patience was waning as she scolded her friend.

Rosalind raised her hips and helped pull her pants down far
enough for the necessary check. But she still refused to undress
entirely, saying, "I'm not doin' it 'til I know for sure you're really
gonna be able to deliver this baby."

The pelvic examination proved Rosalind had not dilated, not one
centimeter; nor did she show any of the usual signs of normal labor.

"God, Rosa, look at me!" choked Anna. "Look at me, dammit, and you tell me the truth this time. I have to know exactly what your doctor told you—and I have to know *now*. Tell me, dammit, 'cause I think this baby's not due yet, and we're in a hell of a lot of trouble here with me trying to induce labor if you aren't ready. God only knows what's happening with the baby!"

Rosalind's own fears surfaced as she lashed out at her accuser. "You tellin' me you can't deliver it? Oh, shit. What a helluva mess! Well, if you can't deliver it then you damn well better get me to a hospital where someone can." She took a deep breath as another pain tightened within her, then went on with her tirade as Anna stood in stunned silence.

"You lyin' quack, I really thought you could do it. I actually thought you could get this baby and get it outa sight before Mom gets here," she whimpered, her pain voicing her fears. "I musta been crazy to listen to you in the first place. I've had enough of your bull-shit . . . get busy now and take me to a hospital."

Anna looked at her with frustration and desperation she could not suppress. "Hey," she said in a determined voice. "We're not going anywhere. We're staying right here 'til we deliver this baby. Now listen . . . listen to me, Rosa! You've got to tell me the truth. Rosa, you must help me if I'm to help you. We've got to get the baby out safely and quickly. Now, tell me!"

Rosalind squirmed away from Anna's painful grip and yelled back, "You bitch, you, with all your pious notions about what's best for me and my kids. Leave me alone! Christ." Her voice became contemptuous. "You and your `good' Luther. Ha!" She ranted on, "Quit foolin' around and get me an ambulance. To hell with this. I'm goin' to the hospital and get me a real doctor." She sank back on the bed, whining, avoiding Anna's eyes.

If she does that I'll be fired, for sure. And . . . why is she being so sarcastic about Luther?

Half in pain, half in fear, Rosalind blurted out, "You're right, you know, the baby's not due for another three weeks."

There was an anguished gasp from Anna as she grabbed

Rosalind with both hands and swung her around. "My God! Why did you lie? Don't you know what you've done? How could you? Three weeks early . . . oh, my God." Fear gripped her and she shoved Rosalind violently back onto the rumpled plastic, her mind in a turmoil.

"That's it," Rosalind snarled. "I've had it. I'm gonna call an ambulance myself. To hell with your precious job. I'm goin'." She started to get up but had trouble trying to pull up her twisted pants.

Anna's mind raced—her thoughts grim and accusing. The baby could be in imminent danger, and she wasn't prepared for an induced birth before term. She knew it. Could she still pull it off? Would her baby be born alive? What should she do now? Couldn't get involved with a hospital. Not now. She'd be arrested for midwifery without a license, and the baby would be lost to her forever.

Can I stop her? Can't let her spoil everything like Mama always did. It's not fair.

She wiped her palms on her lab coat and forced a smile. "There, there, honey, be still. I'm sorry I yelled at you. It's going to be all right. It may be a little harder, but I can still do it. Not to worry. Trust me, honey. Now, please, just relax and let me take care of you," she soothed. "Sorry I got so upset, but I'm okay now, so let's get back to business." She patted Rosalind's arm reassuringly and pointed to the table where she had arranged her instruments and supplies.

"Got another shot ready. It'll work right away. Please be patient a while longer. Come on, honey."

Rosalind moaned. "I don't know. That might not work either. I'm so tired and disappointed. I just want it to be over with."

This time Anna reached for the sodium pentathol.

Something has got to work soon.

"Here, let me help you. If you'll just try this—we'll know if it's going to work in about ten minutes. Then, if it doesn't help and you still want to, we'll go to the hospital. I promise."

Rosalind offered no resistance as Anna carefully positioned her patient's left arm closer to the edge of the bed. She tied off the arm with a tourniquet and quickly injected a hefty dose of the powerful analgesic.

"Just relax now, honey. That's a good girl."

Rosalind did relax a little and rolled away from Anna, facing the wall in offended silence. Her erstwhile immaculate hairdo was lopsided and her expensive perfume mingled with the rancid odor of sweat.

The telephone rang again, but both women scarcely heard it.

Rosalind began to laugh—kind of a low, chuckling rumble as the sodium pentathol took effect.

"It's so funny, really, your Luther. . . . Why, you couldn't hold a man if you had a million dollars." She rolled back, buttoned her blouse, and laughed outright. Anna stood transfixed, staring at her, a sinking chill cramping her gut.

Why is she laughing? All of a sudden intense pain wracked Rosalind as a hard and powerful contraction twisted her body.

"You fool," she screamed. The pentathol controlled her thoughts, now, and her words became foghorns of her guarded secrets. "Don't you know this is really Luther's baby? Ahhh! What do you think he does over here every week—just move the furniture? Do you *really* think you're the only woman he has besides his wife? God, but it's *so* funny . . . you wanting to give him *this* baby, saying it's his . . . and all the time it *is* his! . . . Ha—ha—ha—ah. . . ." Her words trailed off into gibberish.

Anna kept staring down at Rosalind. The scornful, taunting laughter echoed inside her head; pushing against her skull with the abrasiveness of a dull drill bit.

Luther's baby? Luther's baby? Rosa's and Luther's? No!

Oh, no. It can't be true. But the pentathol . . . the pentathol. It must be true. Oh, God! Luther's baby? Headache —pounding—a scream forming in her throat. She drifted in and out of reality. Jumbled memories from childhood stabbed at her. Her mother was saying, "I never wanted you." Dozens of faces out of the past leered at her: faces which laughed derisively as they voiced their rejections of her. Fingers pointed, lips twisted with malice, mouths uttered foul accusations. The terrible laughter!

Her thoughts now became low mutterings as she searched frantically through the medical paraphernalia stacked on the small table . . . subconsciously groping for something . . . anything to silence her tormentor.

"Luther . . . *my* Luther! Mine. But, no, he's not mine, is he?"

Why had Rosa taken him away? Why did she think that was so funny? And why was she killing the baby? She shouldn't be doing that. It was all her fault—Rosa's fault; seducing Luther, losing the baby. No, Rosa was bad: bad for Luther, bad for the baby, bad for everyone.

Rosalind rolled from side to side rocking with laughter. "Shut up!" choked Anna. "Don't you laugh at *me*. You can't do this to me! I won't let you. I won't let her, Papa. Don't you see? She's making fun of me and taking my baby. Oh, Papa, Papa, I can't let her ruin everything like Mama did. I won't let her!"

Rosalind kept laughing and pointing at Anna.

Suddenly Anna's hand felt a sharp blade; and she realized instantly what she had to do. Her fingers clasped tightly around the scalpel. She swung it around in front of her and poised it directly over the bed.

Rosalind roused enough to see into a face less than a foot away from hers—a face contorted with suffering and anger. With her laughter suddenly aborted, Rosalind's pupils dilated with fear. Fear so awful that her heart lurched into her throat, and a silent scream burned into her soul.

And she knew! . . . she knew . . .

CHAPTER 16

Tuesday, July 16, 1974, night.

Anna slept fitfully, tossing from one side to the other on the small bunk in her cell. Her rotund body could not find a restful position on such a hard and narrow space. Welcomed exhaustion claimed her memory of recent events, and, for a short time, sleep obliterated her fearful anxiety.

"Remember, remember," seared into her mind until she pushed upright with sudden wakefulness. With a shaking hand she clutched at her cold, china sink.

"What?" she called out. A guard looked in quickly and asked whether he could get her anything.

"No . . . no . . . I don't think so. . . ." Her panic subsided, but her hands continued to tremble. She sat on the edge of her bed for awhile—again drifting—her mind struggling to grasp the significance of the narrow, sparsely furnished room.

Jail. It must be jail. Oh, sure . . . the trial. But— my baby?

She frowned. Then she remembered; handcuffs, police, the courtroom. No . . . no, the hospital. She should be in the hospital! What had happened?

My baby!

Renewed panic exploded into hysteria. She beat on the iron door of her cell and screamed at the guard, "My baby! Where's my baby?" She reached through the bars, waving frantically.

"It's okay, Mrs. Anderson, it's okay," soothed the special-duty officer assigned to watch her. "Your baby's fine. Really, it's fine. Don't you remember?" he asked softly. He knew he was not allowed to question inmates about their crimes during their trial.

But, all the staff were buzzing about this notorious woman who was in the second week of her preliminary hearing. He was instantly alert and curious to see whether she would finally talk about her bizarre case.

"Don't you remember?" he prodded. "Don't you remember anything?"

No answer. Nor even recognition of his presence. But, she did remember that she had, today, been in a courtroom jammed with strangers. Her recall was re-living Melessa's testimony, every word.

Poor Melly; just doesn't know what to say. Close. She tried to tell the truth, I think . . . but, some of it hurt me. She had no right to talk against me. Some friend! Shouldn't have told about the phone calls. She hurt me!

THE COURT: Counsel, you may call your next witness.

MR. DURBIN: People call Mrs. Birdsong.

MELESSA BIRDSONG called as a witness by and on behalf of the People, having been first duly sworn, was examined and testified as follows:

BY MR. DURBIN:

Q. It is Mrs.?

A. Yes.

Q. And what relationship, if any, do you have to the defendant?

A. She is my adopted sister. I mean, we called ourselves sisters.

Q. So, you are close friends.

A. Right.

Q. Now, Mrs. Birdsong, when did you first learn that Rosalind was dead?

A. On Saturday morning. The 25th, I think.

Q. Sometime after you learned that Rosalind was dead, did you have a telephone conversation with the defendant?

A. Yes, I did.

Q. What did the defendant tell you?

MR. WINGATE: Your Honor, may we have a foundation laid as to where these respective parties were, please.

THE COURT: All right. Will you do that, please.

BY MR. DURBIN:

Q. Well, where were you?

A. At my home.

Q. And the defendant was on the other end of the telephone; is that correct?

A. Right.

Q. What did the defendant tell you?

A. She told me three different stories.

Q. Okay. Could you tell us, please, the first story that the defendant told you.

A. Yes. The first story she told me was that she was in the home with Rosalind, and she, Anna, was hiding in the closet when Rosalind's former boyfriend had come in and killed her. That was Oscar Banks, her boyfriend until two or three months ago.

Q. Okay. What's the next version she told you?

A. The next one, the next time, she told me that *she* had killed Rosa.

Q. Was this in the same conversation, the same telephone call?

A. No. She called me three times that day.

Melessa looked helplessly at Anna, but the defendant was staring at the floor, or, maybe something beyond.

Melessa turned back to face the District Attorney.

Q. Then we'll talk about the first telephone call. In the first telephone call the defendant indicated that she was in the closet when Rosalind's boyfriend, Oscar Banks, killed Rosalind?

A. Right.

Q. What else did Anna tell you concerning the death of Rosalind, in that conversation?

A. That Rosa was in labor, and that she had taken the baby to save its life, and taken it to the hospital.

Q. And that conversation ended? She hung up?

A. I think so. I was very upset that day. So, as far as any other conversation, I really don't remember it at that time.

Q. Now, when did the next telephone conversation take place?

A. An hour, or a couple hours later.

Q. Incidentally, in the first conversation did she tell you where she was calling from?

A. Yes. She said she was in custody in Van Nuys.

Q. Now, what did she say in the second conversation?

A. Well, she told me that *she* had killed Rosa, and the same thing about taking the baby, and taking it to a hospital.

Q. Did she tell you how she had killed Rosalind?

A. Yes. She said she had cut her throat.

Q. Did she say anything about inducing labor in that conversation?

A. She said Rosa had called her to confirm their date for her to come over and induce labor for her.

Q. Did she tell you why she had killed Rosalind?

A. No.

Q. Did she say anything else in that second conversation that you can recall?

A. Only when I started—like I said, I was very upset, and I started crying, and she told me not to be upset, that she didn't feel any pain.

Q. Did she say why Rosalind didn't feel any pain?

MR. WINGATE: No, your Honor, I don't think—she said *she* didn't feel any pain. I think, the connotation I got was that she, the defendant, didn't feel any pain, and not to be upset.

May we have that clarified, please, your Honor?

THE COURT: All right. Will you state exactly what the conversation was, to the best of your recollection, please, in reference to who felt the pain.

THE WITNESS: She said that Rosalind did not feel pain.

MR. WINGATE: Thank you, your Honor.

BY MR. DURBIN:

Q. Did she indicate to you what measures were taken to insure that Rosalind didn't feel any pain?

A. She said that she had sedated her, that she had given her sodium pentothal.

Q. Did she say anything more? Did she go into any details as to how she had killed her?

A. No, she didn't. That was all.

Q. Okay. How about the third conversation? What time did that occur?

A. In the same afternoon. She called me *again.*

Q. And what did she tell you then concerning the death of Rosalind?

A. It was funny. She asked me if Rosa was dead, and I told her, "Yes."

And she said she did not kill Rosa, that she had killed Mattie.

Q. Do you know who Mattie is?

A. Sure. That's the wife of her boyfriend, Luther.

Q. Let's see. You mean Luther Anderson?

A. Yes.

Q. Do you know where he is at this time?

A. No, I do not.

Q. Had you ever met Luther Anderson?

A. Oh, yes, I had.

Q. What race is he?

A. Black.

MR. WINGATE: Well, that's—

(Pause. Mr. Wingate waves comment.)

BY MR. DURBIN:

Q. Okay. Do you know where Mattie is now?

A. No, I don't.

Q. To your knowledge is Mattie—or, was Mattie pregnant on or about the 24th of May?

A. I don't know. I hadn't seen her for over a year.

Q. Was Mattie white or black?

A. Black.

Q. Now, other than what you have told us that the defendant told you in the three telephone conversations, do you have any personal knowledge of the death of Rosalind Delgato?

A. No.

Q. And Anna never mentioned a Caesarean section?

A. No.

Q. Did she ever tell you on the telephone, or otherwise, what she did with the weapon she used to cut Rosa's throat?

A. She told me that there was instruments that had been destroyed on the way to the hospital.

Q. Did she tell you who took her to the hospital?

A. Her daughter, Sandra.

Q. Did she mention anything about taping Rosa's mouth?

A. No.

MR. WINGATE: That's leading and suggestive, your Honor. (Pause.)

But I'll withdraw the objection in view of the answer being, "No."

BY MR. DURBIN:

Q. Incidentally, did the defendant ever say anything else concerning this Mattie? Did she mention any animosity she had toward Mattie, a dislike?

A. Well, of course there was dislike and jealousy.

Q. Did she ever tell you that she was going to get Mattie, or do anything to Mattie?

MR. WINGATE: Your Honor, I object on the ground it's immaterial and irrelevant to the issues of this preliminary hearing.

THE COURT: Counsel?

MR. DURBIN: I'll submit it.

THE COURT: I'm going to sustain the objection.

MR. DURBIN: I have nothing further.

THE COURT: You may cross-examine.

MR. WINGATE: Thank you, your Honor.

CROSS-EXAMINATION

BY MR. WINGATE:

Q. Mrs. Birdsong, today you have told us you had three telephone conversations with Mrs. Anderson on May 25, 1974.

A. Yes.

Q. And did she sound upset when you talked to her?

A. Yes.

Q. Was she crying?

A. No, but her voice, the tone of her voice sounded upset.

Q. And in that conversation she told you that Rosa's boy-friend had killed Rosalind; and that she, Anna, was hiding in the closet at Rosalind's apartment when Oscar Banks killed Rosalind. Is that correct?

A. Yes.

Q. So, the second conversation was an hour or two later. Did she tell you that she had killed Rosalind and that she had taken the baby to save the baby's life?

A. Yes, she did.

Q. And that she had sedated Rosalind.

A. Yes.

Q. Was she upset during this phone conversation?

A. She was very calm.

Q. Very calm?

A. Yes.

Q. So, in the second conversation Mrs. Anderson was not as upset as she was in the first?

A. No.

Q. And then in the third conversation she first asked if Rosa was dead; then told you that she, Anna, had not killed her—that she had killed Mattie, Luther Anderson's wife?

A. Right.

MR. WINGATE: May I approach the witness, your Honor?

THE COURT: Yes.

BY MR. WINGATE:

Q. Mrs. Birdsong, I note that on your written statement that the content of the second conversation is here, in the statement—do you see what I mean? Pointing now to this paragraph, there's nothing about the first conversation, and nothing about the third conversation. Do you see that?

A. Yes, I see.

Q. Who prepared this statement, if you know?

A. Detective Walters.

Q. The gentleman seated in the plaid, green coat?

A. Yes.

Q. Did you sign this statement?

A. No, I haven't.

Q. Well, did you tell Detective Walters about the three telephone conversations?

A. Yes.

Q. But you didn't see this when it was finished?

A. No.

Q. Today, on the witness stand, you are certain that the defendant phoned you three times, and you have given us the entire content of those three conversations. No doubt?

A. None.

Q. What was Anna's condition over the telephone during the third conversation?

A. She was very upset. She started to scream and cry when I told her that Rosa was dead. She said she didn't kill Rosa and then she said if she had, then to let her stay in there because she deserved to die.

Q. You thought Anna said she, Anna, deserved to die?

A. Yes.

Q. Now, did Mrs. Anderson ever tell you that she was glad she had listened to your advice and not gone through with any plan to get any dead fetus and replace a live child?

A. Yes, she did.

Q. Did she tell you that she had never done that?

A. Yes.

MR. WINGATE: No further questions, your Honor.

THE COURT: Anything on redirect?

MR. DURBIN: No.

THE COURT: All right. You heard the Court's order not to discuss any of the testimony given on the stand with any other witnesses?

MR. WINGATE: Mrs. Birdsong, the judge is talking to you.

THE WITNESS: I'm sorry?

THE COURT: Did you hear my order not to discuss your testimony with any other witnesses?

THE WITNESS: Yes, your honor.

THE COURT: You will abide by that order.

THE WITNESS: Yes.

THE COURT: All right. You may be excused. You may leave if you desire.

Anna sat and rocked on the iron bed and stared at the faintly familiar drawings on the jail walls. The trial proceedings faded as she looked around. There was . . . something . . . some other remembrance too terrible to examine. Hallucinations mixed inexorably with reality.

Anna and the awful memory seemed to be spinning, dangling in a deep well—pulling on a knotted, life-saving rope that could lift them up into warmth and safety. A pulley squeaked above her head as she pulled harder on the rope. A sticky, dark spray hit her face and stung her eyes.

The same flat, crudely defined figure that once before had reminded her of Rosalind was bending over the narrow opening at the top of the well. It was sawing at the rope! Sawing, and chuckling in rasping tones, and grinning with vacuous malice.

Anna stared up helplessly at the evil, changing face. The wavering, indistinct outline began taking on her own form, *her* face, *her* malice, *her* hand. That hand now held a knife. She could see the knife clearly—a surgical scalpel. There was blood all over it. Fresh, red blood. There—on the blade and on her hands and up her arms. Then blood was spiraling down the rope onto the figure dangling inside the well.

The rope frayed. The squeaking pulley became a screaming mouth beneath Anna's hands holding the sawing knife. The rope parted! And it was the body of Rosalind . . . falling . . . screaming . . . lost. . . .

Memory echoed back at her from the depths of her illusion.

Muddled pictures surged into clarity as Anna saw her own hand reaching out to grasp the shiny, steel handle of an aseptically clean scalpel. She felt the mugginess of a warm, spring evening. It was May again . . . and . . . someone was laughing.

It was Rosalind. She remembered Rosalind's derisive laughter as she taunted her about Luther. And she remembered about the baby *really* being Luther's! Her body shook as she remembered the sneering glee with which Rosalind had told her about Luther's other affairs, especially the one with her.

"Isn't that a riot?" Rosalind had giggled. "You takin' my baby home and tellin' Luther it's his—yours and his—and all the time it really is his!" She had rolled with shrieks of laughter as the pentothal pumped through her body.

Yes, oh yes, now Anna remembered it all. That awful night, the apartment, Rosalind, the laughter, the scalpel.

Not my Luther, too! Oh, God—no more!

And aloud, in terrible pain, "**NO MORE!**" The scalpel glinted momentarily in the subdued light. Anna held the deadly blade tight and close above Rosalind's face.

The doomed woman looked into Anna's eyes—beyond—into a vapor of horror that engulfed them both. Her scream was aborted as the scalpel sliced clean and savagely deep, finding its way quickly through the trachea and esophagus until it met the jolting resistance of bone. The blade had cut expertly close to the fingers of her left hand, which was pressed firmly against Rosalind's neck, pulling skin and flesh taut.

The severed carotid arteries sprayed blood onto her glasses and spattered the white drapes above the bed as the wound opened up from one ear lobe to the other—bone crunching as her savage thrust slowed and stopped. Anna's right hand clutched the scalpel so tightly that her knuckles showed white through streaks of blood. She had slashed with such force that blood spurted everywhere, creating a myriad of changing patterns, even on the ceiling.

Not until the scalpel became wedged in the neck vertebrae did Anna pause.

Rosa?

For a confused moment her frenzy lessened. Her pupils dilated and her eyes narrowed as she sought to focus on the body beneath her.

"Rosa! Rosa!"

Fear displaced rage. She pulled hard on the blade and freed it from the fractured bone. Absently she sopped up blood with Rosalind's terry towels. Sanity struggled with dementia.

Dead? God, NO!

Her eyes slowly fixed on Rosalind's distended abdomen. A dark-red ooze was seeping down the belly's sides from her slashed neck as the last, pumping spurts from a dying heart pushed Rosalind's lifeblood out onto her body.

Dead? Ohhhh, no, NO! The baby! God, no, not the baby— oh, Lord, my baby—got to save it. God, help me!

Anna called aloud in haggard fear, "Please God, let me save my baby! Please, God, please."

Her fingers closed once again around the flat handle of the scalpel, and she nurtured a dark hope. She dashed over to the door and switched on the overhead light.

Rosalind's severed arteries were draining away not only her own life, but the life support of her unborn child. Also, the pentothal injected minutes before, would now be affecting that new life, slowing its flow of oxygen even more rapidly than the loss of its mother's blood.

Hurry!

Anna yanked downward at Rosalind's badly stretched jeans and underpants; this time stifling her anger so she would not add injury to the unborn life. She grabbed a handful of sponges and again poised the scalpel above Rosalind's body.

Suddenly the hot night stillness was further violated with gurgling sounds bubbling up through the flaccid mouth.

"Shut up!" She quickly tore off enough surgical tape to cover Rosalind's lips and seal off those unbearable sounds of death.

Once again she turned to the task at hand; the task for which

she had come in the first place; the task which now became grotesque in its fruition.   .

She called upon mental pictures of surgeons performing Caesarean sections. It was almost as though she were being guided by
videotaped instructions. The pictures, on total recall, were brought
clearly into focus through her mind's eye, giving assurance to her
fingers. Bloody scalpel in hand, she began.

She drew its razor-sharp point to an exact depth over the large
belly, still warm and moist. Her heart was hurting, its beat pounding, but her hands remained strong and steady. There was blood
everywhere now—too much for the plastic sheeting to contain.
Anna continued to cut precisely and confidently, adhering to the
accepted length and depth for a Caesarean incision.

At last it was done. She put down the scalpel, took a deep
breath, and spread open the door of flesh, exposing the life beneath. Her eyes teared and her lips parted in a smile of delight as
she gently grasped two small feet and lifted the tiny being from its
watery tomb. Holding it slightly downward, yet secure against
her bosom, she raked a finger through its mouth to clear the
miniscule air passage. She then breathed her own oxygen into its
still unopened lungs.

The little form reddened and its head jerked spasmodically.
Every instinct in the tiny body was in total revolt at being snatched
from the warm, soft, hidden existence of the womb. Its arms and
legs thrashed about violently, in desperate motions, as if trying to
find a way back to the calm, quiet safety it had known before. The
quivering lips opened, sucking in the first breath of life on its own,
and with it came its first cry of rebellion.

The puny cries continued with a determined effort to show
disapproval of a cold world; the reddish-brown skin turning darker
with each cry. The sounds of its new environment encompassed,
first the baby's own tiny shrieks of fright, and, then, Anna's whis-
pering voice trying to give it assurance.

"Hush, little one . . . hush."

The primal instinct for survival dominated. Even this defiant newborn accepted the inevitable, and sought a new connection to sustain its life. That connection, at that moment, was Anna Louise Anderson. All of Anna's attention was now focused on her charge. She expertly clamped off the umbilical cord and, with the same, deadly scalpel, cut it cleanly. There was a feeling of triumph as she severed this last bond between the baby and Rosalind. As she cuddled the infant she became vaguely aware of things to be done.

Her practical senses dictated certain mechanical necessities that seemed urgent. She wrapped the baby in a clean towel and laid him gently on a chair under the bold picture of his mother. She then gathered her bloodied equipment, stuffed it all back in the plastic sack, dumped the blood-soaked towels in Rosalind's bathroom sink, and carefully bagged the placenta to take with her.

Leave she must—now. Again, that almost sane sense of urgency. Her baby—premature—she must get him to the hospital.

She glanced around the bedroom.

God, Rosa!

Her thinking clouded again and the consequences of her violent acts were confusing and vague. She stared at Rosalind's body. Suddenly her mind snapped back to reality.

Oh, my God! What'll I do with Rosa? Can't let the children see her like that.

With both hands Anna tugged and pulled the grotesque corpse off the bed onto the floor. She got down on her knees and pushed at the shoulders, then at the hips of the mangled body until she had it well under the bed. She didn't notice the stained drapes, or the blood-soaked bedding, or her own hands, dark with blood and slippery with meconium.

Anna picked up her baby and the two plastic bags, carefully opened the front door, checked the now empty courtyard, and slipped quietly out of the apartment. Soft little jerks pressed into her breasts, and the sucking noises made her smile. She murmered, "Hush, little baby, don't you cry. Mama's gonna love you 'til she dies."

As she left the horror behind, Anna gazed adoringly down at

the vibrant form cradled close to her bosom. Her dream world enveloped them both—shielding them momentarily from gruesome reality.

She whispered, "I love you—my son—my son."

CHAPTER 17

Thursday, July 11, 1974, afternoon.

THE COURT: Mr. Durbin, are you ready to proceed?

MR. DURBIN: Yes, your Honor.

BY MR. DURBIN:

Q. Investigator Walters, going back to the scene of the murder: did you take police department photographs at the scene? Before the body was removed?

A. We did. Investigator Mallory and myself.

Q. How many do you have in your—

A. We have numerous.

Q. Dozens?

A. Dozens. Probably in the neighborhood of 40 to 50.

Q. Directing your attention to 2-A, 2-C and 2-D, could you please identify those photographs verbally.

A. Yes. 2-A is a photograph taken subsequent to the bed being lifted from the top of the body. It depicts the victim approximately from the chest up to the head. It depicts a large gaping wound to the neck area; and shows a piece of tape covering the victim's mouth. The tape is approximately three inches wide and seven inches long, going from cheek to cheek and covering the mouth. There is a large amount of blood beneath the victim's head and shoulder area.

2-C is a photograph depicting the victim from the waist up, again showing the neck, the tape and the blood.

Item 2-D depicts a full length photograph of the victim taken from the area north of the head. It depicts the victim's clothing, a pair of light blue jeans pulled down to approximately five inches above the knees, a pair of multi- colored bikini panties which have been pulled from the normal position to just below the pelvic area. The blouse has been pulled up to just below the breasts.

It also depicts a wound to the abdominal area which is approximately five inches in length, running at the midline of the body directly down to below the navel toward the pubis.

Q. Is that the position of the body undisturbed?

A. Yes, sir, it is.

Q. With the exception of the bed being removed off of it; is that correct?

A. That's correct.

MR. DURBIN: The photographs will be made available to the defense, your Honor, at their request.

THE COURT: All right. The record will so reflect that the District Attorney will make available to Mr. Wingate or his nominee those photos within a reasonable time.

MR.. WINGATE: Thank you, your Honor.

BY MR. DURBIN:

Q. Investigator Walters, I take it that you and Investigator Mallory are and were the ones who are coordinating and conducting the investigation of this matter at this time. That would include investigation of the defendant at the hospital, which you have related. Now, about your meeting with the defendant's children, did Bill tell—

MR. WINGATE: Objection. Improper—

THE COURT: Sustained.

BY MR. DURBIN:

Q. Please answer my first question.

A. That is correct, sir, we are the homicide officers on the case.

MR. DURBIN: I have no further questions.

Saturday, May 25, 1974, 7:20 a.m.

Bobby was certain that most things which venture into the dark recesses beneath any bed become entrapped by the weird, hairy, dust-ball creatures living there in ghostly cobwebs. At this moment he and his sisters were certain there was something more frightening than cobwebs under their mother's bed. He hesitated, as he kneeled beside the disarranged covers bunched over the side of the bed.

With impulsive bravado he lifted the bloodied covers which hung over the edge; while one hand tightly pressed against his closed eyes. The unnatural stillness of the room and the worsening odor in the air paralyzed him with fear.

Corinne tugged at his elbow. "Well? What's there? Is it Mommy? Tell me, Bobby!"

Her insistent pushing grated at him; he knew he had to look. Slowly two fingers parted just enough for one eye to see. His breath quickened into an anguished gasp. He stifled a scream and braced his shaking body against the bed frame as he saw the mangled body of his mother.

Her face, frozen in an expression of terror, seemed to stare back at him. Bobby's eyes were wide and fixed. He saw it all: the grotesque slant of the head showing the deep slash that almost severed it from the body; the wide strip of tape that stretched tightly over the mouth; the gaping hole in the abdomen that exposed an empty womb. The dead stare.

Almost instantly he yanked the covers back down. Gasping waves of shock and disbelief flooded his throat. His head shook uncontrollably as the savagery filled his mind.

"No, oh, no, no, Mom! Oh, Mom . . . please, not Mom."

"Bobby!" screeched Corinne. "Whatsa *matter* with Mom? Lemmie see. Tell me, what's wrong? Is somethin' bad wrong with Mommy?"

As she scooted closer to him Bobby grabbed her arm. "No, Cory, don't. She's dead. Really dead. She's all cut up, I think murdered. I don't want you to see her. It's too awful."

The tears now streaming down his face only heightened Corinne's urgent need to confirm what she had just heard. Ignoring her brother's pleas, she pushed him aside, threw back the covers and peered directly into the unseeing eyes of her mother.

One shrill scream after another drowned out Bobby's sobs, as Corinne knelt there unable to move. Bobby put his arms around her and pulled her back, sobbing out his fears while trying to comfort her.

"Cory, what'll we do? Somebody *killed* Mom!" He glanced over his shoulder. "I'm scared, aren't you? We're all alone. Come on, we gotta go tell someone quick."

He shook her in a frantic effort to get her attention.

"You gotta quit screaming! Stop it, Cory! Come on. Let's get outa here and get help. We gotta tell somebody." Corinne's screams lessened and broke off into crying as she clung to Bobby's waist.

Suddenly they felt Katie hitting them with her tiny fists; and heard her whimpering as she tried to kneel down between them.

"I wanna see too. Is it sumpthin' scarey 'bout Mommy? Wha's unner Mommy's bed, Bobby? Is it Mommy? I wanna see! Can I see unner it?"

"No! You wouldn't like it," sniffed Bobby. "It's too scarey. Get up, Katie. Come on with me and Cory. We're going over to Mrs. Gonzales'—right now! Come *on*. If you're good you can have breakfast with Ramona."

Both girls looked up at their big brother who sounded so much like their mother, and both obeyed him. Corinne sucked in great gulps of the putrid air around her in an effort to stifle her blubbering. She grabbed at Katie's hand and followed Bobby's lead.

Katie dug at her eyes with her fingers and wiped her nose and top lip with a messy swipe of her pajama sleeve. She let herself be pulled out of the apartment; all the while looking back and repeating her pathetic question, "Where's Mommy?"

Bobby, Corinne and Katie, linked in a togetherness which superseded sibling rivalries, ran toward Mrs. Gonzales' apartment.

"Can I play with R'ona 'til you fine Mommy?"

"Sure ya can," answered Corinne.

Bobby tugged at them.

"We gotta hurry," he gulped.

Katie stumbled along, sniffing at the persistent dribble on her lip, while trying to cover her bare bottom with the hanging flap of her pajamas. Corinne kept blowing her nose. Bobby blinked rapidly and tried to pace his half-run to match Katie's short stride.

Several tenants had heard the screams and had ventured out of their apartments in various stages of undress. Since it was Saturday morning most of them were not taking kindly to being awakened so early. But Donald Blake, smiling broadly, sauntered out with a steaming cup of coffee.

"Hey, Bobby," he called to his friend, "What's happening, buddy? Where you kids going this time of day?"

Bobby broke loose from Katie's hand to run to him. He really liked Donald who sometimes let him sit on his motorcycle and who taught him about tools and engines. He had often wished his mother would like Donald instead of the other guys who hung around.

"Quick, Don," he cried. "Come over to our place. My Mom's been hurt real bad . . . m—m—murdered!" Tears, unchecked, poured down his cheeks as he grabbed his friend's arm with both hands.

"Wait a minute, slow down. What the Hell? What do you mean . . . murdered? Where *is* your Mom? And what makes you think she's been murdered?"

"She's home—in her bedroom. Come on . . . I'll show ya. *Please*, Don, she's bloody and all cut up. I told you, murdered. She's dead. Really dead."

Donald set down his coffee cup, hugged the boy and whispered, "Okay, buddy, I'm going to help. Go ahead and cry."

"But, what'll we do? Mom's *dead*."

"Wha's dead mean, Bobby?" asked Katie, pulling on her brother's knee.

"Aw, for cryin' out loud. Will ya just go on with Cory? I'm goin' with Don for awhile." He pushed her toward Corinne. "Keep hold of her. I'll be over soon as I can."

His sisters ran crying across the courtyard, without looking at or answering anyone.

Mrs. Gonzales, with children of all ages and sizes hanging on to her came puffing down her steps. Her long, dark hair, as always, was pulled back and neatly twisted into two, soft rolls on the nape of her neck. Her deep brown eyes focused on the Delgato children as she voiced her concern.

"What on earth's happened to bring all *this* on? What are you kids doing out here so early? Hush, now, hush."

Corinne blurted out, "It's Mommy. Somethin' bad happened to her. She's been kilt . . . an' . . . we're scared!"

Without a word Mrs. Gonzales hugged both girls tightly and looked across at Donald. He gave her a wave of assurance as he and Bobby disappeared into Apartment C. The sluggish irritation of neighbors gave way to realization of some sort of catastrophe, and a wave of movement converged toward the Delgato apartment. Mrs. Gonzales quickly pulled the girls upstairs and out of sight.

Inside Rosalind's door Donald gently patted Bobby's shoulder, nudging him toward the sofa. "Okay, buddy, just show me where to look, and wait right here for me." The boy sank into the couch without taking his eyes off his friend.

"In there," he choked. "There, in the bedroom . . . right there. She's under the bed." He pointed a rigid finger as he blinked back more tears.

"Right. Keep the door locked."

The odor rocked him when he entered the bedroom. His whole body reacted; hands clenched; stomach muscles tightened into a retching spasm; heart beat synchronized at three times the off-beat, clicking sounds made by the oscillating fan. For a moment he, too, was shaken by childhood fears of what might be hiding under the bed. Hesitantly he grasped the bloodied covers, then threw them back over the bed as he bent over.

The sight caused him to gasp and sink down to fight off the nausea. He thought Rosalind's dead eyes were staring at him. With a crazy impulse he reached toward the adhesive tape, thinking she might tell of the terror if her mouth was freed. But, he snatched back his hand, and groaned at the thought that her head was tipped as if she was trying to look into her empty womb.

"My God, Rosa!"

He stumbled from the room and propped himself against the wall by the telephone. It took all his concentration to control his fingers as he dialed the police. There was demanding knocking on the front door while he tried to give concise facts over the telephone.

"Come on, Bobby," he said firmly. "We're going to get out of here. I'll take care of things." They locked the door behind them and jostled through the gathering crowd which threatened to mash them against the wooden siding. A brief explanation of certain death inside was enough to quiet their neighbors for a short time. Bobby gripped Donald's hand as they waited.

Sounds of sirens, squealing brakes, and car doors jarred the eery, Saturday morning stillness of Victory Boulevard. Like a discordant symphony one police car after another careened over the curbing and into the courtyard of the Victory Palms Apartments. Police radios belched out crisp announcements and grating static . . . all at the loudest volume possible.

Donald turned over the keys and led police to the crime scene. Two uniformed officers positioned themselves outside Apartment C while investigating officers started their search for clues to the bizarre murder. The sun was hot already, and it made the inside air oppressive. Donald was quick to exit and join the children.

Curious tenants bunched in toward Officer Piercal and his partner until there were scores of persons in various modes of dress or undress pushing closer to get a glimpse inside. Many didn't even know who lived there, but, they jockeyed for position as if trying to grab a front row at the Pantages. It was nothing new to Piercal to see the morbid fascination that people had toward rumors of horror.

He watched one woman so intent on craning her neck high enough to see over the crowd that she didn't realize one breast was hanging half out of her loose-fitting robe. Nor did she notice that the spent ash from her cigarette had dropped onto the bald head of a squat, sweaty man on tiptoes in front of her. Piercal could see the ash stubbornly clinging to the man's head as if it was a curly, maverick strand of hair on the shiny pate.

Those tenants on the fringes gave up trying to see even the apartment doorway because of the flashing blue and red lights spotting their eyesight. They turned their attention to two setters running joyfully around the courtyard with their yelping adding to the increasing din. The dogs strained at a double leash attached firmly to a robust woman in a ballooning muu muu. Her noisy flip-flops slowed only when her setters lifted a leg to water the police tires. When an officer started chasing the trio, the fringe spectators cheered on the dogs.

A dark sedan was pulling in as a youngster with a giant, pink bubble emerging from his lips rode by too close on his bicycle. When he squeezed on his brakes the bike's back wheel skidded sideways into a scruffy man standing barefooted near the curbing.

"Dammit, kid," growled the old man. "You caught my toe with that thing."

"Sorry. I didn't mean to. What's goin' on, anyway? A fight?"

The man ignored him and leaned toward the open window of the sedan. "Say, don't I know you?" he asked the driver.

A tall, finely chiseled man in a summer business suit unfolded from the automobile, smiled absently, and headed toward the uniformed policemen. He spotted one of his sergeants near Apartment C.

"Hey, Betty, what's with all these looky-loos? For Christ's sake, Sergeant, get them away from here. Tell them we'll see each and every one who lives here, probably before the day is over."

"Yes, Captain."

"Christ, you should have cleared this area before."

"Sorry, sir," answered Sergeant Cordell. "Right away." Captain Arthur Freeley paused before entering Apartment C.

How sad, he thought. How terribly sad that such a vibrant woman would come to a violent, mutilating death. He made an obvious show of checking his notebook, which no one noticed he was holding upside-down, and spoke to the officer on guard.

"Um, Piercal, do you know where the children are?"

"Yes, sir, with a neighbor in Suite E—second floor."

"Has anyone contacted the juvenile authorities?"

"Don't know. I've been out here since I arrived."

"I understand they discovered the body."

"That's right, Captain. And Juvie should be called. I'll check it out. Those poor kids, seeing their mother cut up like that."

"More than that . . . they could have witnessed something to make them a target for more murder. Be sure Juvie picks them up before noon." His hand shook a little, and he knew the officer noticed it. "It's just that those kids are our legal responsibility, and I don't like it. The sooner they're in protective custody the better I'll feel."

"Yes, sir. I'll take care of it." He eyed his captain. "Just a minute, Piercal. Has the Coroner come?"

"Not yet." He shrugged.

"Wonder what the hell's keeping him? *We're* all up and kicking. Well, can't do much until he gets here. I guess I'll go on in." He met his investigators in the kitchen.

"Doughnut, sir?" asked Officer Mallory. "Just eat it with your nose pinched or you'll never get it down. For sure you won't be able to swallow it later. This one's a gut-wrencher."

"Nope. Let's see the body." Sergeant Walters jumped up. "This way, sir." They walked into the hallway and stopped at a closed door. The detective laid a hand on his superior's arm and spoke softly. "Listen, Art, I know you dated her some. Maybe I don't know how you feel about her after all this time, but this is the worst mutilation I've seen in all my twenty-odd years. If you don't want to look I can fill you in on every detail."

"Thanks, Tom, but I have to see for myself." Captain Freeley took off his suit coat and draped it meticulously over a clothes tree which he made sure was clean on top. "Damn, it's like an oven in here." He waved back the detective and entered the bedroom alone.

It was a full 15 minutes before the captain re-joined his men.

He was pale and sweating. There was blood smudged on his white shirt. No one spoke for a long minute. He took a folded handkerchief from his back pocket and wiped upward at the excessive sweat on his forehead and in the thick waves of his dark hair.

Finally he said, "It doesn't add up. That she would just lie there and let someone carve her up. She was too quick—too agile to be calmly lying in her bed if someone was threatening her."

Mallory quickly looked up at his captain with a question on his lips, but Walters kicked his shin under the table.

"You're right, Art. Everything points to her knowing her attacker. She must have let him in."

The captain sat down heavily beside his officers and asked, "Has anyone else been in there since the kids found her body?"

Mallory opened his note pad. "Yup, Cap. A Donald Blake— friend of the son. He called us from this telephone, then had sense enough to lock up the place. Gave Piercal the key. He and his partner were first on the scene, but they waited for us so we would come inside first."

"Spoken with him yet?"

"Blake? Yup."

"Listen," said Sgt. Walters. "While we're waiting for the lab boys and the coroner, maybe I should go check on the kids. We sure don't want them wandering back in here."

"Thanks." The captain gave him a grateful look and picked at Mallory's doughnut. "Might get their story before Juvie comes. Find out if they saw or heard anything—anything at all. "'Course, those kids could always sleep like the dead." He flinched and stared at the wall. "Oh, Tom, go easy, huh? Real easy? 'Specially with Katie: God, she must be, what? Over three by now?"

"Sure, Art. Sure, don't worry. See ya later." He jumped at the chance to get outside, and hurried through the living room, grabbing his tie and fastening his cuffs.

Mallory grimaced and called after his partner, "Still lucky, you bastard."

Within 30 minutes Detective Sgt. Walters had the names of

five persons to investigate: Oscar Banks, live-in boyfriend until three months before; Donald Blake, seen frequently at or near Apartment C; Joyce Cassady, part-time baby sitter; and the Andersons—Luther and Anna Louise. No one mentioned recognizing Captain Freeley as a former visitor, so he made the decision not to list that name.

There was one striking piece of possible incrimination, and the sergeant hurried back to his superior with it.

"This one, Anna Louise Anderson. She was here last evening, made no effort to hide it. Note: Number one, she's a nurse, and, Number two, no one saw her leave."

"Let me see your notes," asked Freeley. He glanced up once at his investigator before handing back the small note pad. "Okay, start with Mr. Hooks and Mrs. Anderson. When you locate them be careful. One of them could be our murderer. Don't take any chances—remember what you've seen here."

"You bet!" said Mallory. "But, listen, this Mrs. Anderson could be in danger, herself. Huh? Suppose she witnessed the crime, or something else to point to the murderer? Or even got kidnapped herself?"

"Good point, Mike," said the Captain. "You and Tom better check on her first. Just be careful."

Sgt. Mallory telephoned his request for a cross-check on the addresses they needed, and got all except for Oscar Banks.

"Let's go, Tom, got her address."

Walters grabbed his sport jacket and police-issue camera.

"Okay, Mike, let's see if we can wrap it up today."

"How the fuck can you be so cocky? Take it easy. Seems like we're always running someplace."

His partner smiled and pocketed his notebook. "So long, Captain," he said. "Don't worry, we'll keep our guard up on this one. Hell, you better believe it!"

CHAPTER 18

Saturday, May 25, 1974, 10:15 a.m.

Sgt. Walters and Officer Mallory read the name above the mail slot for apartment 205 . . . ANNA L. ANDERSON.

"Okay, let's see if she's home." Sgt. Walters tapped his partner on the arm and pointed to his shoulder holster as he led the way up the stairs. Once in front of the apartment Mallory unbuttoned his jacket, checked his pistol, and tucked it into his belt in back. Both men stepped away from the door before knocking. They could hear a baby crying and a woman's voice scolding.

A thin young woman in her twenties opened the door only as far as the safety chain would allow. Her piercing black eyes, framed by loose hanging waves of dark hair, looked them over carefully as they took turns stepping into view.

"Well? What do you want?" she asked.

Both men dangled pictured identifications with badges into the narrow opening simultaneously with their explanation.

"I'm Detective Sergeant Walters and this is Detective Officer Mallory. We're investigators for the Van Nuys Police Department. Is this the residence of Anna Louise Anderson?"

"Yes, uh, I'm her daughter, Sandra. What's wrong? Why do you want to know about my mother?" She scowled, straightened her tank top, keeping her hands busy, and muttered something about the baby needing her.

"Miss, we need to talk with Mrs. Anderson. Is she home?"

"Nope. Are you gonna tell me why you want to see her?" She looked sideways at them with blinking movements, as if she had a nervous tic.

"Miss—Sandra? May we come inside? Don't be nervous. We'd like to ask a few questions and then we'll try to answer some of yours."

"Well, I don't know. Mama isn't here I told you."

"Yes, Miss, but, we need to see for ourselves. While you and I are talking I'd like Officer Mallory here to have a look around so that we can put in our report that we checked out the apartment and Mrs. Anderson was not here. Will that be okay with you?"

"I guess so. Come on in and look, but I told you the truth. She's not here." Sandra pushed the door, unhooked the chain, and let them in.

"Hey! Wait a minute, lemmie see your identifications again," she demanded.

"Okay, here," soothed Walters, "you're right to be certain who you're letting in." He waved his partner on through the doorway of an adjacent room. Noting several overflowing ashtrays he politely asked if he might smoke. He lit his pipe slowly, appraising the nervous young woman who warily sat down while he leaned over to light her cigarette.

"Do you know where your mother is right now?"

"Well of course I know! And you don't need a detective to find her. She's in the hospital. She had a baby last night." The distraught young woman quickly followed Walters into the small kitchen.

"What're you doing?"

"Is this your child, Sandra?" he asked pointing his pen toward a baby strapped in a high chair. She was crying softly while painting the tray with a piece of jam-covered toast. He scribbled a description; close to a year old, dark hair, dark eyes, brown skin, clean clothes, new shoes.

"Gosh, no. I don't have any kids. That's my baby sister, Nancy."

"You mean this is your mother's—Mrs. Anderson's baby?"

"That's what I said, yes."

"Well, well, well." The sergeant paused and made a notation. "She sure is cute. How old is she?"

"'Bout eight months . . . yeah . . . eight," she answered as she counted off the months on her fingers. Just as Walters was about to ask another question his partner came into the kitchen with a young man who was rubbing at his eyes and pushing at his tousled hair. Mallory had re-buttoned his jacket. He shook his head at Walters' questioning eyes.

"This guy was asleep in one of the back bedrooms," he told the sergeant. "Says his name is Bill, and he's Mrs. Anderson's son. Say's he's eighteen."

Sergeant Walters, adept at putting people at ease and off guard, soon sensed this boy was frightened and more than just shy. "Hi, Bill," he began. "Bill, we came out here to try to clear up some things about a case we're working on. Maybe you can help us out."

"Uh, I don't think so."

"Well, you see we're trying to get some information about your mother. You can help with that, can't you?"

"Uh . . ." Bill pushed at his hair again and glanced at his sister.

Sergeant Walters went right on with his rapid questioning.

"First, let's see if I have my notes straight. This is your baby sister and she's eight months old. Is that right, to the best of your knowledge, Bill?"

"Uh, huh, . . . yeah. That's Nancy, right." He looked at Sandra for approval.

"I already told you that," snapped Sandra.

"Yes," Mallory broke in, "but if, as you say, your mother just had another baby last night . . . that's having them pretty close together isn't it?"

Sgt. Walters waved at him to be quiet as Sandra moved in front of her brother and shouted at them.

"The baby last night was premature. That happens you know! What the hell are you accusing her of anyway? Never mind. Maybe you just better leave. I know damn well she had the baby and she *is* in the hospital because I took her there myself!"

"Calm down now, Sandra," the sergeant said, "We only want

to get things straight. You see, your mother has been identified as being at an apartment last night where a young woman was murdered."

Sandra gasped. "How do you know that?" she whispered.

"We know," Officer Mallory volunteered lamely. "Now, we have to talk to her to find out what, if anything she can tell us about the murder. You say she was in the hospital having a baby last night?"

"That's what I said."

"What time did you take her to the hospital?"

"It was the middle of the night, I don't know exactly. What difference does it make?" Her hands shook as she tried to push Bill back into the hallway toward his room.

"Which hospital is she in and what time was the baby delivered?"

"No. Wait a minute. I didn't mean I took her there to have the baby. I said she had the baby last night, and *then* I took her to the hospital. The truth is she had the baby, by herself, out on the road I think. I told you it was premature!" Sandra turned to face the investigators. "Who got murdered? Why do you think any of us are involved?" She was stammering and appeared on the verge of hysteria.

The baby began to cry in a loud bawl while pushing a bowl of cereal off the high chair tray and onto the linoleum floor, sending cream of rice splatters in every direction. Officer Mallory's dark trousers were instantly freckled with gummy white spots. Both men moved back against the sink.

Bill walked over putting his arm around his sister asking, "Are we in trouble Sandra? Mama said not to worry . . . that everything would be all right. Now we're in trouble. I know it."

"Shut up," yelled Sandra, "just shut up, Bill, and get something to clean up this mess. I'll take care of these . . . *po*—lice. You just keep your mouth shut!"

The sergeant tried once more, this time taking advantage of Bill's fears.

"You want to tell us what you know about all this, Bill?

It's really important, that's why we have to ask. You could help us clear up a lot of questions if you'd tell us what happened last night, about your mother and the baby. You know, like what time she got home and was the baby born without any trouble? What did you do . . . did you help out when she got home? Being a good son I bet you were a big help."

His tactic of keeping the subject off guard by bombarding him with questions was working. Bill backed into the high chair and appeared to be near tears, but before he could say anything Sandra yelled at him again, "Don't you answer any of those questions! If they want to know about Mama they can go ask her."

Bill looked like a child who was being punished for something he didn't do and was ready to hide from it all. He freed the baby from its restraints and clutched her to his chest, almost as if he thought she could shield him from the hurt he sensed was enveloping them.

"I don't know what Mama did. You go ask her. She'll tell you. She's at the hospital where she works—that big one. You know, that big one downtown. That's where she's at. Go on and ask her . . . leave us alone. I don't like you askin' all this stuff. You go ask Mama."

"Okay, Bill. You just take it easy." Sergeant Walters directed his next question to the sister. "Sandra, why don't you just tell us exactly which hospital we're talking about?"

"Metro Municipal, here in Van Nuys," she answered curtly. Bill looked down at his feet, realizing he was standing barefooted in the cereal mess, and that the baby was smearing jam all over his bare chest. "Aw, Nancy! . . . . Good God, Sandra, what'll I do? Can't you help me? Why don't you guys please leave us alone and just go on and see Mama?"

"Right, Bill. Take it easy son. We're going to do just that." The sergeant turned to Sandra. "Here's my card and a number you can call if you want to tell us anything. Until our investigation is over you both are to stay available for questioning. Do you understand that? You are not to go out of town without checking with us first. That's important so don't forget."

"Okay, okay, we understand `Off-i-cers,' Sandra answered sarcastically.

"We'll be contacting you later after we talk with your mother. Thanks for your help."

Both men paused in the lobby to finish their notes, then headed for their car. Sgt. Walters stopped and turned to his partner. "Damn, I just wish we could have come up with something more. Anderson's involved, that's for sure. Can't put my finger on it, but my gut pegs her as the murderer. What do you think?"

"Yeah, I'm with you. And if she came directly here, with the missing baby from the murder scene, there could be something, some hard evidence around to point to her. Sure as hell came up empty in the apartment."

"You're right. Tell you what, Mike, let's have a look around here before we go to the hospital. Never can tell, if she did this thing and was in a big hurry, we just might find the fuckin' murder weapon, bloody clothes, or some damn tie-in."

"Sure can't hurt to look while we're here, Sarge. Want me to check out the dumpsters and utility rooms?"

"Good idea. An' I'll browse around the sidewalks and empty lots over there. Meet you back at the car. Good luck with the muck!"

"Yeah, right. Thanks a lot. Dumpsters can be so damn much fun early in the morning. Yuck."

A few minutes later Walters was walking through knee-high, spring weeds, kicking at rusty cans, plastic bottles, fading cardboard boxes and all the other human discards usually found in vacant lots. His mind was still trying to sort out the new evidence in their case, when he spotted a large plastic bag lying in a patch of weeds. It was partially hidden under a squat,bushy looking pepper tree. The season's pollen was already watering his eyes and tickling his nose as he approached the bag. He noted that it was still free from L.A.'s smoggy residue, but damp with morning dew.

His itching nose gave way to violent sneezing as he tried to untie the top.

"Damn it," he muttered, "I would get an early case of hay fever out of this. Shit."

He flipped his handkerchief a couple of times before burying his face into it. With even a greater urge to see inside the bag he tore at the knots and finally worked them loose. He stood there staring down at his prize.

"Well, I'll be damned." Without disturbing anything he could tell the contents were bloody: towels, plastic sheet, syringes, vials and all sorts of medical supplies. The odor indicated that everything had been used recently. Between sneezes, now ignored, he kicked at the bag to change positions of the contents hoping to see a sharp instrument that could be the murder weapon. No luck with that. He marked the spot with brush and stones and secured the bag under a piece of rusting metal; then continued a rapid search of the surrounding area for any other evidence.

There was other suspicious debris which he poked with a stick, but nothing to tie in with the case. Mallory came strolling toward him slapping off the contaminations he'd accumulated on his trousers from the cream of rice and the contents of the dumpsters.

"You're gonna shit, Mike, when you see what I found out here," called Walters, beaming as he waved toward the bag. "We got the goddamn jackpot! You bet we know the murderer or murderers; and what we got here is all the fuckin' evidence to sew up this case.

"Take a look, then you can call in and get the lab men out here. Better get a backup for us to guard this lot. 'Cause the next stop for you and me is Metro Hospital, and we better get over there quick.

"Hey, call Freely too. Have him meet us at the hospital. We can fill him in there."

As they entered the hospital Sgt. Walters and his partner were still speculating on what they were going to find out from their prime suspect when they could confront her.

"My God, Sarge," commented Mallory, "it's hard for me to

believe that a woman, a respectable nurse—a mother herself—could do what we saw had been done to the victim. I mean, shit, how could she do that? Maybe she had help."

"Well, we'll find out soon enough *if* she's going to cooperate. Maybe we can do this the easy way—confront her with the facts and get a confession out of her."

"Maybe. I know one thing for damn sure. I'm not buying the daughter's story that her mother had a baby last night, just eight months after she had her last one."

"That's for sure. But we're no experts about that. Got to take the doctors' word on that score.

The elevator was crowded with happy faces and high pitched voices. Babies was the topic of conversations as the two men were propelled off at the maternity floor. They went directly to the nurses' station and identified themselves to a nurse at the chart rack, explaining that they needed all the information they could get on a new patient, Anna Louise Anderson, and the baby she brought in when admitted.

"I see," said the nurse. She appraised each detective with coy thoroughness, and directed her words toward Mallory.

"I'm the head nurse, Carlotta Perry. I saw Mrs. Anderson on my rounds this morning. What's this all about? Is Anna in some sort of trouble? She's one of my nurses on this floor and if she's in trouble I should know about it."

"It's no secret," answered Walters while his partner smiled broadly and rested an arm on the counter. "Looks like she may know something about a murder case we're on."

Carlotta's eyes widened.

"And we need to find out everything we can about the circumstances of the birth of the baby she claims she had last night."

"I knew it. I said all along she was up to something—just couldn't put my finger on what it was. I've had a lot of trouble with her taking time off because of her pregnancies. There's just something. . . ."

"Yes, ma'am." Sgt. Walters frowned as he posed the next question, "Then most of the medical staff here knew she was pregnant?"

"Oh, yes. Anna talked about it all the time. She was very happy about it. I couldn't believe she'd let herself get pregnant immediately after having the last one, especially at her age. You know she already had six kids?"

"No, we didn't know that. About this pregnancy . . . did she see a doctor here, or somewhere else? Or do you know?"

"Oh, here, of course. We all get a discount as Metro employees." Turning to the file rack she pulled Anna's chart and began leafing through it. "Yes, according to this she has been seen by several doctors during her pregnancy and has been doing very good. A normal pregnancy with no complications. Just the usual entries.

"Let's see now—-here it is, last night—she was admitted at 1:40 a.m. through the emergency ward as a patient with a premature baby delivered out of hospital, umm, complete with the placenta. The baby was placed in our preemie nursery for emergency care and Anna was taken to room 325B here after she declined any examination. Signed the usual hospital release of responsibility That's about all I can tell you. I wasn't on duty last night. "Wait a minute. Wait a cockamamy minute. I just noticed something."

She turned the chart so Officer Mallory could see.

"See this? It says she refused to be examined."

"And that's unusual?" asked Mallory with his eyes holding Carlotta's.

"You bet. Hospital policy. Every admission *must* have a pelvic exam if they come in with an out of hospital delivery. It's just like her to mess things up and act like she's above it all. Humph."

"Thank you, nurse." murmured Walters. "Now, as we understand you, Mrs. Anderson has had no examination at all since she came in—nothing to prove she had delivered a baby?"

"That's what it looks like."

"Then, how could you be sure she was the mother of that baby? Doesn't anyone make sure to examine mothers who deliver before reaching the hospital?"

"Yes, of course. We always do . . . but she, Anna Louise, is one of our own, an OB nurse here. And we have her medical chart with a record of her pregnancy. So, I guess when she came in with her baby and refused to be examined, vaginally that is, well, I guess the staff on duty just didn't pursue it.

"I'm not excusing it, don't get me wrong. She *was* treated however . . . yes, it's recorded here that she was given pitocin."

"And what would that be, nurse, anything that would be harmful if she hadn't just given birth?"

"No. It wouldn't be harmful as such. Might cause some cramping and discomfort but nothing serious."

Officer Mallory leaned over the counter with the intensity of his thoughts evident in his expression. "Miss Perry?" he asked.

"Carlotta."

"Right. Carlotta, how is the baby this morning? What was its condition when admitted?"

"Oh, it's going to be fine. Just borderline premature."

"May we see it?" Walters asked as he scratched away on his notes. He and his partner always took separate notes, then compared them later before typing up their finished reports.

"Sure, look in the window to the left. I'll have the aide hold it up for you."

"By the way, is it a boy or girl? We haven't determined that yet," asked Mallory.

Carlotta primped and smiled at him. "You'll be surprised. It's a boy . . . and he's black." She watched for an effect from her announcement and noted a momentary pause in the notations.

"Okay, thanks for your help. You sure keep on top of things," Mallory said as he smiled at Carlotta. "We'd like to go in and ask some questions of Mrs. Anderson after we see the baby. 325? If you would ask the doctor in charge to meet with us we'll be wanting him to examine her to ascertain if she, in fact, did have a baby last night."

Carlotta raised her eyebrows and came out from behind the

counter to accompany them. She laid her hand lightly on Mallory's arm.

Walters closed his notebook and looked around at a few curious bystanders. "Let's get on with it," he mumbled. "We better shake this audience."

"Okay, Miss Perry," continued Mallory. "We're going to try to get Mrs. Anderson to agree to this examination by convincing her that it would clear up some questions for everyone. Got to find out if she did, in fact, give birth to that particular baby she brought in with her last night.

"You do understand that this is a homicide and kidnapping case, and it's imperative that we get all the facts as soon as we can? Of course it'll be much easier if she cooperates."

"Oh, my God, murder, kidnapping? You know, I always said she was trouble, but I never dreamed she was into something like that. Yes, I'll find Doctor Hanamoto right away and fill him in on all of this. I'll need my supervisor too."

Walters and Mallory conferred as they headed down the hall toward room 325. "We really have to be careful how we handle this," said Walters slowly. "If she did this thing, I mean, killed the Delgato woman and kidnapped that baby, then she must still be pregnant. That must be why she wouldn't let them examine her."

Mallory agreed and added, "One thing's for sure. If she'll let the doctor examine her, and he finds she's still pregnant, then we have our case."

"Yeah, *if* we get that lucky. Otherwise it's gonna be a lot of paper work to get her moved to the county hospital jail ward where we'll have to get court orders to examine her."

The door to room 325 was open and they quietly stepped inside far enough to size up the room and it's contents. On one side there was a made-up, empty bed closest to the door and a half-drawn curtain separating it from the bed next to the window. All they could see were two plump legs until they rounded the end of the bed. Mallory positioning himself between the patient and the window; the other remaining near the curtain.

"Mrs. Anderson? Are you Anna Louise Anderson?" the sergeant asked. Mallory remained quiet, with his note pad poised. The patient looked from one to the other quizzically before answering.

"Yes, I'm Anna Anderson. Who are you and what do you want?"

Both men showed her their badges, identified themselves, and explained that they were there to question her about a friend of hers who had been found dead. There followed a show of tears, questions and agitation.

"But, why are you *here*? Questioning me? I can't help you. I mean, I knew Rosalind—saw her yesterday, but I don't know about a *murder*. I'm just waiting to take my baby home."

"Mrs. Anderson, we're here because you may have been the last person to see your friend alive. In fact, we believe you might even be a prime suspect in her murder."

They both watched her reaction with surprise. She showed no emotion. None at all.

At that point Sgt. Walters put his badge back in his pocket and pulled out his tattered card with the official Miranda warning on it. He began to read their suspect her rights.

"You have the right to remain silent. If you give up the right to remain silent, anything you say can and will be used against . . ."

"Wait a minute! What is this? What are you saying? Why are you asking me all this rights stuff? What do you mean a murder? I've been here in the hospital. I had a baby. What are you accusing me of? There's some mistake here."

The sergeant didn't answer her but continued to read from the card until he had finished.

"Do you understand each of these rights I have just read to you, Mrs Anderson?"

"Of course I understand them! I just don't understand why you read them to *me*, that's all."

"Do you wish to give up the right to remain silent?"

"Yes, yes, but I want to know why you are here."

"Do you give up the right to speak to an attorney and have him present during questioning?"

"Yes, now will you tell me what this is all about?"

The sergeant made a notation for his report. *Suspect appears stable, coherent, apparently not under the influence of any drugs, alert but agitated at being questioned. Sitting up in bed and appears to be in good physical and mental state.*

"Sergeant, whatever your name is, it sounds like I'm under arrest. Did you come here to arrest me?"

"Yes, ma'am," he answered. "You are being taken into custody for questioning about the alleged murder and about a possible kidnapping. You are going to be arraigned as the prime suspect in the case."

"You mean, Rosa's murder?"

"Yes."

"Oh, I get it, I see. And you are threatening me. You are going to get a court order to get me examined, right?"

"I'd like you to freely consent to be examined to prove you had a baby last night."

"No, I don't feel that I have to. The baby is mine. I breast feed him. Could I do that if I hadn't had him? If he's not mine then whose is he?"

"We suspect he's Rosalind Delgato's baby and that you kidnapped him after you murdered her. So why don't you let the doctor examine you and prove what you're saying—that the baby you brought in is yours?"

"But I already told you I breast feed him. That's proof enough."

"We know you have another baby at home, eight months old, and that could be why you might have milk and could nurse this one."

"No, no! I don't nurse *her*. She takes a bottle. You're just trying to pressure me into being examined but I won't do that. It's humiliating and degrading—an assault on my body and I won't do it just to prove he's my baby. You have to believe me! I delivered him myself—he's mine I'm telling you! You're just trying to pressure me into being examined and I can't do that."

Sgt. Mallory sat down beside the bed. "No, Mrs. Anderson,

we aren't trying to upset you. We just hope you will want to cooperate. That's the only way you can prove you had the baby like you
say."

Anna thought that over and finally answered, "Well, I think if
I'm under arrest, and everything, then I'm not going to say anything before I talk to an attorney."

"That's your privilege. You have been warned of your rights
and I believe you understand them fully." Mallory remained just
outside the hospital door while the sergeant met with Carlotta
Perry, her supervisor, and two staff doctors. Walters explained the
situation to them and informed them that they would be moving
Anna to the jail ward at Sybil Brand.

"Is there any reason we wouldn't be able to do that today? She
looks pretty healthy to me."

Dr. Hanamoto answered, "We should examine her to be sure
she's in condition to be transported. I really have to insist upon
that."

"Oh, we agree with that, Doctor."

"Okay, then the nurse and I will see if we can convince her she
should be examined by me so that I can chart my findings before
she leaves here."

"Fine, Doctor. We'll wait in the hall." Both men leaned back
against the wall. Carlotta brushed Mallory slightly and flashed a
warm smile. He grinned before lowering his eyes to his note pad.

Upon entering the room Dr. Hanamoto walked briskly up to
Anna's bed and addressed her gruffly, "Okay, Anna, what's all this
about? You not being examined? You're an OB nurse—and you
know that *any* woman coming in here after having an out of hospital delivery gets a thorough examination to determine her physical
condition. You surely understand that; so what's this business about
you not wanting to be examined?"

She remained silent, turned toward the window. The doctor
glanced toward Carlotta, and tried again. "You know me well
enough to be sure that I always go by hospital rules. Being a nurse
doesn't exempt you from those rules. You might as well under-

stand that right now. "Anna?" Without giving her time to object further he lifted her gown, looked at and felt her abdomen.

"What's this scar?"

"Oh, I had surgery for gall bladder and, and . . . they took my appendix too," she explained lamely.

"Now, Anna, I'm going to do the pelvic exam. It has to be done—either here by me, or at County Hospital. You know the routine."

She started to weep, thrashing around in the bed. Dr. Hanamoto gently pushed her shoulders down and spread her legs. He forced his hand into a tight surgical glove.

"Nurse, give me the speculum," he called over his shoulder. "Hmm . . . hmm." He kept repeating the same examination to be sure of his findings; three times in all. He then turned to Carlotta and told her to chart the results: "No bleeding in the vaginal canal. On manual exam there appears to be no uterus, no fundus and no cervix. On palpation of abdomen I felt no mass. Rectal exam coincides with vaginal and manual exams. Scar at apex of vault. Results of all exams confirm patient has had a hysterectomy several years ago."

Anna looked up at Carlotta and pleaded, "Don't let them take my baby from me. Bring him to me, *please*, Carlotta. I need to hold him."

"Don't ask me to do anything for you, Anna. It's out of my hands. From what I see here you're a disgrace to nursing. I'm sorry I wasn't able to get you off my floor a long time ago like I wanted to."

Dr. Hanamoto scolded, "That will be enough, Miss Perry." He turned to Anna saying, "You didn't tell anyone you had had a hysterectomy. We all thought you were pregnant. You've had a complete hysterectomy, Anna. Why did you lie? You couldn't have had a baby."

Anna began to cry again and yelled at the doctor. "You're trying to take my baby away from me! He's mine, I tell you! I don't care what any of you say. I gave birth to him—he's mine."

Dr. Hanamoto left Anna's room shaking his head in puzzled disbelief. He reported his findings to the two homicide officers in great detail. "I'm shocked. Totally shocked. I've worked with her right here in the labor and delivery rooms—she was one of our best nurses. It's just . . . mind-boggling. Gentlemen, that's all I can tell you. She could *not* have had that baby or any other baby for the past few years."

Walters and Mallory stopped writing and stood staring at each other. Both men had shuddering images of a pretty little baby girl in a high chair, only eight months old. And they both remembered Sandra and Bill telling them, "That's Nancy, our baby sister."

CHAPTER 19

Wednesday, July 17, 1974, 4:10 p.m.

MR. DURBIN: Your Honor, I wish to use my right of recall to clarify a short portion of Sgt. Walters' testimony.

THE COURT: If you can confine your time limit to less than 50 minutes, you may proceed.

MR. DURBIN: Thank you, your Honor. People recall

Detective Sergeant Walters to the stand. You are under oath.

BY MR. DURBIN:

Q. Sgt. Walters, other than what's on your four-page report, is there anything that you omitted that transpired between you and the defendant?

A. Yes. During that portion of the conversation——about the center of the second page—when the defendant said, That's *my* baby. I've been breast-feeding him. How would I be able to do that if he wasn't my baby?"; during that portion of that conversation, we talked about another baby that she claimed was hers. I omitted it because I just forgot. While re-reading my report I remembered that I had not included that part of our conversation in this report.

Q. Did you forget about it because you did not think it was important?

A. No. I just forgot. I remembered it when . . . later on that night. On the way home from the station I was thinking about that other baby. I called the hospital back to confirm that Mrs. Anderson could not have had a baby in a good number of years. Then I remembered what she had said, and that I didn't have it on this report. That's when I telephoned Captain Freely that Officer Mallory and myself should continue our investigation in respect to the other baby, the one in the apartment of the defendant.

Q. So, when you talked to Mrs. Anderson, you were of the opinion that she was definitely not the mother of the newborn in the hospital with her. Am I correct?

A. Yes, that's the way I felt about it.

Q. All right. So, Sergeant, being a good police officer, the mention of any other babies would create a suspicion in your mind, wouldn't it?

A. Yes.

Q. Would you tell us, please, about your investigation concerning the child, Nancy.

MR. WINGATE: Objection, your honor. This line of questioning is irrelevant and immaterial to the case at hand.

THE COURT: I will sustain that at this point.

MR. DURBIN: No further questions.

But the investigators, Sergeant Walters and Officer Mallory,had been concerned enough about who Nancy belonged to that they immediately requested to be left on the case. Captain Freeley agreed, and quickly arranged for two uniformed police to transport his suspect to jail while his homicide team prepared to return to her apartment early the next day.

The two officers assigned to bring Anna in, managed to shuttle the infamous suspect out of the hospital and into their police car before any hungry reporters could corner her. The ride to the station was quiet, quick, and uneventful.

As Anna was being guided through the booking room door she instinctively drew back from the officers and cried out,"Oh, no! Don't do this to me. Please, you've got to understand. I have babies that need me. Can't you just let me go for awhile? 'Til I get it all straight . . . what happened . . . I mean, who got killed . . . need to talk to Luther . . . to tell him about Rosalind, and everything. He has to tell me why! Damn him, he has to tell me why! Maybe he knew all along about Rosa's baby, . . . that it was his baby. Did he know? Gotta see him. . . ." Her voice weakened and she leaned heavily on the counter.

The booking sergeant motioned for Anna to sit down at his

desk. "Look, Mrs. Anderson, we have nothing to do with releasing anyone in here, for any reason. We're booking you for first degree murder. That's it. A routine procedure we'll go through with you, same as everyone else. Now, if you cooperate we'll get it over with as quick and easy as possible, then you and your attorney, if you have one, can talk about bail . . . release, or whatever, with Captain Freeley. He wants to see you as soon as we finish with you in here. You can tell him, the Captain, what's on your mind if you want." He stacked some papers while another officer prepared the fingerprinting equipment. "Do you understand all that?"

"I guess so. What do you want me to do?"

"We'll tell you as we go along. First we have to fill out all these forms. We need your complete name. Do you want to be booked under 'Anderson'?"

"Yes. I am Anna Louise Anderson."

"Do you have any AKA's?"

"What do you mean 'AKA'?"

"Oh, sorry. That's 'also known as.' Are you known by any names other than Anderson, you know, aliases?"

"Well, before Anderson my last name was Dollard, and before that it was Maxwell and for a long time it was Lorenz. My maiden name is Mayer. Do you have to put all that down? I just want to be Anderson. I like being Mrs. Luther Anderson."

"Fine, no problem, we'll book you as Anderson and list the others as AKA's."

The booking went smooth and easy, even the dreaded examination by the nurse. Anna was anxious to get through the ordeal and in to see the Captain. He was the best chance she had to help her get out and see Luther before she was locked up. Yes, Luther was the only one who could explain it all to her.

Captain Freeley introduced himself to Anna, seated her across from him, switched on the tape recorder, then told everyone else to leave. "I want to talk with Mrs. Anderson alone for awhile. Get some coffee or something. No calls. Just give me a few minutes with her. Hell, we don't want to scare her with all your ugly mugs staring at her right away, now do we?"

"Okay, Captain, since you have such a pretty face we'll leave her in your 'gentle' hands."

"Out!"

"Now, Anna, is it okay if I call you Anna? We're going to be doing a lot of talking the next few days trying to get to the bottom of all this."

"Sure. I don't mind. Can I ask you, before we start all the questions, if I can be released on bail or something like that? I mean for a little while . . . to see about my kids and to talk to Luther about what's happened. I *have* to do that or I'll go stark crazy and not be much good to anyone."

"Anna, I realize you've already been read your rights but do you have an attorney yet? You may not want to talk about anything until after you see your attorney. You remember, that's your right don't you?"

"I know. I know! I don't have one yet but I want to talk to you right now. I need to make you understand. *I've got to go home before you lock me up.* You see, Rosalind was my friend and I have to talk to Luther about all this before I can tell anyone what happened to all of us!" She smoothed the uniform skirt and went on. "So, if you will just arrange for me to be released for awhile then I can come back and tell you whatever I can remember, and everything. Just sign some paper that will get me out of here."

"That's not possible. You should know that! Mrs. Delgato was brutally murdered . . . slashed . . . stomach ripped open, her baby kidnapped . . . taken from her dead body . . . and you sit here expecting me to arrange for your release? My God, you must think I'm like one of those damn television cops that can twist the rules to do that sort of thing!

"Well, let me tell you, there's only two kinds of releases. One is called an O.R. which means own recognizance, in other words the court will trust you because of your good character to stick around and report for your trial. The other is bail, paying the court money. Again to insure you'll show up for your trial.

"I have to be honest with you, Anna. It's not easy for me to even sit here and talk with you. You see, I knew Rosalind Delgato, knew her well. And I know she never was a violent or mean person. She was a good woman and a loving mother. She didn't deserve what happened to her. I think you killed her. You mutilated her. You stole her unborn baby from her and you robbed her children of their mother. So you can see that you can't be considered a 'good character' for an O.R. release. And I don't think the judge will allow a release on bail; but even if he did I'm afraid it would be for more money than you could even imagine.

"Now, why don't you just forget all about this release bullshit and tell me how and why you killed Rosalind! That's all we're going to talk about in here and you may as well know that right now! That's what I have to know . . . why you butchered her up like that. And why she just laid there and let you kill her. Goddammit, she didn't even put up a fight. She must have really trusted you!"

"Wait, wait, you don't understand. I loved Rosa. She was my friend. I was helping her. I didn't want to help her but she kept on and on about the baby. She knew I loved babies. She said I had to do it. But . . . but she lied . . . yes, she lied. Everything was a lie. I can't even remember all the lies. The baby, the time, the father . . . she thought it was funny. She *laughed* at me. Well, no more. It's not funny now. Please, Captain, can't you at least bring Luther in to see me? I have to know if he still loves me."

"We've already talked to Luther and he doesn't want to see you. He said knowing you was the biggest mistake of his life. He said *you* turned out to be just one big lie. You see, he already knows that Nancy isn't his, just another one of your lies. How about the truth for a change. Who does Nancy really belong to? Did you kill Nancy's mother, too? Is that how you got her? Was that the reason you killed Rosalind . . . to steal her baby for yourself?"

"No! No! Not for me. It was Luther. Luther's baby. I saved Luther's baby . . . mine and Luther's."

"Not yours, Anna. Not yours! You can't have babies. We know

all about the hysterectomy so don't feed me this crap about the baby being yours. You have to tell me all about Nancy . . . and Rosalind and the baby. Tell me, Anna!"

Anna began to rock, banging her back against the hard chair as she cradled her imaginary baby in her arms. "Hush little baby don't you cry. Mama's gonna love you 'til she dies."

Over and over, louder and louder, she cried out her song as she repeatedly tipped her chair onto its back legs and rocked it violently against the wall.

Captain Freeley yelled at her, "That's enough, Anna. Knock off the crazy act. I'm not buying it. But, he finally gave up on getting through to her, switched off the tape recorder and called for his officers. Pacing the floor, he angrily waved a shaking hand toward Anna.

"Get her out of here. I can't stand the sight of her. Have her put in one of the quiet cells, I guess. She's playing the 'crazy scene' for us. Don't know how real it is, but she's sure as hell not spillin' anything, and she's not giving up who the eight month old baby belongs to. We'll just have to find out the hard way. Damn, I'm wondering now how many of her own kids are really hers. We better check all of them out just to be sure."

"Too bad she wouldn't open up, Captain," said one of the officers as he gave him a knowing squeeze on the shoulder and stood watching as they led the suspect down the hall.

"There she goes . . . rockin' and singin'. That's a hard act to beat."

"Yeah, your right, but damn, I was sure hoping the bitch would fill us in on some answers. Instead she's off to the funny farm. Real or not she'll probably play it out to the end and there's not a damn thing we can do about it."

Freeley kicked the chair away from the wall and rubbed his fingers appraisingly over the pitted marks. "God dammit, how I hate having to deal with a fuckin' prisoner off on a looney trip. It's frustrating as hell. Well, maybe Walters and Mallory will get lucky tomorrow."

Sunday, May 26, 1974, 8:25 a.m.

Again the detectives were knocking on the door of Apartment 205 in seasonally smoggy Hollywood. Walters sneezed. This time he had discarded his tie, leaving his jacket on only to cover his shoulder holster. Their concern for Nancy was evident in their faces, and their knocking was insistent.

"Bill? Open up. We know you're there. We hear you talking to Nancy."

"Who is it?"

"Come on, Bill, you know us. Let us in, son."

"Can't. My sister isn't here."

"Bill, we have a court order to come into your apartment and ask some more questions. If you can't answer, it's okay; we'll wait for Sandra inside."

"Tom," whispered Mallory. "What if we've hit on a bizarre baby-stealing ring here? What then?"

"Shh, we'll play it cool. I think Bill might fill us in on whether there are other kids, and where they are, if we handle him right."

Slowly the door opened. The partners spent several minutes chatting with Bill and admiring the sleeping Nancy before casually asking pointed questions. When they learned Sandra could return momentarily they speeded up the interrogation.

"You say you have five or six brothers and sisters. Can you tell us about them?" asked Walters.

"Yeah, sure, I can do that easy." Bill beamed at them. "There's Noreen, she's the oldest—my half-sister, I guess. She's in Colorado. But the four of us, me and my two brothers and Sandra—we was born in Texas. Our name's Lorenz. And Nancy, well, her Dad is Luther, same as the new baby's. I, well, I don't know what its name is gonna be."

"Okay, son, that's great. Now, are any of these children younger than you? Besides Nancy and the new baby, that is."

"Yep, only one, my brother James. He's fourteen—lives back in Texas with Dad—you know, with *his* dad, *our* dad."

Sandra slammed the door behind her and shoved a bag of groceries at Bill. "Put these away!" she ordered. "You bastards," she choked. "Isn't it enough you had to arrest Mama? Now you come around here messing with my brother. You just better get the hell out of here."

"Calm down," soothed Mallory. "We're very sorry about your Mama, but she *is* a strong suspect in the murder of Mrs. Delgato. We came here this morning to see about Nancy."

"What about her?"

"We have reason to believe your mother might have stolen her . . . kidnapped her."

"Are you crazy? She's my sister! Wait, I'll show you the birth certificate. You are the dumbest cops I ever met!" She ran into a bedroom at the end of the hallway.

"What do you think, Tom?" asked Mallory. "These two seem to really believe that Nancy and the new baby were born to their mother. I mean, they come across as innocent of any knowledge that their mother could be a kidnapper."

"Yeah, I know. Quiet, here she comes." The investigators studied the certificate of birth, then convinced Sandra they had the right to take it with them for further inquiry. They left quietly, neither one able to verbalize their puzzlement, and drove directly to the same Children's Hospital that had issued the certificate.

It took almost an hour to locate the intern who had been on duty in Emergency the morning their suspect had registered Nancy as her own. He was now a junior resident on the medical- surgical unit; at the moment assisting with emergency surgery. They called the station to apprise the captain of their progress.

"Stay there," advised Captain Freeley. "No matter how long it takes, find out who that child's real mother is. We arraigned Mrs. Anderson this morning. Evidence is conclusive. The medical stuff you found near her apartment is enough for the D.A. to agree on immediate prosecution. She'll go to trial for murder one, that's for sure."

"Right. So, we're also going to give him kidnapping on the

newborn. Well, we just may have more kidnappings for the D.A. before this is over."

"You may be right. In this case *anything* is possible. But I don't know whether this other child you've uncovered can be used in our present case. Anyway, your priority at this point is to establish identity of the little girl. Meanwhile I'm working with Juvie on how and when to pick her up from Mrs. Anderson's apartment. We're putting her in protective custody."

"Great. Call you later."

"Hey, Mike," reported Walters, "Cap is having Nancy picked up by Juvie. Wanna bet on how they'll get by Sandra?"

"Nope, and I damn sure wouldn't want their job either."

The young doctor was chagrined and apologetic about his issuing a birth certificate without proper confirmation. "Sure I remember her. She just bowled me over. I took her word for everything—I admit it. Boy, what a mess."

"Yes, sir. Could have happened to any doctor. She's a very persuasive woman. So, can you pin down the day and time of birth any closer?"

"Sorry. I really am. But I recorded what she told me, that the birth was during the early hours of Monday, September 10, 1973. Apparently I thought the examination of the baby fit that time."

"Oh, shit! There's no suit involved, is there?"

"No, nothing like that. Thank you, Doctor. They left for the station with many questions unanswered. There would be hours, maybe days ahead of matching births on that date with the slim facts they already had. Captain Freeley encouraged them.

"Good work. I know it's late, but I need your reports, what is it they say on Perry Mason? 'I need them yesterday.'" He laughed.

"Yeah, right, this is when we rush out of the office with disgusted glances at you."

"Go on with you," grinned Freeley. "You can wait until morning. Here's what I suggest. Start checking on births for September of last year, check with Metro first. Especially where was Mrs. Anderson on the night before she registered the baby girl."

"You bet," answered Walters. "Say, Mike, you take that one, huh? Miss Perry'll give you anything you want." He smirked and slapped his partner on the back.

"You're just jealous, you ancient relic."

"Jealous? Hell! That woman's a barracuda. She's all yours, kid."

It was a restless night for Mallory. The next morning he sauntered into morning report with mischief evident in his bearing. The Captain wasn't there yet.

"So what's with you, lover boy," asked Walters.

"Sir, you are addressing genius. Get a load of this sheer poetry:

"Oh, my darlin' Carlotta, A woman with a whole lotta. "You'd be a great lay, so don't push me away.

"To see you again, I just gotta."

The merriment ceased as Captain Freely arrived. After report the detectives began their research into Nancy's true identity.

"You, Mike," grinned Walters, "you 'gotta see Carlotta,' all right. Just remember, she's a barracuda. See you back here after lunch?"

"Yeah, hope so." The younger man took off amidst the clapping of his colleagues.

He and Carlotta spent all morning pouring over the nurses' log for September. Finally the facts were clear; and Mallory forgot all about his pursuit of Carlotta. The exhilaration of success hindered his usually expert driving on his way back to the Van Nuys police station.

"Got it, Sarge," he shouted into the office. "The whole, bloody ball-of-wax. Come on while I give it to you and Cap together."

The unfolding plot of Nancy's kidnapping touched all three with chilling force. Captain Freeley got the District Attorney and a social worker on the conference line. Mallory repeated his findings to them. In the hospital records on a missing fetus, the same hospital records tell of a shocking, unexplained, stillborn to the Fields—the coinciding time of Nancy's "unattended" birth. And the questionable way she obtained the birth certificate at a different hospital. Captain Freeley congratulated his officers.

"It's all there, Mallory. You and Walters did a great job on this one. All fits together like a jigsaw puzzle. Shows Mrs. Anderson as a diabolic schemer who pulled off two unbelievable crimes. This one might never have been uncovered except for Mrs. Delgato's murder."

Reporters got hold of this latest twist in the case and sped to the telephones. Other officers, subdued and incredulous at first, and then outraged, crowded in together to get every detail of the first kidnapping.

Plans were made to locate the Fields immediately. It was decided that Walters and Mallory should make certain they had a Metro Municipal Hospital administrator to accompany them to the Fields' home. The frenzied arrangements finalized with the agreement of the hospital to have an assistant administrator available by Wednesday.

They were assigned Richard Moses, an austere veteran of the hospital chain for 40 years. He was thoroughly briefed by Wednesday.

The three men approached the Fields' modest home in Arleta with excitement on the part of the detectives, and more than some trepidation for Mr. Moses. Much was at stake for his hospital. Not only a terrible mistake, but damaging publicity for all involved with the Fields' stay at Metro.

Jane Fields opened the door. At first she could hardly believe the bizarre story she heard . . . that her baby might be alive. She called her husband home from work so that both of them could hear and digest the incredible story.

"Alive? Dear Lord, where is she? Where? Where?"

"Easy, honey," said Martin. "They'll tell us."

They all drove over to the foster home where "Nancy" had been placed on Saturday.

When Jane saw her baby she knelt down and opened her arms.

Everyone was unashamedly teary-eyed as the smiling, little girl scrambled over the carpet and reached for her mother. Martin enveloped them both as he wept aloud. There was no doubt about the baby's parentage. She looked exactly like the couple's photo of their eleven-year-old son at his first birthday. Both parents cried aloud with joy and wonderment.

To the hospital administrator it was a moment of anger; and fear, too, about his hospital's accountability.

To the detectives it was an emotional triumph of success, of persistent investigation.

To the Fields it was a miracle from God.

To the baby it was home.

CHAPTER 20

Thursday, March 6, 1975, morning.

Business as usual at the Van Nuys police station. Officer Mallory swiveled his chair to face Captain Freeley emerging from his office.

"Hey, Cap, lookit here—today's the day for sentencing of that Anderson woman. Right here on page two."

"Well, I'll be damned. I'd almost forgotten about her. Christ, what a case that was!" He peered across the room at Sergeant Walters and smiled. "Remember, Tom, how you guys kept calling in to us at the station; building up suspense in that case with every call? Turned into one hell of a thriller, didn't it?"

Mallory grimaced, saying, "God, I guess so. It's made every case since then seem just ho-hum. Anyhow, I got Carlotta out of it."

Everyone snickered at that.

"Humpf, you're just jealous. Go on and laugh yourselves silly. But she's one helluva woman!"

Walters cut the guffaws short to pose a question to his colleagues. "Say, how in the hell do you think that nurse lost it enough to commit such a sloppy, 'give away' murder? She was so damn clever in commiting that first felony. I just can't figure it. That's bugged me ever since I was on the case."

Captain Freeley got up, walked over to the window and reflected back before answering.

"You know, I'm not so sure she was really all that clever. Maybe there's a lesson in all this. I mean, just because she was pleasant, educated and licensed, and in a responsible position, everyone simply trusted her. Nothing she did was questioned. Just shows you we may all be too complacent these days—too trusting. That's how Rosalind bought it."

Walters stepped over to put his hand on the Captain's shoulder. They stood for a moment, each remembering.

"Art, the sergeant asked, "do you ever hear anything about Rosalind's kids? How they're doing?"

"No. As good as can be expected, I guess, without a mother. Last I heard they were with their grandmother, out of state. She sure did a great job of raising Rosalind; so, maybe she'll do as well with her daughter's kids.

"You know, I think I'll take off today and go on into the L.A. County Courthouse. Might give me some measure of satisfaction to see the 'grand finale' to that case."

Anna had been notified that this was the day of her sentencing. For six months she had been at Patton State Hospital as a result of the concerned recommendations of her preliminary trial jurors in 1974. In February she was declared sane, and was free from any particular psychotropic drug which might impair her memory or comprehension.

Time had dimmed the cannibalism of human expectation for horror, so there was no longer a shoving amalgamate of people trying to fit into the courtroom. The press had plenty of room for their revival of the crimes and the reporting of Anna's sentence which would be expected on the 5 o'clock news.

There was little difference in Anna's appearance from the year before at her preliminary trial. As she sat down beside her lawyers, she was aware of hindering shackles and of her two guards from Sybill Brand, the women's county jail. Her blank physiognomy was framed by hanging strands of hair; enhanced by no makeup nor by any noticeable cognizance of her surroundings.

The bailiff closed the doors, motioned for silence, and called out, "All rise."

As soon as the judge was seated the clerk announced the docket. First on the list was the sentencing of Anna Louise.

SUPERIOR COURT OF THE STATE OF CALIFORNIA
FOR THE COUNTY OF LOS ANGELES DEPARTMENT
49 HON. JASON F. TRULL, JUDGE.
THE PEOPLE OF THE STATE OF CALIFORNIA,)
                              Plaintiff.   )
                                 vs.   )
                              No. A-3062146M
ANNA LOUISE ANDERSON,   ) STATE PRISON
                              Defendant.)
_____)

LOS ANGELES, CALIFORNIA,
THURSDAY, MARCH 6, 1975.

Upon the above date, the defendant being present in court
and represented by Counsel, LEONARD WINGATE and
ROLAND STOKES, Esq., and the People being represented by
RALPH DURBIN and JERREL BURR, Deputy District Attor-
neys of Los Angeles County, the following proceedings were held:
(WOLFGANG HUYER, official Reporter.)

THE COURT: The matter of the People versus Anna Louise
Anderson is on the Court's calendar for judgement and sentence.
The Court has read and considered the 22-page probation report
and attached exhibits, and is signing the report.

Counsel, do you waive formal arraignment for judgement?

MR. STOKES: So waived, your Honor.

THE COURT: Is there any legal cause why sentence should
not now be pronounced?

MR. STOKES: It is my understanding that there was a motion of a new trial. I ask that this be heard prior to the probation
and sentence hearing.

THE COURT: Ordinarily such a motion would occur prior
to probation and sentence. That would be a reason for legal cause
as to why these should not now be presently pronounced.

But, heretofore, there has not been either an oral or a written motion for a new trial.

MR. STOKES: Your Honor, may Counsel approach the bench?

THE COURT: With the court Reporter?

MR. STOKES: No, that's not necessary.

(An off-the-record discussion was held at the bench among Court and Counsel.)

(The following proceedings were held in open court.)

MR. STOKES: Your Honor, at this time the defendant would ask that the Court entertain an oral motion for a new trial. I understand the People would waive notice on that motion.

MR. DURBIN: People waive notice.

THE COURT: The Court will recognize a motion of a new trial at this time.

You may be heard.

MR. STOKES: I submit the matter asking only that the Court reduce the charge under which she was convicted of first degree murder . . . to second degree. My basis is the fact that I do not believe that the overwhelming weight of the evidence was such that Mrs. Anderson could have been convicted *beyond a reasonable doubt* of murder in the first. I would ask the Court to reduce it to murder in the second degree.

Submit that, your Honor.

THE COURT: People wish to be heard?

MR. DURBIN: No, I submit the matter, although I will indicate that I am opposed to any reduction in the degree.

THE COURT: I can only say this to Counsel: the Court, in all candor, anticipated the motion of a new trial, and a plea for reduction in the sentence. The Court has reviewed numerous authorities, a majority of its notes, and large portions of the trial transcript.

It is the Court's duty to pass on the weight of all the evidence, to resolve conflicts, and to make an independent judgement. Apparently the grounds of the motion is that the evidence of diminished capacity is such that a finding of conviction in the first degree is not possible?

MR. STOKES: That's correct, your Honor.

THE COURT: In looking at the evidence on that issue it is necessary to weigh all of it, including that produced by the defendant which was the testimony of the two psychiatrists.

In doing so the Court carefully weighed the opinions that there was diminished capacity. However, the reasons given for that opinion were not on the fact that the defendant had a classical type of mental illness. It is clearly stated that she was suffering, at the time of the killing, from an insatiable obsession to have a baby. Their explanation of their reasons discussed the fact that this obsession affected her judgement and ability to reflect on the gravity of her act, and that this obsession existed for most of her adult life, especially following the hysterectomy in the '60s.

The Court cannot accept the major opinions of the psychiatrists. The evidence they presented did not establish to the Court, as a finder of fact, that she was suffering from this type of insatiable obsession for that period of time, or that it existed at the time of the killing.

I might add that I have had both of those doctors in my court in over 5000 cases, and I would hesitate to estimate how many times the Court's decisions were based largely upon their opinions. But here the substantial evidence that the Court has does not establish that at the time of the killing the murderer's motive was just an obsession to have a baby.

The evidence was other than that; the killing was undoubtedly because of her relationship with Mr. Anderson.

The evidence rather clearly establishes that her behavioral conduct prior to the killing . . . all of those things she did over a period of years . . . reflected that her behavior was purposeful and goal directed. It was very decisive and very direct.

The Court has also had the opportunity to observe the defendant over a period of time. Because of that and because of the evidence discussed the motion of a new trial is denied, and the request to reduce the offense from murder in the first to murder in the second degree is denied.

Application for probation for further psychiatric evaluation is denied.

The defendant will be sentenced to the California State Prison for Women on the charge of murder in the first degree for the term prescribed by law.

She will at this time be remanded to the Sheriff to be delivered.

THE END

POEM

LOVE ME

Mama didn't want me.
How can you?
She tried to abort me:
I was too strong.

Do you love me
Just for myself?
Will you accept me
With all my faults?

I started out life
With many defects.
Must overcome them!
I need help.

Please hold me close——
Love me a little,
Let me be me.
Love me. . .for myself.

Norma Jean Jackson
California Institution
For Women, 1979

EPILOGUE

The protagonist of this novel, (Norma Jean Jackson) whom we call Anna Louise Anderson, is presently, in 1999, entering her twenty-sixth year of incarceration at the state penitentiary. She is eligible for parole every one to three years. She accepts the denials, and faults no one but herself. Her conduct is exemplary within the prison.

Anna is sixty-eight years old, repentant and hopeful that her story, for which she receives no remuneration, will serve to help others avoid a similar path to destruction.

We continue to visit . . . two of the three visitors she ever has. We neither condone nor condemn her continued confinement.

She remains our friend.

The Authors

GRAY-JACKET 5.5 X 8.5

9 780738 807645